20

Terminal Value

A novel by
Thomas Waite

Marlborough Press

Paperback ISBN 978-0-9850258-0-9

E-book ISBN 978-1-617509-87-2

Published by Marlborough Press
March 2012

Printed in the USA

www.marlboroughpress.com
www.thomaswaite.com

In memory of my parents

Terminal value:
The value of an asset at the end of its useful life.

Chapter 1

January 7, 2:00 a.m. Boston

Dylan Johnson's mind never reached a deep, rejuvenating sleep that night, but hovered at the edge of the netherworld of sleep paralysis, where faces roamed around his body in an unnerving silence.

He saw faces familiar yet unknown. His mind, its eidetic memory always organizing his thoughts, cried out that he was not asleep—he was awake—but he remained unable to move, even to twitch his little finger. Through closed eyes, he watched as gray shapes floated across the room. Rob's handsome face contorted before him, eyes widening, cheeks sunken. Heather's golden hair, always soft and angelic, blew around her face in a disorganized mess, disrupted by an unfelt tornadic wind that moved through the room and wrapped around her. Tony, Dylan's best friend, howled in silence at some graphic practical joke unintelligible to Dylan. Panic lay next to him on the soft down pillow, refusing to allow him any control.

Voices whispered sounds, but words failed to emerge through the fog, and yet he understood the questions. Why had he called the meeting? What were his partners to expect from him? How had he made decisions without their consent? The inquiries raced past him, swirling through his head. Questions he had no answers for, but questions he knew would be asked. And in the distant background, as always, his father stood in silent disapproval. In his mind, Dylan prayed for the blessed sound of his alarm clock!

• • •

January 7, 7:00 a.m.

He stood in the steamy bathroom, leaning against the sink, staring at his reflection. It was a daily ritual he wished he could stop, and yet every day the practice returned. Today he saw his father's face staring back at him, questioning his choice of careers. Dylan's resemblance to his father amazed everyone. It was as if the day after his father died, Dylan had become him. At six feet four inches tall, with the same tousled brown hair that shimmered like milk chocolate and deep brown eyes with tiny wheat-colored flecks, Dylan was his father in both appearance and gestures. To Dylan's credit, however, he had not become his father in attitude or practice. He remained his own person, pursuing his own dreams.

Dylan sighed and picked up the razor to remove his light brown stubble. He liked the feel of the razor close to his face; it gave him the closeness of the shave and yet the sense of danger as it rode near to his jugular.

"Shit!" Dylan growled as his razor drew blood. He ripped off a shred of toilet paper and slapped it on the cut. He couldn't be late for work. Not today.

"Shit!" he exploded again as the blood soaked through the flimsy bandage.

Monday morning and the clock read 7:25. He had to be out the door in five minutes to make the meeting he himself had called the night before. It promised to be one hell of a session, and he knew it could go in one of two directions—a wild success or a dreadful failure.

Dylan, the twenty-three-year-old President and CEO of MobiCelus, led one of the hottest startups in Massachusetts. In just one year, this mobile computing consulting firm had muscled its way into the limelight, snagging some of the country's most exciting companies as its clients. Positive profiles in *The Boston Globe* and, most recently, *The Wall Street Journal*, blew work through the doors at MobiCelus, keeping its hundred-plus employees overworked and well-paid.

Now, Dylan was about to close a deal to sell MobiCelus to a bigger and better-known technology firm. If he succeeded, he and his three partners would emerge with bank accounts as big as some of their clients' egos. Plus, they would have the resources they would need to do the large-scale, innovative projects that, to this point, had been beyond their reach.

Dylan had met Art Williams, the head of Mantric Technology Solutions, at a Silicon Valley conference the previous fall. What Dylan thought of as simply a polite conversation quickly escalated, and, several telephone calls later, a proposal Dylan could not refuse unfolded before him.

He rubbed a towel over his thick brown hair and brushed it into place. He threw on a shirt, then sprinted to the door, grabbing his black leather jacket off its hook. He jumped into his silver Toyota Prius parked in the alley behind his condo and glanced at the clock. Seven thirty-five. It was going to be close.

The night before, he had e-mailed each partner and told them to meet him at eight o'clock—no excuses. "I'll explain tomorrow," the e-mail said. "It's a sensitive matter, and I want you all to hear about it at the same time." Since then, he'd avoided the phone, not wanting to deal with their questions.

Dylan's ability to compartmentalize every aspect of his life startled people when they first met him, but, as relationships grew, friends, acquaintances, and even lovers appreciated the way he focused his attention on any immediate problem at hand. He spoke to everyone as if he or she was the only person in the world. His ability to focus his attention, coupled with his startling memory recall, were skills he put to their best use now as he went over the agenda for the meeting just minutes away, while at the same time juggling traffic and avoiding stops and goes.

Rush-hour traffic seemed unusually heavy for a cold January morning. Dylan glanced out through the frosty window at the Public Garden Lagoon. In the summer, swan boats and tourists filled the park. Now it was empty of water and people—a sure sign of a prolonged winter. He and his friend Tony had discussed the mobile computing revolution during many strolls through the garden.

Dylan and Tony Caruso met at the Massachusetts Institute of Technology, where both had earned degrees in Computer Science. Tony was barely seventeen when he entered MIT, but his irreverence and acute understanding of business and technology had allowed him to cruise easily through every class. His curly brown hair usually looked like it needed a good scrub, and his T-shirts screamed out his cocky humor. His favorite: "MIT: A great party with one hell of a cover charge."

Tony intimidated Dylan at first, but soon a deep friendship evolved. They planned to go on for their master's degrees together after graduation in the spring of 2009, but the breakthroughs in mobile technologies changed those plans. The astounding success of Apple's iPhone and Google's Android smartphones captivated their imaginations. It wasn't just the money they envied; it was the *cool*. They ached to be in on the action.

Dylan and Tony had met their partners, Rob Townsend and Heather Carter, nearly four years earlier at a party on Beacon Hill. Rob, finishing up his MBA at the Harvard Business School, was top-of-the-class smart and knew it. Six feet tall and wiry, Rob was forever sweeping a shock of blond hair off his face. Offers poured in from such renowned companies as Goldman Sachs and McKinsey, but Rob wasn't interested. Too old-school. His goal was twofold: to do something incredible as part of a new venture, and to make a killing. The success of mobile computing entrepreneurs had not gone unnoticed, and Rob bet he would be on top.

Heather finished her degree with a concentration in digital media at RISD, the Rhode Island School of Design—or "Riz-dee" as it's universally known. Her artistic skills notwithstanding, she was always intrigued by the intersection of design and technology. Heather's astute intuition quickly recognized that mobile phones were replacing computers in many still uncounted ways, and she focused on landing a job that would allow her to work on cutting-edge displays and visual apps. Her comments in board meetings were often insightful, raising issues that others had overlooked.

Heather's striking beauty showed in her green eyes, blonde hair, and lean, athletic build, but her most outstanding feature was a nose just a shade off-kilter. No one ever asked her about it, of course, but they didn't need to. She loved to tell the story of how she and her three brothers walloped a group of neighborhood bullies in an epic street hockey brawl that left her with a broken nose. The end result only added to her allure. In fact, Dylan was just about to ask Heather out when Rob barged in to introduce himself and beat him to it, placing Dylan in the back seat for her attention.

As the introductions and typical small talk gave way to post-graduation plans, the four discovered their shared passion for mobile computing. Engrossed in their conversation, they looked up to see an empty room and a mildly annoyed host waiting for the stragglers to leave so he could go to bed. They had, by that time, already decided to go into business together.

Lost in his thoughts, Dylan was startled back to reality by the sound of a horn blaring behind him. He stepped on the gas and darted into the left lane to avoid the caravan of delivery trucks that always double-parked at this time of the morning. He glanced again at his watch as he headed across the Fort Point Channel towards MobiCelus's warehouse offices. He wheeled into his parking space, bolted from his car, and ran inside to the old freight elevator. The contraption burped twice before beginning its slow grind to the fourth floor.

Dylan stepped off the elevator at one minute past eight and hurried toward the conference room. He and his partners had conducted many meetings in this room. Tony almost always arrived early, busily fiddling with a prototype of some new smartphone or tablet. Heather and Rob always arrived together—and late. Today, though, all three sat in anticipation, each staring in different directions, trying to focus their attention while they waited. All conversation stopped the moment Dylan walked through the door.

As he looked around the room, Heather smiled and motioned mysteriously to her face. "What?" he mouthed to her, when he realized he still had toilet paper stuck to his chin. He sheepishly removed it and sat down at the head of the table.

"So Dylan, what's the big mystery?" Rob asked, breaking the silence.

"I have some big news, incredible news, really," he began. His eyes darted around the room from one to another, and he cleared his throat. "And I know you're going to be very excited when you hear it."

As Dylan fumbled and hesitated, Tony piped up, "For God's sake, Dylan, just tell us already!"

Dylan took a deep breath and blurted, "Mantric Technology Solutions has offered to buy MobiCelus for two million dollars in cash and 300,000 shares of common stock. The deal could be worth a total of fourteen million dollars. Maybe more."

Heather gasped. Tony let go of his smartphone and sat up straight in his chair. Rob quickly tapped on the calculator app on his own phone and began doing the math as his mouth fell open in amazement.

"Our dream is about to come true," Dylan continued.

Tony screamed, "No way! No *fucking* way! You're kidding us— right?"

"Oh my God!" Heather said loudly. She glanced at a now-grinning Rob and clapped her hands together.

"Mantric—that's Art Williams in New York—right? The guy who took ProTechSure public?" Rob asked.

Dylan exhaled. "Yeah." Their excitement came as a huge relief. In the back of his mind, he had harbored a fear that they might have a desire to maintain total control of their brainchild, à la Bill Gates and Paul Allen at Microsoft or Mark Zuckerberg at Facebook. Just as ProTechSure Group, the most successful technology services firm to ever go public, had wowed the group of friends, they saw themselves following that same path. Hundreds of people became millionaires. Like so many technology companies, the name was a compilation of everything it professed to be: Profit + Technology + Assurance = ProTechSure.

Tony immediately saw why Williams must have selected the word "Mantric." It was the adjective form of mantra, and so was meant to suggest that the company had mystical powers. Tony, of course, had been the one to come up with MobiCelus, though he initially wanted to call the company MobiCelu$—or so he'd said. He recalled the name had elicited groans from the partners. "It's still just so fucking unbelievable," Tony said now. "Jeez, to think we could be doing really cool stuff and rolling in the green before we're even thirty."

"Yeah, and we haven't even suffered yet," Heather grinned.

Mantric, which specialized in using cloud computing and other web-based technologies to run systems for major corporations, was said to be planning an initial public offering. Rumor had it Mantric would float its IPO within the year.

"So here's the deal," Dylan resumed. "Besides access to their kick-ass resources and technology, we're talking an incredible upside opportunity with the stock. Based on what Art told me about Mantric's growth and comparing the company to its public counterparts, I think the stock could be worth forty to fifty dollars a share within eighteen months. And who knows how much higher it'll go after that?"

"So you're saying, Dylan, that the deal, all told, could be worth maybe seventeen million dollars, or even more?" Rob spoke without looking up from his calculator.

"That's right. No guarantees, of course, but even a worst-case scenario winds up being pretty impressive. Let's say the stock ends up being worth just thirty dollars a share. That's nine million dollars, plus we get some cash up front." Dylan let the numbers sink in for a moment. "So what do you all think?"

"Are you crazy?" Tony yelled, raising his hands in the air. "What's to think about? We get to do the coolest work in the world and we're going to be rich!"

"Heather? Any thoughts?"

"I like this deal. I could design some great stuff with more resources. And the cash alone comes to almost half a million, up front, for each of us—right?"

"It's 400,000 dollars before taxes for the three of us," Rob quickly interjected, "and 800,000 dollars for Dylan," factoring in Dylan's majority stake in MobiCelus. "Anybody wanna bet on where the stock will end up?" Rob's question elicited smiles across the table.

"And if, after the IPO, the 300,000 shares become worth, say, fifty dollars a share," Heather calculated, picking up on Rob's question.

"That's at least another three-point-five million dollars for each of us."

"Fucking A is what I say!" Tony exploded.

Everyone burst out laughing.

"Then I can assume everyone is in agreement? If that's a go, I'll contact Art and we'll move this forward as quickly as possible," Dylan said.

Everyone nodded quickly.

Dylan added, "I'm going to go let Rich and Matt know what's going on."

He left the conference room and smiled as he heard an explosion of laughter behind him. The last comment he heard was Rob making a bet about how quickly Dylan could consummate the deal.

• • •

January 7, 9:30 a.m. Boston

Dylan poked his head around the partially opened door in Rich Linderman's office to see him hunched over a side desk, working his computer with one hand and an old desk calculator with the other. The young man's attention was focused on the current financial status report.

Dylan had hired Rich soon after they launched MobiCelus to run the administrative side of the firm. As it grew and they hired a few more staff people, Rich asked if he could be put in charge of the firm's finances. His partners, particularly Rob, had been concerned about putting him in such an important role, and Dylan thought it would be a stretch, but Rich had proven himself. Sure, he was a bit quirky. But when he cut the operating costs of MobiCelus in his first year by 20 percent, even Rob had to admit he was wrong.

As MobiCelus's controller, Rich did not hold a chair at the conference table unless invited, but Dylan valued Rich's opinion on the financial health of the company. He graduated tenth in his class at Wharton, and Dylan had snapped him up after their first interview. An introvert, Rich dedicated his time at the office to the business of MobiCelus, and Dylan was convinced Rich was one of the lynchpins that kept the others on the straight and narrow. There were never any questions about fuzzy financial reports—every piece of information presented by Rich Linderman could be counted on for its accuracy and reliability.

Dylan coughed in order to get Rich's attention but not startle him. Rich raised his hand, but did not turn around for another fifteen seconds. When he did, he shoved his glasses—which had slid down to the end of his nose—back up toward his forehead, where they perched precariously, ready to slide back down with one errant move.

Rich smiled. "Oh, hi, Dylan. Sorry, I didn't realize it was you. I was working on a touchy problem. What can I do for you?"

Dylan walked over to the desk and sat across from Rich. He noticed Rich had on the very same shirt he had worn the last time he'd seen him. "Just wanted to alert you to something big that's going to be happening in the next few weeks."

"Would that be the Mantric offer?" Rich asked.

Dylan sat up, startled. "How in the world did you know that? I haven't even accepted the offer yet."

"Oh, their financial person, Christine something or other, called late Friday and said she was going to want to access our financials. She was pretty vague, but mentioned the offer. Of course, I refused to give her access to anything because I don't know her from Adam—or Eve." He smiled at his weak attempt at humor.

Dylan stared at the wall behind Rich, wondering why in the world anyone from Mantric would go around him, especially before the offer was even accepted.

"Er, that's what I was working on when you came in." Rich stumbled over his words. "It was late Friday, and I tried to contact you, but you weren't around. I guess I should have e-mailed you or something. I just figured since I wasn't giving her any information it could wait until today, and then I got tied up this morning in reviewing the financials to make sure everything was okay. I hope I was right in not giving any information out."

"Oh, yes, absolutely, you were right. Um, did she say she would be calling again?" Dylan asked.

"Yeah, she said she'd get back to me, but didn't say when."

"Okay, Rich. Do me a favor—if she calls back, direct her to me. Okay?"

"Sure. Hey, this looks like it could really be good for the company and all of us—right?"

Dylan heard some trepidation in Rich's question. "Yeah, it could be just that. Thanks for letting me know about Christine's call."

He rose to leave, not sure whether to call Art or Christine or just wait. He considered his options as he wandered down the hall to see Matt Smith. Matt was one of MobiCelus's senior consultants, well respected by his peers and clients alike. Matt graduated near the top of his class at Stanford before moving east, and when it came to dealing with problems and sorting out answers, Dylan was comfortable bringing pithy issues to Matt's attention. But this information about Mantric's CFO left him baffled, and he decided not to pursue it with Matt at this time.

Matt's office sparkled with organization. He knew where every file, every document—hell, every paper clip—was located. Dylan walked in and chuckled because he saw a wet ring of coffee on the table just as Matt raised the cup to his lips.

"Hmm. Getting sloppy in your old age?" He pointed to the coffee ring.

Matt quickly wiped it with a napkin. "Oops, sorry 'bout that," he said, smiling. "What's up?"

Dylan sat across from him and told him about the pending acquisition, but left out the part about Christine's call to Rich.

"Hey! That's great news. Do you have a date when this will happen?"

Dylan just shook his head. "Not definitely. I'll be calling Art Williams as soon as I get back to my office and start the ball rolling. I just wanted to let everyone know what was in the wind so no one would be blindsided." Dylan questioned the veracity of his own words.

"This is exciting. To be in on something like this at the very beginning!"

Dylan heard the energy in Matt's voice. "Yes, it is."

"Then great! I'll look forward to it. Let me know what I can do to help make it a smooth transition."

Dylan rose to leave. "I'll be sure to do that." He walked back to his office and sat at the desk, his hand hovering over his computer keyboard. He called Art Williams's private line.

"Art Williams here."

"Art, Dylan Johnson. I just wanted you to know I spoke with my partners, and we're a 'go' if you are."

"Hey, that's great! We'll start to carve out the details. Can I get back to you in the next day or two?"

"Absolutely. And, by the way, my controller tells me your CFO, Christine Rohnmann, called and asked him for our financials. I thought that was a little premature and wondered why she didn't come to me for that information."

Dylan heard a brief silence before Art responded. "Oh—sorry about that. I don't know what Christine was thinking. I'll be sure to mention to her that in the future she should use better judgment."

"Thanks. I appreciate that, and I'll look forward to talking with you again soon."

He released the call just as Rich Linderman came in and approached him. "Dylan, I don't think I mentioned it, but I did say something to Rob about Christine's call. He was the only person here on Friday night, but he seemed to be in a hurry and I don't think he paid much attention to me. And I was a little frazzled by the call."

Dylan thought for a moment and then asked, "How did Rob respond?"

"Basically, he waved me off. Said he had some place to go. Something about meeting a filly, if that makes any sense. Maybe he had a hot date."

"Thanks, Rich. Let's just keep this to ourselves. I don't want too many people knowing about this acquisition until it's finalized."

Rich gave him a thumbs-up sign and nodded, leaving the room as quietly as he had arrived.

Chapter 2

Art Williams hung up the phone, then dialed Christine's private line. "Christine, what in the hell are you doing, calling MobiCelus's controller? I just got off the phone with Dylan, and he wanted to know why you didn't go through him."

"Calm down, Art. That snarky little controller refused to give me any info. So no harm, no foul."

"Christine, don't go rogue on me. MobiCelus has some valuable clients, and we don't want to fuck anything up until this deal is signed and sealed."

"Okay, okay. When are you going to tell the rest of the staff?"

"No time like the present. I'll gather them in the conference room in thirty minutes. Be there."

He hung up the phone and called his administrative assistant. "Michelle, gather up the managers and have them meet in the conference room in thirty minutes. I have an announcement, and I want everyone there."

Thirty minutes later Art and Christine walked into the conference room, where a startled and nervous group of managers gathered around the table, sitting in silence.

"I'll make this short so everyone can get back to work," Art said. "You may have heard some rumblings about some changes, so let me set you all at ease. Mantric has made an offer to buy MobiCelus. Since you are all surfing the web constantly, I'm sure you know of this company. I've spoken with the CEO, Dylan Johnson, and his team has agreed, in principle, to our offer. We'll be finalizing the contract in the next few weeks, so many of you will be seeing new faces around here. They are Boston-based and will keep a presence in that office—at least for now. Eventually we hope to move all aspects of the company here, but that will not be in our first phase. Some of you will be doing some traveling

11

back and forth over the next few months, so be prepared for that. Any questions?" He scanned the sea of wide eyes staring back at him.

Sandeep Nigam, Chief Technology Officer, slowly raised his hand. "Excuse me, Mr. Williams. Can you tell us how this acquisition will occur with regard to our departments?"

Sandeep was a legend. Born in India, he had attended the prestigious India Institute of Technology. After moving to the U.S., Sandeep quickly established himself as a technology genius and became legendary in technology circles. He was one of the original engineers at Apple, where he made his initial mark before establishing his credentials at Google. Then Art Williams had recruited him to join Mantric. And yet, as smart as he was, Sandeep's lack of self-confidence hindered his growth into other opportunities. He'd climbed to his current position and seemed perfectly happy to remain there, but he was always looking over his shoulder.

"I don't have a lot of details because we haven't finalized them. However, in your case, we will be bringing Tony Caruso into the department. He is currently your counterpart at MobiCelus, and he will be reporting to you. My understanding is that he is brilliant in mobile computing, especially in the design and development of new products, so I'm sure he will be an asset. Any other questions? If not, Christine and I will be filling you in as we bring this down to the wire. Shouldn't be much longer. As you know, we are also working on the IPO, and so you can all expect some very busy months ahead. Thank you for your time."

Art did not wait for any further questions. He nodded to Christine, who gathered up her papers and rose from the table, not acknowledging anyone.

• • •

Sandeep hurried out of the conference room, close behind Art and Christine, and rushed back to his office. He closed the door and sat at his desk, where he immediately spun around to the side table and opened up his browser.

He Googled "Tony Caruso." Several hits appeared before him, and he began with the first—a reference to MobiCelus and its officers, with a brief history of the company. The second and third hits displayed papers Tony had published regarding the fallibility of some mobile devices. Sandeep scrolled through five more postings but garnered nothing specific about the man, only that his brilliance would bear watching.

Sandeep closed his browser and pushed himself back to the desk, where he remained deep in thought for the remainder of the day.

Chapter 3

With the terms of the acquisition set, things moved quickly. Positions changed, some for the better, some not. Dylan had watched as Art skillfully placed people in the roles he felt best suited them in the growing organization, and although Dylan did not agree with everything, he stood by and quietly watched.

The plans had moved with swift accuracy since earlier in the month when everyone agreed to the acquisition. Art Williams had just completed the initial registration with the SEC, and while they awaited approval, the positions in the Boston office seemed to be on a merry-go-round.

Dylan looked out the window of his office, watching the winter storm pelt the windows. Large snowflakes banded together in heavy clumps that slithered down the frosted glass. He had received a request from Christine Rohnmann for the financial information, which he provided through Rich. Dylan found her to be aloof and removed, but thought she was probably annoyed with him for mentioning her premature request for financial information to Art.

His distant thoughts muffled the knock on his door.

"Hey!" Tony called.

Dylan spun around to see his best friend, disheveled and unkempt, standing across from him. Tony Caruso stood five foot seven in his stocking feet. He was thin to the point of being described as "gaunt," and his light brown hair and skin told of his northern Italian background.

"Hey!" Dylan said, smiling. "What's up?"

"Just got off the phone with Sandeep Nigam at Mantric. He tells me I will be reporting directly to him."

Dylan showed his surprise. "I was not aware of that." He chewed the inside of his cheek. "Is that a problem?"

"Nope, not at all. He has a great reputation, and besides, if I don't have to make the heavy decisions, it opens me up for some of my own work."

"You got something going on the side?" Dylan asked with a smirk. Tony always had something going on the side.

"Actually, I do, but it's in such a preliminary stage I'm not ready to talk about it. Doing some research with a guy in New Jersey. When I get it a little further along, I'll send you something on it. I value your comments, you know."

"Thanks. I'll look forward to giving you my thoughts. And you're sure you're okay with being second banana?"

Tony threw a wad of paper in the air and caught it. "Yep. Not a problem. Just thought you should know." He threw the wad of paper at Dylan, who caught it with his left hand. "Nice catch," Tony said, and turned and left the office.

Dylan had not met the full Mantric senior staff, and yet his own staff members were getting calls without his involvement. He wondered about this as he turned back to watch the snow drizzle down the window.

• • •

January 21, 10:00 a.m. Boston

Rob Townsend had been named Senior Vice President of Operations for Mantric. While it was a new role at Mantric, and he hadn't even been given a formal job description, he really didn't care. He felt it fit well with his Harvard MBA. Rob was sitting behind his desk working on a spreadsheet when Heather walked in.

"What are you doing?" she asked, smiling. "Planning on how you're going to spend those millions?" The team continued to reel over the potential windfall of earnings they anticipated as a result of the acquisition by Mantric.

Rob quickly closed the spreadsheet and looked up. "Yeah, this is almost too good to be true. You don't think anything can happen to jinx the deal, do you?" He took the papers he had been working on and threw them into the top right-hand desk drawer.

Heather scrunched up her crooked nose and considered his question. "Why would you think that? Have you heard something that might indicate a problem?"

"No, no! I've just been working out some different scenarios, and it sometimes seems almost impossible."

"You've been doodling with numbers ever since Dylan told us about this. He's working with Art Williams—jeez—those Mantric people have been all over this building. Of course, nothing is going to go wrong. Dylan wouldn't let that happen to us."

"Right. Dylan." Rob quickly looked up at Heather and realized she was annoyed with his line of questioning. "How about lunch?"

Heather smiled. "Sounds good!"

Rob locked his desk, rose, and quickly walked around to take Heather's elbow and direct her away from the office.

"Were you working on something specific?" Heather asked.

"No! Quit bugging me!" Rob snapped.

Heather removed her arm from his hand and stepped away from him.

Across the hall, Dylan watched as Heather pulled away from Rob. *Hmm,* he wondered. *What's that all about?*

• • •

January 21, 11:00 a.m. Boston

Tony Caruso watched over the Hyperfōn account like a mother hen clucking over its chicks. Before MobiCelus was acquired, Hyperfōn was MobiCelus's biggest client. With the acquisition all but official, it transferred to Mantric, but Tony remained at its helm.

Hyperfōn presented a slick new business design geared to transform the way consumers used their smartphones. Hyperfōn members would create their own personal "hyperspace" with informative and custom-designed interactive applications called "tiles" that reflected their personal interests and lifestyles. The concept advanced beyond Apple's iPhone, which had generic websites crunched onto a mobile screen. These "tiles" could easily be sent via phone to other Hyperfōn members, allowing communities of friends to quickly embrace, share, and use whatever suited their unique interests. And since new smartphones were being launched every month with different technologies, Hyperfōn had cleverly developed a state-of-the-art adaptive platform that would work on any phone.

Dylan and Rob had worked hard on developing Hyperfōn's strategy, and before the acquisition, Dylan transferred total control of the client to Tony. Tony selected Matt Smith as his second, to focus full attention on the imminent web-based marketing campaign. But it was Tony's extraordinary programming skills that had made Hyperfōn's technology possible. Rob and Dylan remained involved, but in the background.

Tony scratched his head, unsure of something he had just noticed, when Matt walked into his office. "Hey—Tony. You left a message. You wanted to see me?"

Tony looked up from his computer. "Yeah. Did you do something to the account report for Hyperfōn?"

Matt frowned. "No, I haven't done anything with Hyperfōn in about a week. There have been so many Mantric people stopping into my office without notice, just to ask a question, I haven't really had a chance to do anything with Hyperfōn. Why, what's up?"

"I'm not sure, but I went into the account files today, just to get ready for the next few weeks when we launch the campaign, and it seems like some of the information has been accessed. There are very few of us who have access to those files, and I can't imagine who would be opening them."

"Did you talk to Dylan?" Matt asked. "Maybe he needed to do something."

"Not like him to keep me out of the loop. But hey, listen—maybe it's just my imagination. I'll talk to Dylan and Rob and see if they did something."

Matt nodded his head. "I tell ya, there are so many things happening all at once, it's hard to tell what's being done to what! Let me know when you want to get back into this. That campaign is going to be on us before we know it."

"Yeah, let's plan on getting back into it tomorrow. Let's meet here at nine a.m."

Matt pulled out his smartphone and noted the appointment, then shoved it back into his pocket. "See you then. Let me know if you want me to bring anything."

"Right." Tony watched Matt as he left the office. Sure he was alone, he turned back to the computer and looked at the file list. *Matt's right. Too many things happening at once—too many people involved,* he thought, and closed the file.

Chapter 4

A late-winter storm had formed off the coast of the Carolinas and strengthened dramatically as it moved up the coast and raged through Boston. A classic nor'easter.

The weather became the lead story on every news station imaginable, with the forecasters absolutely giddy about the prospect of the storm racing up the coast, dumping not inches but feet of snow in its aftermath—snarling traffic, closing airports and train stations, and making life generally miserable for everyone. In this case, their forecasts were spot-on. Rob parked his new blue Ferrari California in the first-floor garage of the MobiCelus building, taking a spot farthest away from any other vehicles. As he exited the car, he stamped his feet on the concrete floor of the garage to ward off the cold air that swirled around him. He lifted the trunk lid and retrieved a soft woolen cloth from a plastic bag and began brushing the snow from the car.

"Damn!" he said to no one in particular. "I can't believe we're getting a storm like this right after I bought this beauty. That ass in the KIA almost slammed into me!"

He stood back and looked at the car, dabbing here and wiping there to remove every vestige of snow from its shiny exterior. "Yeah, a magnet, for sure!" He reopened the trunk, laid the cloth flat on the carpet inside to dry, and locked the car.

He hurried through the cold garage to the far side of the building, where he rang for the old service elevator. It lumbered slowly down toward him. He pushed the button for the fourth floor, and as the elevator began its crawl up, he fingered the car keys in his pocket and smiled.

The elevator stopped at the fourth floor and Rob exited, turned left, and walked to his office. The storm had left the bullpen almost empty, except for the few brave souls who lived close to the building. Rob looked around at those who now worked double assignments. Every day, as the date of the official announcement of the acquisition approached, he knew there could be no mistakes, no last-minute problems that might arise and upset the final deal. He had not worked this long and hard to watch everything fall around him.

He entered his office, removed his silk scarf and camelhair coat, carefully hung them up in the closet, and rubbed his hands together to ward off the final remainder of cold. He ran his fingers through his blond hair, turned on his computer and saw three messages—Heather, Dylan, and Molly—his secretary. He dialed Molly.

• • •

February 15, 10:00 a.m. Boston

Heather scanned the multiple flat-panel displays on a table that occupied much of her office, scrutinizing the various designs. Tony and Matt stood on either side of her, following the graceful line made by her slender finger as she drew their attention from one design to another.

"I like this one best, but you two have to select maybe three designs to present to Joe Ferrano. Hyperfōn is his baby, and he will have to make the final decision on the overall appearance of these tiles."

Matt leaned forward and studied all of the samples on the screens. "I agree with you. I think this one is the best, but there are going to have to be a lot of tile styles once this thing gets moving, so we do want to present him with some initial choices and still have a lot of designs as backup."

"Hey, you guys, I leave this decision up to you. I'm the geek, remember?" Tony remained removed from the two of them, but kept his eye on the displays.

Heather and Matt looked at each other, then at him. Heather laughed. "Yeah, right. Like you wouldn't put your two cents worth in if you didn't agree. Seriously, Tony, we all have to be in agreement on this. Joe's been really cool about letting us go with our ideas and not hovering over us, but he's no fool. If we don't give him something exceptional, he'll nail it immediately."

Tony nodded in agreement. "Of course, you're right. I don't disagree with anything you've got here. Have you talked to Dylan or Rob about these choices?"

"Not yet. I wanted some strength in numbers. If you guys don't agree with me, then I have to go back to the drawing board." She looked at her watch and then let her eyes wander over to the computer on her desk.

Tony caught her glance. "So why don't you call one of them? I saw Dylan earlier this morning when he arrived. Haven't seen Rob yet. Have you?"

It was an awkward moment. Tony knew Heather and Rob were an item, but the atmosphere around them recently seemed cool. He hated getting into personal lives and avoided asking the obvious questions. Now he felt intrusive.

Heather smiled. She knew what was going through his mind. "No, I haven't heard from him. He told me he was picking up a new car last night, so I expect he will be driving very carefully, if you know what I mean." She nodded toward the window where enormous snowflakes clumped and slid down, pulled by their own weight.

Tony changed the subject. "Okay, I think we agree with you on the best designs to present to Joe. Let me know when you talk to Dylan and Rob, then e-mail me the designs, and I'll put them in the presentation folder. In the meantime, we'll leave you and get back to our other projects."

Heather knew what Tony meant by "other projects." He always kept one step ahead of technology, and although she did not know what he was working on, she was sure it would be huge and he would tell them about it when the time was right. She did not question him.

"Right. I'll probably get back to you later today." She walked them to the door and listened to their conversation until they disappeared down the hallway toward their offices. She looked at her watch again. Ten-thirty, and she still had not heard from Rob. Their conversation the night before had been terse, and she regretted sticking her nose into his business, but she felt the car purchase was premature. He made a point of telling her, in very short sentences, that it was not her business, and their conversation ended abruptly.

Heather walked to the end of the hallway and looked around the corner. At the other end of the hall, she saw Rob in front of his office. His back was to her, but she noticed the very pretty Molly standing by him, laughing. She watched as Rob touched her lightly on the shoulder.

• • •

February 15, 10:30 a.m. Boston

Dylan looked up at the sound of a knock. He did not often close his door, except during a meeting, so it startled him that someone would knock.

"Hey, got a minute?" Tony said, walking in without being invited.

"For you? Always. What's up?"

Tony hesitated. "Have you given the Mantric people any access to our files?"

Puzzled, Dylan shook his head. "No. Why would I do that? What's up?"

Tony sat down across from him and took a deep breath. "There are just so many people here, total strangers showing up, asking questions. It just feels odd."

Dylan looked at his friend for a moment in silence. "Tony, what's up?" he asked again.

"It's probably nothing, but several times over the past few weeks, since the Mantric group has been here, I've sensed that someone has been meddling with files. My major project is Hyperfōn, and a few times I've felt like things in the files have been out of order, or someone has accessed them. I've waited to tell you, thinking it was just my imagination. Matt doesn't know anything about it, and I'm sure if you or Rob were doing anything, you'd let me know."

"Well, I certainly haven't had the time to do anything other than focus on the transition. Is there anything missing?"

"No, not that I can tell. It just doesn't feel right when I go into the file. This is a really important account, and I want to be sure nothing goes wrong. Do you think any of their techno-geeks could have hacked in?"

Dylan sat forward and thought about Tony's words. "I can't imagine why they would do that. Hyperfōn and all of our other clients are becoming part of Mantric, and there will probably be a lot more people with access. I've confirmed with Art that you're the primary and Matt the secondary on that account, and he's agreed you two are the best ones to handle it because of your experience and your relationship with Joe Ferrano."

Tony sat back and nodded. "Yeah, you're probably right. I guess I'm just anxious about this whole thing. It's pretty important to all of us."

"Thanks for asking about this, Tony, but I really don't think we need to worry."

He smiled and left the room. Dylan sat back and wondered.

Chapter 5

It was an unusually warm day for early March in Manhattan. People were dressed more for spring than for winter, bringing a smile to Dylan's face as he walked through the maze of high-rise buildings.

Mantric's New York headquarters occupied five floors of a forty-six-story green glass skyscraper located in downtown Manhattan on West 19th Street, not far from the Hudson River. The company shared the building with an assortment of financial services and management consulting firms. With its modern design, sleek furnishings, and river views, it made MobiCelus's Boston office look like little more than the run-down factory it was.

Gossipy stories about the firm's beginnings were the talk of the technology world. CEO Art Williams had pitched Mantric's first deal to a major global insurance firm. Although everything Art described was essentially hypothetical, the insurance firm bit anyway, heady at the thought of the money to be made in the "clouds," so to speak, and in thirty days he had assembled a staff of nearly 500 low-cost Indian software engineers to launch the project. True to form, Williams also hired a publicist to play up the win and the enormous cost reductions the insurance firm would realize. It worked, and Mantric's phones rang off the hook.

Now, the firm had grown to some 10,000 employees around the world, including India and China. But the two-year-old company had a mixed reputation. Its innovative new client solutions, incorporating technologies such as cloud computing, made it a business media darling by leveraging low-cost labor to achieve huge savings for clients and equally huge profits for Mantric. But liberal politicians and the public media lambasted the firm for shipping thousands of U.S. jobs overseas and for incorporating itself in tax-friendly Bermuda. Nevertheless, its success was real and its IPO imminent.

Dylan stepped into the elevator. The doors closed behind him, and the voice sensor blinked in acknowledgement as he announced, "Twenty-fifth floor." He smiled, remembering his bewilderment the first time he rode this elevator. Had another passenger not entered directly behind him, it could have been embarrassing as he searched for a way to make it rise.

The elevator glided smoothly up to the twenty-fifth floor, and when the doors opened, Dylan stepped into the reception area: a virtual shrine to the very latest technological marvels—from a 3-D high-definition screen that occupied nearly an entire wall to a voice-activated computer consisting of nothing more than a razor-thin flat HD panel.

Stenciled on the wall across from the reception desk were famous quotes from visionaries like Gordon Moore, the Intel cofounder who, back in 1965, stated his famous law that the number of transistors that could be placed on an integrated circuit or chip would double approximately every two years while the cost of a given amount of computing power would fall by 50 percent. At the time, Moore was thought to be crazy, but his prediction proved to be spot-on.

Silence ruled in the reception area, where thick carpets absorbed all sound, and the absence of human beings grabbed the visitor. Dylan walked over to a wall-sized screen displaying a rotating art collection, where an attractive female avatar appeared.

"Welcome, Mr. Johnson." A female voice spoke with a faint metallic ring. Soft music played in the background as she announced, "Mr. Williams will be with you momentarily."

Dylan found this "Big Brother" welcome somewhat disconcerting.

"While you are waiting," the avatar continued, "I will update you on how we are doing."

The avatar evaporated, replaced by a slowly spinning globe where the continents looked like integrated circuits. The globe began to pick up speed until it became a whirling blur that finally exploded to reveal the Mantric logo. The avatar's voice resumed, "In two short years, Mantric has grown faster than any other technology company in history." The logo pixelized into multicolored floating currencies that dribbled down into an enormous pile on the screen. "To date, our clients have saved over twenty billion dollars by entrusting their technologies to us."

"Hello, Dylan," a deep baritone voice called from behind, and Dylan spun around to find Art Williams walking toward him with a beaming smile and outstretched hand. At five feet ten inches tall and with a round protruding belly, the fifty-one-year-old did not look the part of a successful CEO. Streaks of gray wandered through the disheveled brown hair that brushed lightly across his collar. He wore the attire of technology geeks twenty-five years his junior. In his dark gray mock turtleneck pullover, blue jeans, and Nike running shoes, nobody would confuse Art Williams with the cool young techies he apparently aspired to be. Dylan mused that the costume didn't work.

"Pretty impressive, huh?" Art remarked as he motioned toward the screen.

"Very," said Dylan, attempting to hide his continued discomfort at the "Big Brother" effect.

"Come," Art said, taking Dylan's shoulder. "The team is waiting for you."

They entered the conference room where the executive committee had assembled, as well as Frank Crowley, Mantric's master internal technologist, who would be handling the virtual worldwide meeting. Art directed Dylan to a seat at the middle of the table.

"Dylan, I think you've already met a few of these people, but let's go around the table and have everybody introduce themselves."

Christine Rohnmann, tall and slender, with short brown hair cut in severe layers, was dressed in an expensive, conservative pinstripe suit. She wore a small pearl choker and pearl and diamond earrings—her statement of wealth, class, and control. After she had guided ProTechSure through the stages of going public, she earned her reputation as the female version of Attila the Hun and became Art's trusted first lieutenant. She was about to do the same at Mantric, cementing her role in the company.

"Hello, Christine," Dylan said politely. "Good to see you again."

She nodded, did not look at him, and said nothing.

"Hello, Dylan," said an Indian man who got up, walked over to him, and shook his hand. "I am Sandeep Nigam, Chief Technology Officer. It's a great pleasure to meet you. I admire the work you have been doing, and I'm very happy you are now part of our team."

"It's a pleasure to meet you. Tony Caruso speaks highly of you and your work." Dylan shook Sandeep's hand, wondering if he should have stood up as well. He observed that the wrinkled white button-down shirt, faded jeans, and Nikes that Sandeep wore worked, in this case, just fine.

"I return the compliment. He is quite brilliant."

He sensed a lack of enthusiasm in Sandeep's words, but wondered if it was just the heavy accent. Dylan watched the soft-spoken twenty-nine-year-old Indian, with hair so black it was almost blue and dark eyes that hovered between sad and humorous, and wondered how misleading appearances might be. Something about Sandeep set an uncomfortable tone, but Dylan could not put his finger on it.

Across the room away from the doorway, Ivan Venko, Mantric's Chief Security Officer, stood in absolute contrast to Sandeep. Ivan, pale and matchstick thin, was dressed totally in black—black suit, black turtleneck sweater, black shoes highly polished enough to reflect things in close proximity. In this digital world, he was responsible for keeping all Mantric's data secure. His pockmarked face, slicked-back hair, and constant scowl gave him a mysterious and unpleasant air. A headset curled around his left ear and extended halfway along his jaw. He had been trained as a security specialist in Prague, which in those days meant working for the Slovak Intelligence Service, or SIS: an organization accused of kidnapping, torture, and most infamously the assassination of Róbert Remiáš, a key figure in the trial against the SIS for the kidnapping of the president's son. Rumor had it that, following the break-up of Czechoslovakia in 1993, Ivan had fled the new republic to avoid retribution from the now-free Slovaks. Ivan made no attempt to move forward to meet Dylan, but remained away from the group, his dark eyes quickly glancing around the room in search of any problems.

One person remained at the table, and before she could speak, Art stepped in and introduced her. "Dylan, I'd like you to meet Stephanie Mathers, our Chief People Officer." At forty-one, Stephanie stood out like a sore thumb. She was short and overweight, and her hair was bleached several shades too light; the jacket of her business suit was one size too small and pulled tight over her ample chest.

"Welcome to Mantric," she said, shoving her hand toward Dylan with a bit too much enthusiasm. "I'd love to tell you all about the really special culture we have created here. We're all really, really looking forward to working with you and your staff. And if there is anything I can do—"

"Okay then," Art interrupted abruptly, cutting off the conversation. "Frank, let's get things started."

Since Mantric employees were scattered across three continents, the meeting was conducted over an encrypted virtual private network, or VPN, eliminating the possibility of access by any outsider.

Frank adjusted Art's chair to make sure Art was in view of the minicam perched on the table. Art sat down in front of his laptop, and the minor adjustment to his chair gave him the appearance of being taller than he was. He gave the nod to begin.

"Hello everyone," Art said. "You all know why we're gathered here today, but I want to make it official. I am very happy to let you know the initial registration with the SEC has occurred, and we now expect to go public with our IPO the week of May second. I have no doubt we will absolutely be the hottest offering in our sector."

Cheers resounded throughout the room and through the monitors.

"I don't need to remind you that, given our stock option plan, each of you watching or listening to me today have a—well, let's just say you all have a strong incentive to hear the details of our offering." Knowing chuckles erupted. "So here they are. We've filed to offer three million shares of common stock, and we expect the initial offering price to be between ten and twelve dollars per share."

With a click of the mouse, the room lights dimmed, and the plasma screen hanging on the wall behind Art, as well as on everyone's displays all over the globe, sprang to life. The program started with a slowly spinning Mantric logo, and soft strains of music floated in the background as animated images began to appear on the screen.

"Joining us today is Dylan Johnson, the former head of MobiCelus and now Senior Vice President of our mobile division. As you know, given the migration of computing to mobile devices, the acquisition of his company is a crucial element of how our offering will be viewed on Wall Street. Not to mention the addition of their revenues!" Art paused and smiled at Dylan. "Thanks to Dylan and his team, many of whom are watching this, we now have the capabilities we need to be the clear leader in the world market.

"We generated eighty-three million dollars in revenues in the second half of our first year of operations, a 670 percent increase over the first half." A chart appeared with a revenue curve shooting upward quarter by quarter, literally blowing the roof off the chart at the end. "As you know, we were projecting revenues for the next quarter of ninety-four million dollars, about a forty percent increase over last quarter. More importantly, we've become profitable a full quarter earlier than we expected. But, with the addition of MobiCelus, I think we can now hit 100 million dollars next quarter." The incline of the curve increased even more.

Dylan leaned forward and studied the chart. Would they really be able to add that much revenue that quickly? He made a silent note to himself to check these figures with Rich. Quickly, the chart dissolved, and the spinning logo returned.

The animated chart flipped over, revealing a NASDAQ listing of companies on the other side. Mantric was on it, with the trading symbol

MNTR, and rose off the page into large type. "You know, I'm not a greedy man," Art said, "but I think by the time we go public we'll be the hottest offering in our sector." The listing turned into a stock chart, with a starburst signifying an initial offering price of ten dollars a share, then rising up to twenty dollars, then forty dollars, and then it burst through the roof of the chart again. "And within three or four months, based on comparable valuations we've looked at, I expect our stock will be trading at about sixty dollars." Everyone applauded again.

"We are now officially in our quiet period. No one, and I mean no one, is to discuss our stock offering or our firm's performance with any outsider. Not to a reporter, not to an analyst, not to an investor, not to your mother. If that happens, the SEC will prohibit us from going public. I want to remind all of you that we must concentrate on our clients and our projects. I know this is an exciting time for us, but the worst thing we can do right now is take our eye off the ball.

"So the next step is to prepare for the road show, which will be the last ten days of April. The management team will be visiting investors in London, Los Angeles, San Francisco, Chicago, Dallas, Boston, and New York."

Dylan smiled at the mention of the road show. As the head of the mobile division, he would play an important role in Mantric's show as perhaps the world's most renowned expert on the future of mobile computing technologies. He had already started working on his presentation.

As Art began a discussion of the history of the company, Dylan felt a light buzz against his chest. He retrieved his cell phone and flipped it open to see Tony's signature response on the screen. A short text message darted across the screen, reading: "something odd, need 2 talk 2U." Then the message ended. Dylan's mind raced through what could be important enough for Tony to send such a cryptic message during this event. He snapped the phone shut and returned his attention to the meeting.

"This is only the beginning. Everyone knows the future lies in constantly developing and capitalizing on emerging technologies to achieve enormous competitive advantage—"

Art's voice droned on and on in the distance, while Dylan's mind returned to Tony's mysterious message. Dylan tucked the message into the back of his mind as Art completed the virtual meeting. Dylan pushed away from the desk and slid out of the chair. He wanted to talk to Rich about the numbers Art had rattled off, and then he had to find Tony.

"Good meeting, Art," he said and rose.

Art did not respond but wafted a casual wave through the air as he walked toward Ivan. Dylan watched as Ivan held out his cell phone toward Art. Art looked at the face of the phone, then looked back at Ivan, and just raised his eyebrows and pursed his lips as if contemplating some deep thought. Simultaneously he and Ivan slowly raised their eyes toward Dylan. Art smiled and waved again.

• • •

March 5, 2:00 p.m. Boston

The meeting ended at 11:15 that morning, and Dylan grabbed a cab to the airport. He'd called Tony but, as always, got his voice-mail. Dylan was anxious to get back to Boston and pursue his questions with both Tony and Rich. The twelve-thirty p.m. shuttle touched down just sixty minutes later, and by two o'clock, Dylan had settled in at his desk and dialed Rich's extension through the computer keypad. The screen opened, and Dylan saw Rich with his right side turned to the screen, his attention drawn to another computer on the credenza at the side of his desk. Dylan chuckled at Rich's ability to multitask with such focus.

Rich turned and smiled when he saw Dylan. "Oh, hi, Dylan. Meeting over? I only caught part of it."

"Yeah. Listen, Rich. Just a quick question. Did you hear Art's announcement about the revenue levels once Mantric goes public? Now, I'm not a financial wizard like you are, but did the numbers he announced sound solid to you?"

Rich waited for a few seconds before answering. "Well, I thought that part of the speech, which by the way I found terribly boring, was a wee bit of a stretch, but that's what Art does well, isn't it?"

Dylan chuckled. Only a number cruncher would find the meeting boring. "Yes," he said. "It is his strong point."

"Why do you ask?" Rich asked.

"Well, like you said, I thought that was a bit of stretch as well. Could you just do a cursory glance at the numbers?"

Rich leaned in toward the webcam. "You think there is something fishy about the numbers?"

"Good Lord, no!" Dylan responded quickly. "I just wanted to be sure, and you're the person I trust to do that research best."

Rich sat back. "Oh! Okay. I'll check into it and let you know what I find out, but I think he was just doing a little exaggerating to jazz the meeting—not that it worked for me." He mumbled the last comment half to himself, half to Dylan.

Dylan chuckled. "I'm just curious, but don't put a priority on it—just when you have a few minutes."

"Yeah, like *that* will happen anytime soon." Rich responded. "But I'll check the numbers for you."

They both clicked off the call at the same time. Dylan wasn't sure if he would understand the numbers, or what he was going to do with that information, especially if the numbers were exaggerated. He just had a nagging itch he couldn't scratch, and he needed to satisfy his curiosity. His fingers returned to the keyboard, and he deftly dialed Tony's number, which rolled into voice-mail again.

"Tony, don't you ever answer your phone? You sent me an odd little message. Want to talk about it? Call me."

"Dylan." The soft voice filled the quiet room. Dylan turned to see Heather standing in the doorway.

"Hi!"

Heather walked into the room and sat on the sofa. Dylan couldn't help but admire her slender legs as she crossed them. She looked out the window, then back toward Dylan. She noticed him looking at her legs, and her green eyes bored into his. "So," she said with a sly grin. "How do you think the meeting went?"

Dylan turned beet-red. "I think there may have been some exaggerations, although minor, but they were probably made to 'jazz' the audience." He could not believe he had just stolen a comment from Rich.

Heather laughed. "Yeah, I'd agree." She leaned forward and licked her lips. "But it is exciting, isn't it?"

A noise from the doorway caught their attention, and they both turned to see Rob standing at the door.

"Not interrupting anything, am I?" he asked in a peevish tone.

"Not at all," Heather interjected.

Dylan sensed a lowering of the emotional temperature in the room and wondered if it was reality or just wishful thinking on his part. Rob entered and threw himself into the chair across from Dylan. "We were just discussing the meeting," Dylan said.

"Yeah, I'll bet that was the most boring meeting you've ever attended." Rob did not address either person directly.

"Yeah, well, maybe for you, but not for the new people who haven't been in on this thing from the very beginning. Others might find it a bit more interesting." Heather responded. The chill deepened.

"Whoa," he answered, throwing his hands up. "I didn't mean anything by it!"

Dylan watched their reactions with interest. "Well, anyway," he said in a vain attempt to warm the room. "We should be preparing for the offering and making sure we have everything in place that we need to handle on our end. We also need to make sure Hyperfōn is brought on-line without a hitch."

"Hey!"

All three turned at the sound of the nasal voice at the doorway. Dylan asked, with the sort of exasperation one friend displays to another, "Don't you return your calls anymore?"

"Did I ever?" asked Tony, grinning. He stepped into the room and looked at Heather and Rob.

Heather rose first and walked to the doorway, then turned. "Looks like you guys have something to talk about, and I have work to do. Ciao!"

"Hey, wait a minute! How about lunch?" Rob jumped up and dashed out the door after Heather, who had disappeared down the hallway.

Dylan remained quiet for a moment, gathering his thoughts. "So—what was that mysterious message you sent me while I was in the meeting? You said there was something odd going on and you wanted to talk about it."

Tony stared out the window, then moved his chair closer to Dylan. He looked around to be sure no one else was there to hear him. "Listen, I don't usually pat myself on the back, but I'm pretty confident I know what I'm doing when it comes to technology."

Dylan raised his eyebrows high on his forehead and gave his friend a lopsided grin. "Yeah, I think I could agree with you on both those things!"

Tony glanced around again. "When the newest technology comes out, I'm always on top of it. I like to think my knowledge gives me an edge. Like, I'm virtually always around, even if you don't know it. I'm a teeny tiny software script in your electronic life." He pointed to Dylan's pocket where he kept his cell phone. "I see you, but you don't see me. But, when you need me, voilà! I magically appear."

The smile left Dylan's face, replaced with a frown. "I'm not following you, Tony."

Tony lowered his voice to a hushed whisper. "I'm beginning to sense I'm not the only one with a tiny software script in our collective electronic lives."

Dylan looked from Tony to his own pocket and back to Tony. "I'm still not sure I get you. Are you saying—?"

Tony grabbed his friend's wrist, pointed to the computer, and shook his head without further comment.

Dylan nodded and the conversation stopped. Tony left the room, and Dylan knew better than to push Tony for any explanation of his comments. Tony would give him the information when the time was right, and Dylan would just have to wait. He sat back and thought back to the meeting that morning and how it ended.

Chapter 6

The moment the acquisition closed, the various MobiCelus projects had transferred to Mantric at a breakneck pace. Dylan and his team were able to keep up. Tony and Matt continued their work on Hyperfōn and kept Joe Ferrano happy. Dylan looked at his watch as he walked into Tony's office. "You want to get something to drink?" he asked.

"Sure. What the hell." Tony put his work away. "How about that new place, Tamo? They have excellent sashimi!"

He and Tony were the last people in the building to leave as they stepped into the old elevator that grumbled and creaked as it slowly descended to the street. They hopped into Dylan's car for the short drive to the restaurant. They ordered beers, and then Dylan said, "So tell me. What's it like working with Sandeep instead of having complete autonomy?"

"Dylan, we've talked about this before, and, really, I'm good with the situation as it is. He leaves me to my own devices. I actually think he's avoiding me most of the time. Just asks me some short questions, then I don't hear from him for another week. He doesn't include me in a lot of meetings, but I am so okay with that! I'm knee-deep with Hyperfōn, and I'm involved with a new invention I've been working on and don't need the distractions that come with being the boss. Hey, don't worry, man!"

"The virtual keyboard?" Dylan asked, scanning the menu.

Tony took a long swig from his beer. "What? That is so passé. I'm working on something so revolutionary, if I can pull it off, it'll blow your mind."

"You want to give me a hint?"

"Nope, not just yet. Still too early. But remember I was telling you about when I was in Jersey catching up with an old friend—Brandon? He's the one who was fired from Microsoft for inventing, from scratch, an operating system that runs on anything, takes up next to no space, diagnoses and fixes itself, and even allows constant upgrades so you wouldn't have to buy a new version every couple of years."

Dylan raised his eyebrows in surprise. "What? You're kidding—right?"

"I know, it sounds crazy. Freakin' Microsoft!"

"Sounds too good to be true. What happened?"

"They hated it, of course. It would totally ruin the way they made money. So they gave him the golden handshake, but with a gun to his head. Okay, not literally. Bought him out, then booted him out the door. He can't do anything with his invention because Microsoft says they own it."

"Well, technically—"

"Yeah, yeah, yeah. So he tried to get a job at Apple, but, whaddaya know, they wouldn't talk to him either. No one would. He'd played with fire once too often. He turned bitter and tried to get even by posting a modified operating system on the web for free, like Linux. Microsoft sicced the Feds on him for copyright violation. Then he turned kinda crazy. I wanted to see if he could help me out with something—"

Dylan loved Tony, but this was the kind of behavior that sometimes infuriated him. "Honestly, Tony, as your best friend, I'm telling you, I think it's time you grew up a bit. We're in the big show now. If Art found out—"

"Oh, man! You're not going all tight-ass on me, are you? Don't worry about Art." Tony set down his beer and changed the subject, his way of avoiding conflict. "Seriously Dylan, I know you think I'm crazy, but I'm working on two really cool things. The first is an amazing smartphone. Imagine you set it on a desk, and, at the push of a button, it becomes a virtual notebook PC. On the desk it projects a full working keyboard, and on the wall it projects a 3-D image. And it runs as fast as a jaguar. I'm telling you, it'll be huge!"

"If you're right, you'll make a fortune."

"How long have you known me?" Tony punched Dylan in the arm. "I'm talking about being a technology genius, and you're talking about a fortune."

"What's the other thing?"

"I'm not ready to tell you. That's a surprise for later." He took another sip of his beer and stared out the window.

Dylan shook his head and laughed. "Sounds good, but don't get yourself into the same fix as your friend from Microsoft. Remember the contract you signed with Mantric. They might own any ideas you have while you're employed with them."

"Hah!"

Dylan sighed. He knew he had to refocus Tony. "Tony, what's going on? Does your visit to New Jersey have something to do with that cryptic little message you sent me last month?"

"Remember a few weeks ago when I asked you about who had access to our files?"

"Yeah, you had some concerns about Hyperfōn." An alarm bell went off in Dylan's head as his mind revisited that conversation, word-for-word. "Has something else happened?"

"I've been doing some digging, and I'm getting close, but I always feel like I'm being watched, like someone else has gained access to the file. I know I sound like a conspiracy theorist, but I can't help it."

Dylan looked across the table at his friend and then let out a long sigh. "Tony?"

"Yeah?"

"Joe Ferrano's getting panicky. You know, you're one of his favorite people. I don't know how you won him over, but he trusts you. You *are* coming with me to meet him tomorrow, aren't you?"

"Of course! What time?"

"Ten o'clock at their offices in Waltham."

"I'll be there with bells on!"

"Thanks," Dylan said, relieved, as the waitress set down their sashimi platters. "And don't worry about the files. I think you're just as jittery as Joe about this campaign."

• • •

April 6, 8:30 a.m. Boston

Hyperfōn was set to announce a breakthrough in mobile phone technology, and with the launch little more than two weeks away, Joe Ferrano wanted reassurances.

Dylan pulled into a parking space in the technology office park in Waltham. As he walked to the front door, he noticed Tony perched on the steps, wearing his usual sport coat and jeans for a client meeting. They took the elevator to a reception desk at the front end of a large, open room on the second floor.

A young woman greeted them and told them Joe would be with

them shortly. Dylan went to examine the old "brick" cell telephone on display—the very one Michael Douglas so famously used in the movie *Wall Street* and recovered when leaving prison in the sequel. He smirked. How times had changed. He returned to Tony and sat down.

"You're making me nervous," said Tony.

"Well, Hyperfōn is my division's biggest client."

"Don't worry," Tony said, reaching over and patting him on the shoulder. "We'll settle him down, no problem. Trust me. It'll be a piece of cake."

Joe Ferrano came around the corner. The CEO of Hyperfōn carried his early fifties with dignity. He kept his dark hair cropped short; his steel blue eyes bore into every person he met with an intensity and interest that spoke volumes. At six feet four inches tall, he carried his taut body like a professional boxer, strong and determined. His entire appearance was a study in confidence, and yet his demeanor was warm and friendly.

"Hi, guys, good to see you," he said, shaking their hands. "Come on in."

Tony and Dylan followed Joe across the open space towards his office. They walked past the twenty employees, most of them glued to their computer screens. This was one aspect of Hyperfōn's distinct advantage. A small company with very little overhead was about to change the way people viewed smartphones forever. The inexpensive price tag assigned to the product would undercut their bigger competitors, with their massive buildings, elaborate distribution systems, exclusive contracts, and enormous executive salaries.

For the next hour, the three of them hovered around the conference table in Joe's austere office and reviewed every detail for Hyperfōn's impending launch. By ten o'clock, with all questions asked and answered, Joe cocked an astute eye at Dylan.

"So, how's life at Mantric treating you?"

"Great, Joe. It's as if nothing's changed."

"Yeah," added Tony, "except now we've got the technological resources to guarantee Hyperfōn will stay in front of the competition for years."

"Well, boys, that's nice to hear," said Joe, folding his arms and leaning back in his chair. "Our advertising campaign starts at the end of the week, which means we're about to spend a hell of a lot of our venture capital money."

"I know, Joe," Dylan said, smiling. "And we're ready for the launch. You're going to blow the doors off this market. And then you're going to be seen as the greatest mobile genius since Steve Jobs. We can't wait to see it happen."

Joe leaned forward and stared into Dylan's eyes. "Launching the marketing campaign is only the beginning, Dylan. What concerns me is how important I'm going to be to you once it is up and running. We're going to need a lot of help figuring out what's working and what isn't. Screwing that up could make or break us."

"We know that, Joe," said Tony. "And that's why I'm here. I wanted to personally reassure you I'm not going to take my eyes off the ball. Not for a minute."

"So, does that mean I can count on you to stay personally involved in this project?"

"Absolutely!"

Dylan shifted uneasily in his chair. He knew Joe was especially fond of Tony, but Tony was walking a fine line. His new responsibilities at Mantric wouldn't allow him to spend the same kind of time he had on Hyperfōn in the past. His mind went back to the conversation the previous evening, when Tony talked about his two new projects. In order to succeed, Tony would have to drop some projects or delegate. On the other hand, if Tony could attend all the key meetings with Joe, that might be enough. After all, the critical work was really in the hands of the mobile application developers now. And they'd assigned their very best to Hyperfōn.

"What about you, Dylan?" Joe asked. "How do I know you're not going to be preoccupied with your own IPO? When I heard the IPO had been moved up to May, I figured you'd be taking off just about when we launch."

So that was what had triggered Joe's anxiety. Dylan took a deep breath. "Joe, we may be owned by Mantric, but you're MobiCelus's flagship client. Without you, we wouldn't have become the success we did. I owe you this one."

Joe got up and paced his office. "You know, that sounds great. That really does. But the fact is, I haven't seen much of you guys lately."

"Matt Smith has been managing the launch," Dylan said cautiously, "and we meet with him constantly. And Rob has remained involved as well."

"Matt's good. In fact, he's very good. But I've been around the block a few times, guys. I know what happens in business when companies get bought. I know about Art Williams and his reputation. Promises get broken because the people who made them have new bosses. Personal integrity goes out the window when big money comes in the door. I've got a lot of good people out there who have been working their asses off for me for practically nothing. They get paid peanuts, and hell, even the secretary owns a bunch of stock. They're like family to me. I owe them everything, and I want to be damn sure they get the riches they deserve." Joe stopped his pacing and looked directly from Dylan to Tony. "So tell me. Do I have your personal guarantee to help me make that happen?"

Dylan composed himself, stood up, and tried not to think of the fact that he was already pretty stretched. The important thing was that the Hyperfōn work would be done—and done by the best. He could put the IPO aside; he would figure out how to make it all work. "You have my word, Joe. We're gonna help you rock the world and nuke your competition."

Joe paused for a moment and then laughed. "I'm a pacifist, Dylan, so I'll just stick with rocking the world. What about you, Tony?"

Tony stood up as well. "Are you kidding? I wouldn't miss this revolution for anything!"

"All right then. Just keep your heads firmly attached to your shoulders—all right?"

"We will," Tony and Dylan said in unison.

"Well, thanks for coming by, boys," he said shaking their hands. "And I look forward to seeing you both again real soon."

Tony and Dylan left Joe's office and walked back across the open space. As the elevator doors closed, Tony turned to Dylan and grinned.

"See what I mean? Piece of cake."

But something in his tone raised a concern in Dylan's mind. He mulled over Joe's cryptic comment about Art Williams. A sideways glance told him Tony apparently thought nothing of it. Dylan realized this was a situation to keep a close eye on.

• • •

April 6, 11:45 a.m. Boston

Dylan and Tony drove separately to MobiCelus's former headquarters. Dylan headed across the Fort Point Channel towards the converted warehouse, not far from what was now the booming seaport area of the city. He pulled into his parking space in the garage, entered the old freight elevator, and hit the button for the fourth floor. The elevator jumped and then slowly creaked its way up. Dylan marveled at the difference between this elevator and the one at Mantric's office in Manhattan, and yet he felt a comfortable closeness with this old one. He knew that once the lease was up, Mantric would dump this property. He already missed the slow churning of the elevator.

The smell of fresh paint lingered in the building, a reminder of the cosmetic revamping that had occurred in the weeks following the acquisition. More vivid reminders were the new faces that ignored him as he crossed the floor.

Dylan walked past Tony's workspace—a jumble of computers, mobile devices, and assorted electronic toys scattered everywhere. That at least was the same, but only because Tony had no interest in redecorating it.

Dylan turned the corner. "Hey, Dylan," Sarah Forrester called from her new desk outside his office. "Christine wants to see you. Pronto." Before the acquisition, Sarah had been receptionist, office manager, and support person for all four MobiCelus partners. Now she was Dylan and Rob's personal assistant in the Boston office. Even though Rob had technically moved over to Mantric and had a New York office, he retained an office in Boston.

"Thanks." Dylan sat at his desk and turned on his computer. As he waited for it to boot up, he checked his voice-mail on the speakerphone.

"Good morning, Mr. Johnson," said a chipper female voice. "This is Arlene calling for Ms. Rohnmann. She would like to see you at your earliest convenience."

"Hello, Mr. Johnson. This is Arlene again. Ms. Rohnmann asked me to give you another call."

"Hi again, Mr. Johnson—"

"I told her you were at a meeting," said Sarah, leaning on the office door and smiling.

Dylan returned a wry smile. "Have we received the itinerary for the road show yet?"

"Nope."

"Okay. Why don't you call Arlene and tell her to tell Christine I'm in and will be over shortly." Christine Rohnmann also kept an office in Boston—another part of the transition.

"Have you been a bad boy?" Sarah asked with a grin. "She seems mighty impatient."

"She just wants to talk about the road show."

Sarah sighed and shook her Gibson-girl head. "You really need to get a life, Dylan."

• • •

April 6, 2:00 p.m. Boston

Christine Rohnmann's home page, always set on CNBC, flickered as charts neatly tracked the daily fluctuations of the NASDAQ and the performance of Mantric's competitors. Christine multitasked in a myriad of ways, primarily by keeping watch on the incoming messages during meetings in her office while asking detailed questions of those in attendance. And she was infamous for keeping a close eye on the firm's employees' personal as well as professional lives.

Christine thrived in her role as CFO. She had dived into the furor of the past three months with relish. She led the effort to register Mantric with the Securities and Exchange Commission, and after submitting it to the SEC, she had responded to a large number of questions and requests for revisions. This action had chewed up valuable time, as their technology sector of the stock market was the one hot spot. She enjoyed being in the spotlight, and she let everyone know that complications such as being required to spend valuable time in Boston, working with the menial Rich Linderman on the acquisition, did not please her.

As Dylan walked across the open space, he had a good view of Christine through the new glass wall of her office—glass walls designed to represent fiscal transparency and unity with the employees on the floor, yet maintaining a distinct separation. As Dylan watched her expressionless face staring at the huge LCD display in front of her, tapping the lethal fake nails of her left hand on her desk, he could not help but think transparency was not the picture. Dylan rapped on the glass door and entered as she looked up and waved him in.

He was uncomfortable with this new office style, which was so out of character for MobiCelus. Christine had done the room over in steel and glass, giving it a sense of ice. She then covered every available surface with stacks of papers, spreadsheets, and notes. The shelves on the side walls overflowed with binders, and more stacks of papers were piled high on top.

"Morning, Christine," said Dylan, mustering up civility.

"Have a seat," said Christine, pointing to a hard-backed chair on the far side of her desk.

Dylan settled into his chair as a winter-like chill washed over him. "You've made some interesting changes to your office," he said, attempting to start a conversation.

Christine neither nodded nor shook her head, an ingrained habit of hers. "I hope you're not planning on starting all of your conversations today like that."

Dylan smiled. He found Christine's abrasiveness odd but refused to let it bother him. Through his acquaintance with her over the past few months, he realized she used that technique with everyone, to get them on the defensive and off balance. She was the polar opposite of the affable Art, and together they formed a corporate good cop/bad cop team. The trick was not to accept her terms.

"I had a meeting with your people here this morning in preparation for the road show."

Dylan sat back and wrinkled his brow. While it wasn't his company anymore, being kept out of the loop just didn't sit right. It was still his division. "Well, Christine, I'd appreciate it if next time you want to communicate with my division about any issue, you'd work through me." He silently wondered if she was still angry about the incident with Rich several months ago.

"You were out of your office."

"I'm often out of my office, Christine. It's part of my job." Christine raised her eyes, but not her head. Dylan felt the room closing in on him. "What can I help you with?" he asked, changing the subject.

"We've decided to limit the road show to only Art, myself, and Sandeep—with our support staff, of course."

"What?" Dylan responded, shocked. Even though they had never discussed the road show except in the abstract, he had always assumed he'd be part of it. "Are you serious?"

"I'm sure you were hoping to go with us, but we don't want you distracted from running our mobile computing division. The last thing we can afford is to stumble while we're out selling ourselves to investors." She continued to watch the scrolling information on the screen.

"But, Christine," Dylan protested, "a huge piece of what makes us attractive to investors is our mobile computing business. And the MobiCelus reputation is an important asset for our offering. I really need to be there."

"Our success isn't going to be determined by just our IPO. We need you and your team to make sure our numbers continue to improve so our stock value will go up over the long run." She did not raise her eyes toward him but kept her famous multitasking activities moving.

Dylan struggled to maintain his composure while his anger seethed just under the surface. His numbers were fine, and taking ten days to go on the road wouldn't be a problem. Christine was wrong. Showcasing their phenomenal mobile computing expertise and clients was absolutely critical to the stock offering. "Christine, you can't do this. You know how important our expertise will be seen on the street. Given the acquisition of MobiCelus, I think people will be really surprised not to see me there. Besides, who the hell else is going to describe our work?"

"Art will handle that," Christine said. "And he'll need you to help get him prepared." She stared at him for just a moment, then her eyes returned to the charts flicking along the bottom of the screen.

Dylan felt the blood rising above his collar, and his anger surged. "Art knows nothing about mobile computing—absolutely nothing. As one of the world's foremost experts in this field, I have proven myself many times over. This is an incredibly stupid decision." For the first time since selling his firm, Dylan knew he didn't like having a boss. "Art will get slaughtered if he can't answer a tough question."

"You don't think Art can handle it?" Christine stopped multitasking and looked up at him, a glimmer of a smile curling her lips.

The moment she asked it, Dylan knew it was a loaded question. He refused to answer it. "I guarantee you my going on the road show won't impact my division at all. And it'll do great things for our IPO."

"I'm sorry." Christine returned her attention to her computer monitor and tapped at the keyboard. "Art and I talked it over. The decision is final."

Dylan stared at her and then turned his attention toward the window. He took a deep breath. "I'm asking you to think about it for a couple of days. Let me talk to Art—"

"There's no point," she countered, her deadly nails continuing to tap on the keyboard. "He wants you to help him get prepared, and he wants you to continue to focus on your division. The road show is at the end of this month, so you'll need to have some intense meetings with Art. I'll take care of the rest."

Dylan was being cut out of the game, and he didn't like it. "Jesus, Christine. This is just stupid."

Christine didn't say anything. She sat across from him. Staring. Silent. Smiling.

Dylan stared back. "You're making a mistake. A big mistake." He shook his head. "But Art's the boss. I'll pull together some material for him. But don't blame me if he gets blindsided by a technical question he can't answer."

"That's just it, Dylan. I will blame you," Christine said, standing up. "Thank you, Dylan." She held out a hand.

Dylan did not take it. "I'm returning to New York." He felt her stare burning into his back as he turned to leave the office.

"Have a safe trip," Christine said, and returned her attention to the computer.

Dylan walked out of the office in a daze.

• • •

April 6, 4:00 p.m. Boston

Dylan's mind replayed the meeting with Christine over and over. His anger continued to rise. He paced back and forth in the elevator as it climbed up two floors to the nerd herd, where he sought out Tony. There was no mistaking this was where the technologists liked to hang out. The open space found on the other floors wasn't open here at all. Clutter defined the area, with boxes piled against walls and chairs, bookshelves in a state of disarray, small mechanical devices in various states of creation spread everywhere—a hoarder's paradise. Most boxes were unopened and contained computers, assorted cell phones, smartphone components, plasma screens, routers, printers, and other equipment. The rest were empty pizza boxes. By the elevator, a poster showed a man dressed in a suit in a circle with a slash painted over it.

Dylan walked towards Tony's office. As he turned the corner, a small, silver robotic dog bounced off his right foot.

"Ah, sorry dude," said a young man with a pierced nose and orange hair holding the remote control. Dylan didn't know his name, but he'd seen him before. Enormously talented, the young man had a reputation for playing during the day and working all night. He also changed his hair color every week. Last week was his purple period.

Dylan said nothing as he stepped over the metallic dog. He heard it skitter across the hardwood floor and down the hallway behind him. Dylan walked to Tony's office and glanced inside. Empty.

"Dylan!"

Dylan looked up and saw Rich walking towards him with a stack of papers in his hand. Since the acquisition, Rich was now working under Christine.

"You okay?" asked Rich. When he got no answer, he caught Dylan by the elbow and steered him into Tony's workspace. "What's up?"

"Nothing." Dylan pulled himself together. Unsure of the working relationship between Rich and Christine, Dylan decided this wasn't

41

something to talk about with Rich. "Where the hell is Tony?"

"That's what I was wondering. I came up here to find him. He hasn't submitted his time and expenses for two months."

"Jesus," muttered Dylan. He looked around the mess that was Tony's workspace. It was just as well he was not there. It was a mistake to come running to him when something went wrong with his job. Things were different now. Better to tough it out.

"How's it going, working under Christine?" asked Dylan.

Rich shrugged. "She's a first-class S.O.B. Or would that be D.O.B.? But she gets it done. I wouldn't fuck with her, though, if I were you."

"Perish the thought." Dylan headed back to his office.

Chapter 7

Art walked into Christine's office and closed the door. Her head remained down; only her eyes moved as her glance followed him from the door to her desk.

"How have your 'classes' been going with our quasi-resident teacher, Dylan?" she asked, a smirk creeping across her face.

"His knowledge really is amazing. It would be an advantage to have him on the road show."

Christine shook her head; an errant tress of hair swirled across her face from one side to the other. "No. We agreed we did not want him on this trip."

"I know, I know, I'm just commenting on his knowledge. Did you know he has perfect recall? His mind compartmentalizes everything, and he can remember even the smallest details. Amazing." Art pursed his lips as he thought about the two weeks he had spent with Dylan, learning all he could about mobile computing.

"Yes, I do know about his memory. That's one of the reasons we decided not to include him. Perhaps you should hone your own memory."

Art took a deep breath as he considered her snide comment. "My comments are rhetorical and don't require a response." His annoyance with Christine showed, thinly veiled, throughout the conversation.

"What is it you want, Art? I'm busy with my own preparations."

"I got a call today about Hyperfōn. We need to make a decision about that proposal."

Christine stopped tapping the keyboard and sat back in her chair. She raised her head and stared beyond Art at the back wall of her office. "I was surprised the proposal came to us from that source."

Art nodded his head. He too had been surprised, but recognized the lucrative end of the proposal was too much to reject. "So? Yes or no?" he asked.

Christine did not take more than a moment to reflect on the "lucrative" side of the proposal Art mentioned. Her answer was short and terse: "Yes." She returned her attention to the keyboard and the numbers that scrolled across the monitor screen.

Art smiled. "I'll pass that along."

The sound of a cough at the door caught their attention, and they turned to see Tony standing in the doorway, fidgeting with a handful of papers.

"Sorry to bother you, Christine, but Rich asked me to bring these to you. He would have sent them interoffice package, but he knew I would be returning to Boston on the shuttle this evening and asked me to bring them back with me." He shuffled his feet and held the papers out toward her.

She snatched them from him, signed them, and shoved them back in his hand.

"Thanks." Tony turned and left the office with no further discussion.

"Close the door on your way out!" Christine demanded.

When the door closed, Art turned to Christine. "How long do you think he was standing there?"

"I don't know, but I'm sure even if he heard anything, our conversation was too general for him to suspect anything."

"Right." Art walked to the door and turned back to face her. "I'll take care of that matter today." But he had already lost her attention.

• • •

April 19, 4:00 p.m. Boston

The road show fast approaching, Dylan sat in his office waiting for his three ex-partners to join him. After many long and harrowing hours, they found themselves in Boston with enough time between appointments to be together. While Dylan waited, he thought back over the past two weeks.

Dylan had shuttled back and forth between Boston and New York, spending long hours briefing Art on MobiCelus's clients and on the state of the current, and emerging, mobile computing market.

He found Art to be a quick study, with an almost uncanny ability to pick out the latest buzzwords and use them to his advantage in a casual, conversational manner. But Dylan recognized one flaw—that Art's knowledge of technology was mired in smoke and mirrors. Dylan wondered if Art would be able to answer detailed questions about the technology and stay apprised of the ever-changing new developments. He seemed more like a brilliant manipulator—a con artist who focused his abilities on making a great deal of money.

Aware he was still angry at being left behind, Dylan was jarred out of his thoughts by a knock on the door. Heather walked into the office. "These two puppy dogs followed me home. Can I keep them?"

Tony and Rob trotted in behind her, giving their most mournful look. Dylan laughed for the first time in two weeks. "Hey, c'mon in. It's been a long time since we had a chance to talk. How's everybody doing?"

Heather jumped right into the discussion with an exciting report. "We've got some beautiful new intuitive interfaces in development at the L.A. office." She filled them in on the rapid growth of the experience design group—the folks who concentrated on making sure any mobile device was intuitive, easy to navigate, and attractive. "Our clients will be blown away by what they see. We designed a new mobile interface for a smartphone screen, and our testing showed the client would likely see an increase in revenues of over thirty percent." Her enthusiasm blew through the room, infecting Tony and Rob, while Dylan remained quiet, observing his friends.

"That's incredible. Have you got a demo?" asked Tony.

"Not with me," she replied. "I could send the application via e-mail, but then I'd have to convince Ivan it's not a breach of company security." She rolled her eyes. "That man is a menace."

"It's the quiet period," said Rob. "He's trying to be extra careful."

"Is there really any danger?" Heather asked.

Rob turned on her. "Heather, you know damn well the SEC takes this stuff very seriously. The 'quiet period' is a restriction. It's meant to keep companies from improperly hyping the stock before it goes public."

"Right," Heather said, her voice dripping with sarcasm. "Thanks for the reminder."

Dylan noticed the tension between them but remained quiet.

Rob turned to Dylan. "What's the news on the road show?"

Dylan took a deep breath. All the members of the team had duties that kept them busy, and he had kept the news of his lack of participation to himself. Now he was glad of that decision because he knew he'd only have to tell it once.

"I'm not going on the road show," he announced.

"What?" they all said in unison. Tony and Heather crowded around the desk; Rob remained seated across from Dylan and leaned forward.

"Christine gave me the news earlier this month. Of course, it was Art's decision, but he had Christine tell me. I'm guessing he doesn't like to give bad news."

"Is he friggin' insane?" Tony demanded. "Doesn't he know that our mobile computing capability is what's going to drive our valuation?"

"I tried to explain that."

"And?" said Rob.

"She made it crystal clear Art is going to handle it."

"You're fucking kidding me!" said Tony. "Art can't talk knowledgeably about the mobile computing world. That's not his strong point. Has he lost his mind?"

"Tony, I pushed as hard as I could. I told both of them it was a huge mistake, but neither of them would budge."

"Jesus," said Heather. "That decision could really hurt us." She knew they all had visions of their IPO being like Google's, not some old tired dog. When Google went public, the company's market value had skyrocketed to over twenty-three billion dollars, making many employees instant paper millionaires.

"I know. It's unbelievably stupid," Dylan said.

"So why won't they let you go?" Rob asked.

"She said they don't want me to be distracted from running my division."

"What a load of crap," said Tony, slamming his hands on the desk.

A moment of silence draped over the group. Rob finally said, "Dylan, I know you're not going to like my saying this, but this isn't our firm anymore. It's a stupid decision, but Art's in charge now."

Dylan stared at Rob. He felt his anger rising again. "I'm well aware of that fact, Rob. I've spent the last two weeks educating Art, beating this stuff into his head, and, frankly, it's difficult to educate someone in that timeframe about stuff that's taken me years to learn. I just don't want to see him fuck this up." His last sentence trailed off into oblivion.

The room dropped into a stony silence as Dylan realized he had stooped to shouting at his friends. He didn't know why he was suddenly so angry with Rob. "Listen, I'm sorry," he said. "I guess I'm angrier about this than I realized. Of course you're right. There are going to be changes, and this is just the beginning."

Rob nodded his head but said nothing more.

"I don't know, guys," Heather said, breaking the mood. "This doesn't seem right at all."

"Maybe," said Rob, "but it isn't the end of the world. Look at how many people Art's made wealthy. Our employees are going to be ecstatic when we go out."

"Unless Art fucks up," Dylan added, allowing his anger to reappear.

"Just keep telling yourself that becoming famous and getting rich in the process is the best revenge," said Rob.

"It's not all about the money, Rob!" Heather raised her voice. "It's about changing how people interact and making our employees happy." She paused. "Look, Dylan, they're completely wrong, that's all. Don't let these guys get to you."

Dylan sat back against his chair and sighed. "I know." He looked at Heather. She said nothing more, just slowly shook her head.

"You know the old saying, Dylan," said Tony. "You can't fight City Hall." He glanced at his watch. "I have a few things I have to clean up, and then I'm heading home."

"Yeah, me too. I'm on call for any last-minute questions from Art." Dylan turned to Rob and Heather. "I suppose you two have plans for this weekend?"

"I'm going to a friend's art opening," said Heather. She glanced at her watch. "And I'd better be on my way. See you all Monday." She grabbed her jacket and rushed out the door.

"I'm out of here too," Rob said. "I've got to see Rich before he leaves."

Tony strolled over to the door and waited for a moment, then turned back to Dylan. "Why do you really think Art and Christine cut you out of the road show?"

Dylan considered the question. "I think they just don't like having any competition. Maybe Art wants to be the big shot—you know? Doesn't want one of the new kids around showing him up."

"Well, maybe there's more to it than that. Maybe there are other forces at play here."

"What the hell is that supposed to mean?" Dylan asked.

"Hey, forget it. I've just got a lot on my mind. Shouldn't have said anything." Tony turned and walked out the door without further comment.

Dylan returned to his desk and flopped down into his chair. Jesus. So many cryptic comments. *Why doesn't he just speak so I can understand him?* Dylan stared at the door, wondering exactly what message Tony was really delivering.

• • •

April 19, 4:45 p.m. Boston

Tony's rubber-soled shoes trod silently across the thick carpet as he approached his office. The technology team had departed, except for the young man with the orange hair, who was settled in a cubicle at the other end of the building. Tony tossed a wad of paper in the air and, as he caught it, his attention was drawn to the closed door of his office. A thin strip of light oozed out under the door. Tony stopped. He never closed the door of his office, even when he left for a prolonged length of time. The few personal items that he considered his own never left his possession, so there was no reason to close the office door.

He approached quietly and placed his ear against the door. Inside he heard the sound of papers being shuffled. He placed his fingers on the doorknob and turned it, very slowly. As it opened, he saw a man bending over the desk, rifling through the right-hand drawer. Tony opened the door wider until he stood in the office.

"What the hell are you doing?"

The man shot up straight and spun around. Sandeep Nigam stood facing Tony, unable to speak.

"Did you hear me? What the hell are you doing?" Tony demanded.

"I—I, was looking for some paper clips." Sandeep's eyes darted around the room, perhaps searching for an escape.

"That is the worst excuse I have ever heard." He pointed to a small dish on the desk. "What do you think those silver things in the dish are? Staples?"

"I'm sorry, Tony. I didn't see them." He picked up two paper clips and placed them in his pocket.

"What's this really about, Sandeep? You're no more looking for paper clips than I am!"

Sandeep stood up. "No, no! Really, I just needed some paper clips. Thank you very much." He backed against the wall and sidled like a crab until he got to the door, where he spun around and hurried away.

Tony watched Sandeep scramble down the hall and then turned and looked back at his desk. He moved his hands across the papers that lay scattered in every direction until he found a crumpled yellow sheet of paper, which he thrust into his pocket. He reached into the right-hand drawer and retrieved a key that he tossed in the air and caught. A deep frown furrowed Tony's forehead. *This is so wrong,* he thought. This was the first time he ever even considered locking his office, much less actually doing it. He turned off the light and walked into the hallway, turned around and locked the door. *Yeah, this is so wrong,* he thought again.

• • •

April 19, 5:00 p.m. Boston

Sandeep reached his office and slammed the door shut. He leaned against it and raised his head, staring at the ceiling. As the embarrassment and fear subsided, anger began a slow climb up his spine. He paced from the door to the windows, then made a large circle around the room, ending up at his desk. He yanked the chair out from under the desk and flopped down.

"Damn!" he said out loud. "How stupid am I? I should have waited until I knew he was definitely gone. I know he wants my job. He wants to be in the driver's seat and see me out in the cold. I am not going to have that happen to me. I don't care what I have to do to prevent him from taking over. I have not worked this long to lose out at this point."

Sandeep looked at his watch. *5:10 p.m.* He grabbed his jacket and walked out the door, considering his options.

Chapter 8

Art and Christine met at the New York office early on that Wednesday, getting ready to start the road show. They reviewed their schedule: first London, where most American companies went to warm up, before returning to America at the end of the week. They hoped to attract a few European investors and were confident their presentations would be well received by the investment banks. They would then continue with the second half of the road show, beginning with San Francisco and Los Angeles, then Chicago and Dallas, and finally working their way east to Boston and New York. Satisfied they had not discounted any important stops, Art called the airport for their private jet.

"Do you have everything?" Christine asked him, as though he were an errant child.

"Of course I do," Art snapped. As he closed the office door, his cell phone rang. "Yes?" He stopped and motioned to Christine, who had walked ahead of him toward the elevator. "Yes, it's all taken care of. Are you sure the security is in place? We don't want this going wrong, especially while Christine and I are out of town. Okay, stay on it. We'll be back late on Friday."

"What was that about?" she asked, tapping her foot.

"Just an update on that other little issue we discussed. Everything is in place. At some point that's going to be big news, and we need to distance ourselves when it happens."

"We don't have time for that right now, Art. We'll deal with any blowback when we get home. Let's hope there won't be any. I assume you made arrangements for the money?"

"All taken care of."

• • •

April 20, 7:15 a.m. Boston

The halls of the Boston office were quiet. Employees didn't begin to arrive until around eight o'clock, so the trip down the hall went unobserved. The tall man shut his cell phone and turned the corner at Tony's office. He retrieved a small leather case from his inside breast pocket and removed a thin, bladed instrument, which he inserted delicately into the lock, twisting it until he heard the lock click open.

He slid into Tony's office, where his first reaction was that it was the epitome of disorganized clutter—the area around the computer seemed to be the worst. Papers lay across the top of the desk in no particular order.

"How can he work in such disarray?" the man whispered to himself.

He quickly removed the back of the computer and inserted a small device. "Okay. That was simple," he mumbled. A cursory glance down the quiet hall confirmed that the fourth floor, home of the nerd herd, was still vacant, and the intruder departed in silence, locking the door behind him and moving on silent steps toward the front door and the trip back to New York.

An hour later, Tony arrived in his office, preparing for a meeting with Dylan and Matt to discuss the Hyperfōn launch. As he approached his desk, he knew something was out of order. Others may have seen his own personal version of organization as unsystematic, but he could locate every paper, every pencil, every clip on his desk blindfolded. When asked, he could find an errant note within ten seconds—it was his filing system, and although others might not see it, he certainly did. So he knew when something was out of place, and as his glance roved over the desk, he definitely knew someone had been there.

"Hey, Tony!" Dylan called as he walked into the office. Dylan clucked his tongue against his teeth and shook his head. "How in the world do you live with this mess?" he asked, laughing through his own curiosity. "You ready to talk Hyperfōn?"

"You notice anything out of order here?" Tony asked, ignoring Dylan's question. His eyes scanned the top of the desk.

Dylan laughed. "You're kidding—right? I don't see anything *in* order here." Dylan realized the joke was lost on Tony, whose eyes now roamed around the room in search of something out of order.

51

"What do you think is wrong?" Dylan asked.

Tony turned to his friend. "An odd thing happened last night after we all met in your office. I came back here and found Sandeep rummaging through my desk."

Dylan turned and stared at Tony. "Sandeep? I didn't even know he was in Boston. What did he say?"

"I didn't know he was here either, although he doesn't exactly give me his schedule. He said he was looking for paper clips. When I pointed to the dish on top of the desk, he grabbed a few, threw them into his pocket, and then high-tailed it out of here."

Dylan remained silent for a few moments before continuing. "Do you have any idea what he may have been looking for?"

"Not a clue. I was really angry about it." Tony turned to Dylan. "You don't think this acquisition was a mistake, do you? There just seem to be lots of strange things going on these days, not like when we were just a small business."

Dylan took a deep breath and raised his eyebrows. "I'm sure there is an explanation for this." He did not answer Tony's question.

Tony stared at him for a moment, then shrugged and said, "Okay. Let's go do this meeting."

Tony followed Dylan out the door and then turned and locked it. Dylan stared at Tony, asking himself: *What in the hell is going on here?* But he followed Tony to the meeting.

Chapter 9

The warm spring air of Tuesday morning wafted through the conference room windows. The initial public offering of Mantric, following on the tail of the outrageously successful road show, was slated to open on the NASDAQ stock market in fifteen minutes. Fortunately, emerging technology sectors—including mobile computing, cloud-based technologies, and social media—were still hot despite the turbulence of the overall market.

In every Mantric office, employees stared at the scrolling ticker on the wall and waited and watched as the offering numbers scrolled across the large screens before them.

The night before, WMR Capital, the primary investment bank that was taking the firm public, had priced the offering at fifteen dollars per share, above the twelve-dollar price the bank had originally expected shares to sell for on opening day.

Now the moment of truth had arrived. Art paced the sleek, computerized NASDAQ trading floor near the WMR Capital station. Christine stood nearby, undeterred and cool. Art stopped pacing for a moment, then turned to Malcolm Pierce, a top executive with WMR Capital. "Talk to me."

Malcolm shot a quick glance at Christine and then said to Art, "I think today's going to be your lucky day. The futures are up." He pointed at his computer screen. "It's a good day to go public."

"And the orders?" asked Christine.

Malcolm peered at the bids showing up on his computer. He read the numbers aloud. "Seventeen dollars for 15,000 shares. Eighteen dollars for 50,000 shares."

The prices continued to rise. The group stared at the computer console next to Malcolm. The computer clock read nine twenty-nine.

Malcolm turned to Bob Gianno, a trader who mastered the art of picking the right opening price that made their best customers happy, while allowing the stock to sustain itself during the day. Bob entered a number on his keyboard.

"And the answer is?" Malcolm asked.

"Twenty and a half," Bob replied.

"We're opening at twenty dollars and fifty cents a share?" said Christine, showing surprise for the first time.

Before Malcolm could answer, the opening bell went off and Bob rose to his feet. The trading floor sprang into action. Traders jumped up and down, waved their arms and shouted out orders.

"Twenty-three for fifty," one trader shouted.

"No way," Bob responded. "But I'll take twenty-three for a hundred."

A hundred thousand shares at twenty-three dollars a share. "Jesus!" Christine cried out loud, looking at Art, just the hint of a smile crossing her lips.

"What did I tell you?" Art said, gripping Christine tightly by the shoulder.

She nodded, her heart pounding. It was working. The stock was definitely moving in the right direction.

Malcolm turned to Art. "Congratulations, Art. It looks like you've done it again. This is a great sign!"

Art wandered around, shaking hands and accepting congratulations.

• • •

May 2, 9:15 a.m. Boston

Dylan had spent the previous week working with Matt Smith and his team on the Hyperfōn marketing launch. Now he hovered over his computer, reviewing information on the project.

"What the hell are you doing here?" Heather cried, marching into his office. "Don't you know we go public in fifteen minutes?" She grabbed him by the arm, gently but firmly, and led him out of his office to the main conference room, where the entire office staff had gathered to enjoy breakfast and watch the real-time ticker.

Dylan sensed the excitement that filled the air. Employees laughed and called to each other about the emerging technology sector performance, their predictions on how Mantric's IPO would go, what they thought it would be worth by the time the first 25 percent of their stock options were vested, and how they would spend their newfound fortunes.

As nine-thirty approached, the crowd quieted down and gathered around the screen that displayed two lines. On one was the overall number for the NASDAQ; the other line simply said MNTR. The group watched and waited for the opening price to scroll before them.

Nine-thirty came and went. A ripple of concern ran through the room, and then, suddenly, the MNTR symbol started flashing.

"Here we go," someone shouted out. There was a pause as MNTR momentarily disappeared. Then it reappeared, reading "MNTR ... 20.50."

"Jesus," someone else muttered.

I'll say, Dylan thought. They had opened at twenty dollars and fifty cents a share, and the room erupted into loud cheers and whistles. "MNTR ...20.50" started flashing again, and the room quickly quieted down as the ticker scrolled from right to left, as if chasing the NASDAQ number above it. Everyone leaned forward at the same time in anticipation.

The numbers began to race across the screen. "MNTR ...21.00 ... MNTR ...21.64 ...MNTR ...22.24 ...MNTR ...23.50." The room burst into deafening cheers, and then a steady chant emerged. "Go! Go! Go!" "MNTR ...24.75 ...MNTR ...25.00 ...MNTR ...26.33," the ticker continued.

This is unbelievable, Dylan thought. He looked around the room at Heather, and their eyes locked for an awkward moment. They smiled, then quickly looked away. They both knew what this meant. From a risky idea born at a party on Beacon Hill to a crazy vision for revolutionizing the mobile computing world, they now were about to realize their dreams.

"Holy shit!" someone yelled out from behind. Dylan spun around and looked at the ticker again. "MNTR ...35.50" Silence crept through the room. Some people covered their mouths with their hands; others spoke silent words of encouragement to the screen as they watched the price continue to climb. "MNTR ...36.25 ...MNTR ...37.50."

Corks popped out of champagne bottles, and flutes of the golden liquid moved through the crowd. The staffers laughed and toasted each other. The celebration continued through the afternoon, with little work accomplished. Matt and Sarah and half a dozen other members of the MobiCelus division dragged Dylan over to Matt's workspace, where an active IPO drinking game was in progress. Every time MNTR rose another point, a raucous group toast erupted. When the price broke above forty, another round of cheers, celebrations, and champagne toasts exploded in the crowd. Then, as it bounced up and down in the forties, the noise stabilized to a soft hum.

The market closed at four o'clock, and Mantric's stock finished at $41.25 in a stunning début. The market value of the firm closed at over a billion dollars.

Dylan found his way over to Heather. "When does your flight to L.A. leave tonight?"

"Not 'til eight."

"Good. The guys are supposed to join us online in about fifteen minutes to celebrate. But Tony—well, where do we think our errant young inventor is, anyway?"

"I have no idea. I haven't heard from him all day," she said, her eyes looking deeply into his. They clinked glasses and turned away from the partiers.

Dylan felt something stir inside him as her shoulder brushed his. "I wish all of us could be together. Tony and I have dreamed of this moment for years. Let me just check my voice-mail. Maybe that rat has checked in."

Heather smiled and nodded. "So, seriously, do you have any idea where he is?" she asked, sitting at the side of his desk.

"Beats me. This type of celebration would never interest him. He always seems to have something better to work on." An icon on the lower right corner of the screen began to blink, and the time and date flashed with Tony's name. Dylan nodded and held up a finger. "Yep, a message from Tony!" he said as he clicked on it.

Tony's voice came over the phone. "Dylan! Hey, it's Tony. How come you're never there? Look, things are sort of crazy around here, y'know? I got sort of caught up in something big. Ha! So you're coming back to Boston tonight—right? Listen, stop by my place on your way home and I'll show you what I've found, like I promised I would. And look, this is hush-hush, so don't tell anybody—okay? Heads are gonna roll when this gets out. Oh, and hey—I'll be online just after four for the IPO celebration. Promise!"

Dylan set his jaw and frowned. "Now what do you think that was all about?"

Heather shrugged. "He is who he is, Dylan. His life is about technology, not money."

He turned in his chair and fussed over his screen, turning it so both he and Heather could see it. Then he saw Rob's icon flashing.

"Rob!" called Dylan as he made the connection. "Can you see us? We're here!" He felt flushed from the champagne.

"Yeah, I see you." Rob sat close to the screen, his face distorted by the closeness; deep shadows surrounded the little bit of light that shone from behind him. "Where's Tony?" His voice came across in a hoarse whisper.

Dylan glanced down the list of "buddies." Tony's name was grayed out. "Who knows? Probably developing something none of us would ever dream of." He laughed and added, "Can you guys fucking believe it? Who would have bet our little start-up would ever turn into a huge, publicly traded corporation? I guess selling the firm wasn't such a bad idea after all."

"Always the master of the understatement," Heather said, and smiled at Dylan.

"I can't believe we went out so strongly today," said Dylan. At the moment, at least on paper, Dylan was now worth over six million dollars, and his partners close to three-point-five million. Dylan raised his glass. "I'd like to make a toast. To my co-founders and friends. With apologies to the Grateful Dead, what a short, strange trip it's been!"

Dylan and Heather raised their glasses; Rob just nodded.

"I have something I want to say," said Heather in a serious tone. "I know we've sometimes had our differences over the past year and a half. But I want to take this opportunity to tell all of you that the best decision I've ever made in my life was agreeing to partner with you to launch MobiCelus."

"Hear, hear," murmured Dylan. He turned to the computer. "Your turn, Rob."

Rob looked back and forth between them and then pushed his hair off his forehead. "I don't know what to say." His voice, digitized, choked a little. "To good friends!"

Dylan took a long drink of champagne, draining his glass. "Hey, Rob, when you get back from New York, call me. I'm going to stop by Tony's later. Maybe we can all go out for dinner?"

He looked at Heather, who shook her head and tapped the face of her watch. She mouthed the words *plane to L.A.*, and he remembered. He shrugged and mouthed *when you get back*. Heather nodded, blew him a kiss, and quickly left the office.

"Er, yeah, sure. I'll call you when I get back there."

A sheepish smile crossed Dylan's face as he realized Rob had watched the exchange.

• • •

Dylan sat alone in his office completing the details for the Hyperfōn project. Now Dylan wanted to spend time with Tony, his best friend. He needed to spend time with him, to get drunk with him and celebrate achieving their goal, but every time he tried to reach Tony, he went right to voice-mail. Tony's unexcused absence annoyed Dylan. He looked at his watch. *Time to find out where my friend has wandered off to,* he thought as he shut down his computer. He walked out the door and glanced throughout the quiet office. All the celebrations had either stopped or moved offsite. He smiled as he thought of the success of the day. Just then a movement at the end of the hallway caught his eye. In the distance, he saw a shadow that looked like Sandeep enter one of the offices. What was he doing here?

He continued to the old elevator and listened to the loud grumblings echo through the empty building as it slowly descended. A light rain fell over Boston; with a shake of his head, Dylan hurried to his car and drove the dark streets of Boston to Tony's address on Hancock Street.

At nine-thirty, Dylan stepped out onto the damp cobbles of Beacon Hill. The unusually warm spring temperatures foretold a hot summer ahead, and after a brief shower, the resulting mist wrapped eerily around the lampposts. Dylan admired the old neighborhood, with its Federalist and Greek Revival brick row houses, most of which were built between 1800 and 1850. After the turn of the century, many of the wealthy residents moved to the suburbs, and the old houses were subdivided into small apartments and, later, condominiums. Tony had moved into one of the roomier apartments shortly after their initial MobiCelus success. True to his character, his eclectic furnishings barely filled the space.

Dylan climbed the stairs unsteadily, still feeling the effects of the champagne. He reached for the key in its usual spot on top of the light next to the door.

"Tony!" he called as he turned the handle of the door.

He walked into the dark apartment, wondering if Tony was in the workroom designing his next work of genius. Dylan fumbled for the light switch on the wall next to the door. The dim light illuminated the room, casting shadows across the dark walls, and Dylan's initial reaction was to smile at the disorganized mess in front of him, but, as his eyes became accustomed to the light, he stopped in horror.

In the middle of the room, Tony lay on his back, a tangle of burnt electrical cord wrapped around his body. His lips, a dark blue—almost purple—were in sharp contrast to the ashen tinge of his skin. His left arm extended into the acrid air; his lifeless eyes stared at Dylan, an expression of terror and pain frozen in ghostly silence.

Chapter 10

The police station on New Sudbury Street, built in the 1960s, shared its ugly appearance with the other government offices nearby. The unsightliness trailed inside as well. Building renovations in the surrounding neighborhood had bypassed the police station. No modern windowed cubicles here, just a warren of tiny offices connected by faded linoleum paths and echoing hallways, painted in a muted brown that had dirtied through years of greasy hands and endless scuffles.

Dylan sat alone in a bleak nine-by-twelve room, at a table that had been secured to the floor to ensure conflicts did not involve furniture. A large, round clock anchored high on the wall emitted an audible tick each time the second hand moved. He shifted his gaze from the clock to the pink and black linoleum tiles on the floor; his eyes picked points of damage where the linoleum had been slit, or where it curled away from the floor in a corner, the result of too much water when the floor was washed. The events of the last few hours played over and over in his mind—shouting Tony's name, adrenalin surging through his veins, his fingers fumbling to dial 911. He watched himself stand by helpless when the paramedics arrived, practiced in controlled speed, then the arrival of the first police, slow and cautious, and the sound of his own voice—strangled and high—asking if he could go with Tony in the ambulance.

This was what people meant when they said it felt like a dream. It was a wish, really: a desperate desire to reverse history but knowing he could not; he could only affect the future.

Then he thought of Rob and Heather. Rob had arrived from New York several hours ago and was somewhere in Boston—somewhere within reach—and Heather was on a plane to California. Dylan pulled out his cell phone and hit the speed-dial for Rob, who didn't answer. Dylan paused for a moment, grimaced, and left a voice-mail letting him know the news. Not very personal, but he'd expect the same if the situation were reversed.

He placed his cell phone in his pocket just as a door opened and a tall woman dressed in a mauve pantsuit entered. He looked at her bony face, not much softened by a cursory application of lipstick and eye shadow, then trailed down her thin figure, all shoulders and hips—almost to the point of emaciation. A round-faced African American man followed close behind her, the buttons of his suit jacket pulled taut across his belly.

"Mr. Johnson?" the woman said in a deep voice. "I'm Detective Melanie Baldwin. This is Detective Jackson." She sat next to Detective Jackson at the table. "We're sorry about your friend."

Dylan cleared his throat. "Thanks," he said, fighting back tears.

"I've read through your statement," she continued. "You say you received a telephone message from Mr. Caruso today around four o'clock." She flipped through the report but did not look at him.

"Right."

"What did he say?"

"Asked me where I was. Said he was busy, that he'd gotten caught up in something. Asked me to stop by this evening to talk about something that was bothering him."

"Four o'clock. Is that when you listened to the message, or when he sent it?"

"When I listened to it. I don't know when he actually called. It must have been between about one and four. I can get the time, though, if you want it."

"Please. As soon as possible. And give me a call when you do."

"You don't have to wait." Dylan took his cell phone from his pocket and flipped it open. He had all the numbers he called most often on shortcut. He hit keypad number three—the number that called his office voice-mail. His throat tightened as he skipped through the messages until he got to Tony's.

"Dylan! Hey. . . ."

His chest tightened; his breathing constricted. He punched in the number to get the detail of the call. A mechanical voice spoke: "This call from . . . Tony Caruso . . . was received at two . . . seventeen."

"Two-seventeen," Dylan repeated, hoarsely, closing his phone.

"Thank you." She pulled a pencil case from an inside pocket and opened a notebook. An audible minute ticked by on the old clock on the wall.

Dylan wiped his mouth. Emotions swept through his body—fear, pain, disbelief, anger. He wrestled with his memory of finding Tony. "Look," he finally burst out. "Shouldn't you be out there trying to find whoever did this?"

Detective Baldwin spoke calmly, without looking up. "Why do you think someone else was responsible, Mr. Johnson? Mr. Caruso appeared to have accidentally electrocuted himself, don't you think?"

Dylan's hands shook. "No. I don't. You didn't know Tony. He would never in a million years make a mistake like that."

"It happens, Mr. Johnson. He had a wide-open electrical box in his apartment."

"That may be, but he wouldn't have been hauling that great tangle of cable around with him with the circuit closed. I'm telling you—I watched him work with electronics in that apartment for years, everything from microscopic circuitry to microwaves. And he did not work in his living room. He has a fully equipped workroom with a rubber mat on the floor. And did you see the bruise on his head?"

"Yes. He appeared to have struck his head on the coffee table as he fell." She turned to her partner. "Isn't that right, Bill?"

"Yep. Skin tissue and blood were noted on the corner of the table."

"Please, Mr. Johnson, trust us to do our jobs."

"Actually, if you think this was an accident or suicide, then I don't trust you to do your job." Emotions surged, sapping what little strength he had left. He stood and turned, walking unsteadily toward the door.

"Mr. Johnson," Detective Baldwin called.

"This is a total waste of time."

"Please sit down."

"You can't convince me."

"I won't try. Please," she repeated.

Baldwin's cool manner washed over him. He realized he was losing control, while she was wholly unmoved. He took his seat again and stared back at her, silent and angry.

"Mr. Johnson, where were you this evening?"

Dylan's eyes opened wide. They wanted an alibi from him? His mouth opened slightly, then he realized they did think there was something else going on, that this was not an accident. "I was in our local office. Our business went public today, and there was a lot of chaos. By the time I finished work, got into my car, and arrived at Tony's, it was about 9:15."

"You realize we have to check these things, don't you? Can anyone verify your story?"

Dylan choked back tears. "Just about every one of our employees. I spent most of the day with one of our partners, Heather Carter."

"Where can we reach this Ms. Carter?" Baldwin did not look up from her notebook.

"She's on a plane to Los Angeles. I can give you her cell phone number." He repeated the number while Detective Baldwin continued to take notes.

"Thank you, Mr. Johnson. This is a requirement. No one is above suspicion, no matter how close they were to the victim."

Dylan winced at the use of the word "victim"—it sounded cold and aloof. The image of Tony, dead, reappeared in his mind. Tony was gone, and Dylan was convinced someone had killed him. If the police were not going to do anything, then he would.

As if reading his mind, Detective Baldwin added, "The best thing you can do for your friend is to keep quiet for a week or so. We'll put out a statement that this is an apparent accident, but the medical examiner is still investigating. Let us handle it. We'll advise the family and begin collecting information."

"I don't know. You don't seem—I don't want this fucked up. It means more to me than to you." His sentence ended in a whisper.

"I'm a homicide detective," said Baldwin. "Every questionable death means something to me. Do you think I'm in the habit of letting killers go? He was your friend. Do you have any idea who might do something like this?"

Dylan shook his head and sighed. "I don't know." *Was his friend.* Dylan's mind focused on the past tense. "Everybody loved him. He drove you crazy, but nobody—I don't know. I'm not thinking too clearly right now."

Baldwin rose. "You need to get some sleep. Here's my card. Call me when your head's clearer."

Dylan took the card and allowed himself to be walked to the door.

"Now, do we have your word that you won't tell anyone these details? I'm not asking you to lie, just to tell your associates the cause of death is under investigation. Okay?"

"Okay."

Dylan stepped through the door and heard it close behind him. He stood for a moment, long enough to hear the detectives talking within.

"Ya think he'll keep his trap shut?"

"I don't know; hard to read these business types. But he will if he thinks about his friend for half a minute. I believe him, but let's call this Heather person and see what she has to say."

Dylan moved away from the door, walking alone down the long corridor in a daze of shock and disbelief. He looked at his watch. Seven-twenty in the morning.

"Dylan!"

He looked up as he walked across the main lobby of the police station and saw Rob hurrying toward him, a haggard look on his handsome face. The two men embraced—a brief moment of shared raw emotion, then Dylan pulled back. "What are you doing here?"

"I got up early to go to the gym, and then I heard your voice-mail, so I came here as fast as I could. Jesus, Dylan, is it true? Are they sure?"

"They're sure."

"I still can't believe it."

"Yeah," Dylan said blankly. "Me either. How are you doing?"

"I think I'm still in shock." Rob paused for a moment. "How did it happen? You just said it was horrible."

Detective Baldwin's words rang in his head. "I'm not sure. And I don't really want to guess until his dad is notified."

"What was it? Suicide?"

"What? No!" He stopped in his tracks, taken aback by the comment. "No. He had no reason to do something like that." Dylan looked at the floor, then mumbled, "Some awful accident, somehow he electrocuted himself." Detective Baldwin's words echoed again through his mind, and he found himself wondering who he could trust.

"Oh my God." Rob closed his eyes. "It must have been awful for you to see him."

"You can't imagine," Dylan said softly.

He took Rob's arm and led him out of the building. A pink and grey sky began to appear in the east. The mist from the previous evening had disappeared, leaving only small puddles on the streets. The noise from heavy traffic on nearby Cambridge Street echoed in the day.

"I've got my car," said Rob. "I'll take you to yours."

"Thanks. The police are going to call Tony's dad, but I want to talk to him."

"Right."

"They're going to call Heather also, but I don't want her to hear it from them. I think you should call her, Rob."

"Me? Why?"

Dylan gave him a puzzled look and then glanced at his watch. "Given your relationship, you should be the one to—"

Rob cut him off with a terse answer: "No, Dylan, I shouldn't." He pulled into the Beacon Hill neighborhood and stopped at Tony's building in front of Dylan's car. He turned to Dylan. "Look, Heather and I are history. We agreed we wouldn't discuss it in public, but, given the situation, I'm telling you it wasn't a pretty break-up."

"Why?"

"Because—well, let's just say it was a mutual thing." Rob paused. "Fuck it. The truth is she broke up with me and I didn't take it well. We're barely speaking outside of the office. So trust me, it should be you."

"Okay." He glanced at Rob's angry face. "Sorry."

"Yeah, me too. But that's water under the bridge compared to this, so—"

"Okay, I'll call her."

"I'll go to the office and call Art," Rob added.

"Fine. Thanks. Rob, I mean it. Thanks for everything."

Rob shook his head. "Okay, go. You look awful."

Dylan stopped for a moment in front of Tony's building before getting into his own car. Then he drove to his apartment, where exhaustion displaced shock and anger. He took a quick shower, wrapped himself in a robe, and retrieved his cell phone to call Heather. He knew he should let the police call her, considering she was his alibi, but he did not give a damn. Heather should hear about this from a friend, not a stranger.

Grief rocked him as he stared at the phone. He sank down onto the sofa, and all at once the hold he had kept on his emotions and thoughts let go. Tony was dead. Tony had been murdered—any doubt he might have had of that had been removed by Detective Baldwin's reaction to his questions. But who—and why?

Tears washed down his cheeks, and he pressed back against the soft sofa as wave after wave of grief hit. He struggled to stifle the emotions that flowed over him—the memories, the fights, the laughter. The grief eventually ebbed, leaving him feeling numb and alone. He sucked in dry gulps of air, then sat up. He hit number three on his phone and retrieved Tony's archived message. Head throbbing, he listened again to his friend's last words to him:

"Dylan! Hey, it's Tony. How come you're never there? Look, things are sort of crazy around here, y'know? I got sort of caught up in something big.

Ha! So you're coming back to Boston tonight—right? Listen, stop by my place on your way home and I'll show you what I've found like I promised I would. And look, this is hush-hush, so don't tell anybody—okay? Heads are gonna roll when this gets out. Oh, and hey—I'll be online just after four for the IPO celebration. Promise!"

Dylan tossed the phone on the sofa. What the hell? Yesterday he had assumed Tony was wrapped up in one of his projects, that he had wanted Dylan to stop by to show him the latest on his super smartphone, maybe even a prototype. But now. Now Tony was dead, and the words of his message took on a whole new meaning. Tony had wanted to talk to Dylan about something. Something hush-hush. Something big—but big enough to die for?

Dylan considered for a moment that the killer might be someone he knew. A shiver ran down his spine. Of course, there was no reason to think Tony's death had anything to do with MobiCelus or Mantric. What had Tony said about that guy he visited in New Jersey—the disaffected guy from Microsoft? Was it possible Tony had gotten into trouble with some shady characters? Dylan thought about it for a moment, but he knew his brain was in no shape for critical thinking.

He took a deep breath and picked up his phone again. He needed to call Tony's dad. But first. . . . Four. That was the shortcut to Heather's cell. She picked up on the fifth ring.

"Hey," she said, stifling a yawn. "Why are you calling at this hour?"

• • •

May 3, 5:00 p.m. Boston

A chiming sound echoed through his mind, as if from a far-distant place. Dylan opened his eyes. He had nodded off on the sofa. The sound of his home computer repeated itself. He got up and staggered to his den on uneasy legs. He glanced at the clock. Five o'clock in the afternoon.

The icon identified Art as the caller to Dylan's computer. He cleared his throat and swallowed as he shook the mouse to activate the screen and clicked on the "answer" button.

"Hello."

"Dylan! My God! Are you all right?" Art's voice shouted through the speaker.

"I'm fine," he answered, his tongue thick with sleep.

"Rob is on the network from Boston."

"Hi Dylan," Rob said. "Is your video on?"

Dylan ran a hand through his hair, then tapped a couple of keys. Video images of Art and Rob materialized next to each other on the screen.

"I want you to know we'll do whatever you need us to do," said Art. "Anything. What about Tony's family?"

"Tony grew up here, and his mother's buried in Cambridge. I spoke with his father last night. He's in Florida. He's going to try to get a flight out today."

"We can fly Mr. Caruso up on a private jet," said Art.

"I think he'd appreciate that."

"Stephanie?" Art spoke to Stephanie Mathers on another line.

"I'll get right on it, Mr. Williams," said Stephanie. "Dylan, can you message me Mr. Caruso's phone number?"

"I'd like to call him myself," said Art. "Such a bright young man." He shook his head. "Such a shock."

"Yeah," Dylan mumbled.

"Did you reach Heather?" asked Rob.

Dylan nodded. "She's flying back tomorrow."

"How did she—?"

"She's hanging in there." Not for the world would he have described the anguish in Heather's voice when he had told her the news Tony was dead, or how he insisted there was nothing she could do in Boston at this time.

Art nodded. "I don't mean to pry, Dylan, but how—"

"I stopped by his place last night and found him."

"Rob says the police told you it was an accident."

Dylan thought he noted a flash of coldness in the comment. "Yeah." *Heads are gonna roll when this gets out.* He could not get Tony's words out of his mind. A queasy feeling assailed Dylan. Whose heads? He wondered if he was seeing guilt where it did not exist.

"This is such a tragedy," said Art. "Look, Dylan, I want you to take as much time off as you need—okay? Do you know anything about the funeral arrangements?"

"I really don't know anything about that yet."

"Of course not," said Art. "Look, we shouldn't be bothering you. I just wanted to say how sorry I am. This is a terrible tragedy, and, I've got to admit, I've never had to deal with something like this before."

"Neither have I."

"Well, I guess the best thing to do now is try to move forward and be as sensitive to people's needs as possible." He turned his attention to Stephanie. "If anyone who knew Tony well wants to take tomorrow off, you tell them that's fine."

"I think that's the right thing to do, Mr. Williams."

"All right. Thanks everyone. Take care, Dylan. I mean that."

Dylan clicked off. He stared at the dark plasma screen, then snatched suddenly at the mouse. He hadn't checked his e-mail for a while. Maybe Tony had sent him something.

He accessed his e-mail account and ran his eyes down the list of e-mails. One short message from Tony read: 'file for your eyes only—will forward.'

Dylan reread the short, cryptic message. He scanned his e-mails for anything else from Tony, but nothing appeared with an attachment. That meant those files could be on his home computer, but with Tony, who was connected to half the planet by every known type of electronic communication, it could be anywhere. Still, the place to start was in his home.

He pulled Detective Baldwin's card out of his pocket and tapped in her number. She was not available, and Dylan left his number for her to call back—he said it was important.

Silence, broken only by the distant sound of late afternoon traffic two blocks away, drifted through the open window. Emptiness weighed on Dylan. He put his head in his hands and felt an overwhelming wave of sadness crash over him.

He thought of Heather. He had encouraged her to go through with her client meeting in L.A., argued that she could do nothing in Boston that day. She had tried to tell him how she felt, but he hadn't listened. Of course, it was different for him. Tony was his best friend. . . . *Was.*

Exhaustion enveloped him like a blanket. He staggered to his bedroom, dragged his clothes off, and climbed into bed.

• • •

May 3, 9:00 p.m. Boston

The ringing sound startled him, and Dylan fumbled on his bedside table for his cell phone. He rolled over and looked out the window into a darkness yellowed by streetlights. Then he glanced at the screen of his phone: BPD.

"Hello?"

"This is Detective Melanie Baldwin returning Mr. Dylan Johnson's call."

"This is Dylan." He sat up and shook his head, collecting his thoughts.

"How may I help you, Mr. Johnson?"

"I went back and listened to Tony's message to me yesterday." Dylan repeated the message, stressing the part about Tony having prepared a file for him. "I was hoping you would get me into Tony's apartment so I could try to find that file. It might give me a clue as to who—"

"Thank you, Mr. Johnson. Actually our computer people are in the process of securing all of Mr. Caruso's equipment. They will look them over and see if they can find this file he mentioned. We'll follow it up, rest assured."

"Good." Dylan paused and then added, "Look, he said the file was for me. Don't I have some right to see it or try to find it? Not to keep it from you, of course, just—"

"I'm sorry, Mr. Johnson. That's not the way it works. If there is a personal communication, you may be able to retrieve it in due course."

Dylan stared out the window. Not what he wanted to hear. "Okay."

"Thank you for understanding." Her deep voice was tinged with sympathy and an ounce of apology. "While I've got you on the line—"

"Yes?"

"Have you had a chance to think about Mr. Caruso's relationships with his co-workers?"

"A little." The sleep had helped. "He didn't have any enemies, if that's what you're thinking."

"Who were Mr. Caruso's closest friends?"

"Myself. Our other two partners, Heather Carter and Rob Townsend."

"We spoke to Ms. Carter and verified your statement as well as her being on the plane to Los Angeles. Do you know where Mr. Townsend was yesterday afternoon?"

"Rob was in the New York office. He returned last night."

"Anyone else Tony might have communicated with?"

Dylan thought for a moment. "There's Ivan Venko, he's the head of security. And Sandeep Nigam, he's Tony's boss. And Art Williams is the CEO of Mantric. Those are the people he would have interacted with at the company. I would not call them friends, more like business acquaintances."

69

"And where would these gentlemen have been found?"

"I think Sandeep may have been in the Boston office. Ivan and Art were in New York."

"Are you sure?"

"Our company went public yesterday, and they were at the NAS-DAQ in New York. And I saw Art myself."

"You saw him?"

"Well, technically I only saw and heard Art on a teleconference call."

"I see," she answered. "You saw him sitting in his New York office?"

"Yes, I did," he answered, but his mind rushed back to the conversation. He saw Art's face, but not the background. The computer conversation could have occurred from anywhere. He shook his head and removed the question that was forming. Art would have no reason for hurting Tony.

Chapter 11

Dylan, victim of restless dreams, awoke at midnight in a cold sweat. His normally organized mind was mired in a fog of uncertainty. Had he turned on the alarm? He got up to check, then crawled back into bed and stared at the ceiling. His thoughts assailed him like no-see-ums at the beach. He got up and retrieved his laptop. Propped up in bed, he fired up the computer and watched his home page paint onto the screen: the business front page at Boston.com. He scrolled down to the technology news, where a headline caught his eye:

"Local Technology Wiz Kid Found Dead.
"Brookline native Tony Caruso, 24, was found dead last night in his Beacon Hill apartment due to an apparent accident involving faulty wiring, Boston Police Chief Harlan Bloom announced this morning. The medical examiner is expected to make a final ruling on the cause of death in about a week."

Dylan scrolled back up the page without reading the rest. He remembered Tony's dead face. His scorched skin and lifeless eyes were emblazoned in his memory. Dylan closed his eyes. Tears slipped between his eyelids and ran down his cheeks. He did not know how he would get beyond these memories.

"Fuck," he said, and wiped his tears away. He focused on his computer and went to a web page he frequented: a page that provided links to Internet businesses divided by type and sector. He trolled the Internet, looking for information about his clients' competitors and checking new ideas. Maybe it was disrespectful of Tony, but concentrating on his work was his coping mechanism.

May 4, 8:00 a.m. Boston

The spring morning greeted him, cloudless and warm. Dylan drove across the Fort Point Channel to MobiCelus's office. He had driven this route thousands of times, but today an odd sense of surrealism rode with him. Sounds echoed in the distance, muffled as if wrapped in cotton.

At the old warehouse, heads turned and nodded as he headed for his office. He checked his voice-mail. Twenty-four messages. The first call was from Joe Ferrano. If there was trouble with Hyperfōn. . . .

"Dylan. Joe Ferrano. I just heard the news about Tony. I wanted to call and tell you how sorry I am. What a great guy he was. If you need anything, I'm here. Take care."

Dylan hung up the phone without listening to any more messages. He was not ready for that yet. He headed for Rich Linderman's office.

Wrapped up in other thoughts, he came around the corner and thought he was in the wrong place. Other than the phone and computer, the office was empty. He must have been moved, Dylan thought. He backtracked and went to Faith Navitsky's desk. Faith was the administrative assistant for the financial department and would know where Rich could be found. "Morning, Faith."

She looked up from her computer. "Dylan! What are you doing here?" She half-stood and leaned on her desk.

"Working."

"Oh, Dylan. You should take some time. I'm so sorry." She looked sorry, and worried, too.

"Work is good for me. I'm not staying the whole day. I've got to pick up Heather at the airport. Listen, I'm looking for Rich."

Faith took off her reading glasses. A strange expression came over her face. "So you don't know?"

"Know what?"

"Rich doesn't work here anymore."

"What?" Dylan said, astonished. "What are you talking about? Since when?"

"They escorted him out of the building yesterday morning."

"What?" Dylan repeated, louder. "Faith, what the hell is going on?"

"I don't know. Dylan, I'm so sorry about this. The timing—I know Rich is a friend of yours. I thought they would have told you."

Dylan shook his head. "Well, whoever the hell 'they' are didn't. This is unbelievable." He stormed back to his office and slammed the door, then pulled out his phone and dialed Rich's cell, where he got a message saying the number was no longer in service. Shit, they'd already shut off his phone! Dylan dialed Rich's home phone and let it ring.

On the fifth ring, Rich picked up.

"Hello?"

"Rich? It's me. Dylan."

"Dylan! I was wondering if anybody was gonna call."

"I just found out, Rich. I went to your old office. It's empty. What the hell happened?"

"They didn't tell you, huh? What a gang. They took my computer, my office phone, even my cell phone. That bitch Christine actually had me escorted out of the building! They disabled everything. I just bought a new house with my pregnant wife and son, for Christ's sake. Notice how they waited until after the IPO?"

"So what the hell happened? Why did Christine fire you?" Dylan asked.

"I wasn't fired," Rich said indignantly. "They eliminated my position. Christine said the division didn't need a financial director, that the scope of my work simply duplicated what was already being done by the accountants."

"Is that true?"

"In terms of accounting? Probably."

"Okay. So what about another job at the firm?"

"I was told there wasn't one that fit my skills."

"That doesn't make sense. We're growing so fast. Stephanie keeps saying she's pressed to find good people."

"I know. But to tell you the truth, I'm happy to be out of there."

"Why?"

"This running back and forth to New York stinks. And Christine— well, she's a real piece of work."

"Why do you say that?" Dylan asked, wanting Rich's take.

"The finance department's organization is archaic. She has some people focused on revenue projections, but only for one or two offices. Others look at expenses, but only for certain categories. There are fire- walls all over the place, so that the left hand doesn't know what the right is doing. I don't think she has a clue how the firm is really performing. My skills were not utilized, and frankly, I felt like I was intentionally being left out of things."

"Come on, Rich. Mantric's a big firm and—"

"Excuse me, Dylan, but this isn't fucking rocket science. Plus she didn't even know how to account for a reserve properly."

"What are you talking about?"

"She forgot to include the reserve for the acquisition of MobiCelus in the prospectus, and that's illegal."

Dylan was stunned. Improperly recording or classifying an acquisition can be a way to manipulate a company's financial statements—a very serious and criminal offense. It was one of the factors at the heart of the Tyco scandal. "Are you sure?" Dylan's thoughts scrambled back to Tony's mysterious comment about something big happening and heads rolling.

"Yes, Dylan. I'm sure."

"Why didn't you tell me about this before?"

"I dunno," he said, a bit sheepishly. "Everything was happening so fast, and Christine is so intimidating—I guess I just let it pass, thinking she had other things on her mind as well."

Dylan's thoughts raced from one scenario to another. If this was true and the SEC found out, they could have cancelled the IPO.

"Anyway, I don't give a shit. They gave me a nice package, and I'm happy to be the hell out of there."

"What kind of package?"

"Two years' pay, plus my bonus, and they'll let my stock vest for the first year. And they'll cover the cost of COBRA for my health insurance for the full eighteen months as well."

Dylan was stunned. No one at Rich's level got a deal like that. Hell, no one *ever* got such a deal. The norm was more like one month for every year employed, and if you were let go, you didn't usually get to keep any unvested stock options. "That's rather surprising," he managed to say.

"Yeah, and they said they wouldn't contest me if I filed for unemployment, either. Said I should represent it as being a lump sum in exchange for signing some stupid release. Guess they thought I might sue or something."

Dylan said nothing. He kept wondering why Christine would have been so generous.

"Dylan?"

"Yeah. Sorry. So what are you going to do now?"

"Cruise on my severance and unemployment, take a long vacation, and then find another job."

"All right. I'm sorry it ended like this."

"Don't worry about me, Dylan. Worry about yourself. You and Tony."

Dylan was brought up short. "God. Rich. Haven't you heard?"

"Heard what?"

Dylan closed his eyes and told Rich about Tony's death. All the while, questions nagged at him. Ten minutes later, as he hung up the phone, Dylan felt a wave of anger. He was supposed to be one of the most senior executives at Mantric, but he was continually made to feel like an outsider. Could these events have something to do with Tony's death?

He knew Art was in Boston today. He bolted to the guest office he used. "I need to see Art."

The administrative assistant shook her head. "He's wrapping up a call right now. Is there something I can help you with?"

"No." Ignoring her, he burst through the door. Art spun around and looked at him.

"We need to talk."

"Dylan, can't you see I'm in the middle of—"

"Now!" he demanded, slamming the door behind him.

Art stared at him for a second. "I'll call you back," he said, hanging up the phone. "What's your problem?" he demanded.

"You're joking—right? For starters, you can tell me why Christine fired Rich Linderman without talking to me first!"

"Look Dylan, need I remind you, Rich didn't work for you anymore."

"So you think it's fine I heard about it from the goddamn receptionist?"

Art paused. "I suppose she should have notified you first."

"Ya think?" Dylan said sharply. "And why the hell did she have him hauled out of the building in front of everyone else?"

"Because he had access to confidential information." Art raised his eyebrows and stared at Dylan, waiting for a response. "In situations like this, we have to protect the company from potentially disgruntled employees."

"So," Dylan said, his voice brimming with sarcasm, "I guess that means you both face this sort of situation a lot, huh?"

"Unfortunately."

Dylan blinked. "And you haven't learned that waiting a few hours until people have left is a better option?"

Art bit his lip. "That's a good point," he admitted. "Maybe we should have done that."

"And maybe you should have found him another job."

"That was my call. Based on Christine's recommendation, I felt Rich didn't have the right skills for any other opening. Frankly, he lacks the sort of experience and know-how we're used to seeing in our finance people."

"Well if he did a bad job, how did he qualify for two years' severance?"

Art flinched then quickly caught himself. "I would have thought you'd be happy we did that for him."

"Oh I am. It just doesn't make any sense."

"Maybe that was our way of acknowledging it was a difficult situation."

Dylan paused for a moment. He didn't know if what Rich had told him was true. But if it was, Mantric had illegally manipulated its financials in advance of the IPO. He decided to tuck that information in his back pocket.

"As a senior member of this management team, I should have been informed, and I think I should be included in all future financial reviews."

Art remained silent for a moment, then smiled and said, "I'll certainly bring that to the board's attention. We'll get back to you on it." He said nothing more but reached for his phone.

"Fine. Please let me know their answer." It was a weak response, and he knew it. He turned on his heel and left before Art could say anything.

Art waited until Dylan closed the door, then dialed Christine's number. "Have you made arrangements to get Tony's computer? I don't think it should be lying around here. Be sure to send Ivan to get it. Oh, and Dylan was just here demanding to be given access to the company financials. I told him I thought that would be a board decision. I don't think there will be any problems, but we should meet and discuss this before it goes any further."

• • •

May 4, 3:50 p.m. Boston

Heather's four o'clock flight arrived ten minutes early at Terminal C at Logan Airport. Dylan spotted her before she saw him and moved quietly to her side.

"Heather."

She whirled and reached out to him. Dylan pulled her close and hugged her, feeling her body shake as she sobbed. He stroked the back of her head, trying to comfort her.

"Come on, Heather. Let's get out of here," he said, taking her bag in one hand and holding her hand in the other.

"I still can't believe it," she said, sobbing.

"Neither can I," he said as he guided them out the door and towards the parking lot.

A warm blast of dry air swept across the road. Heather sat in the passenger's seat, reached into her purse, and pulled out a tissue. She wiped her eyes and blew her nose. She looked straight ahead, staring into the distance. Dylan put his hand on hers, and she turned and looked at him through red, puffy eyes.

"Are you hungry?" he asked. "Do you want to get something to eat?"

She shook her head. "I don't want to be in a public place."

"Shall I take you home?"

"No. I need to talk. I want to know—"

"My place?"

She nodded. "That's where we always used to meet and talk, the four of us."

The four of us. Dylan started up the car. They drove away from the airport and into the tunnels of the Big Dig. "You okay?" he asked as they pulled onto Storrow Drive.

"I'm just glad I'm back." She turned to him. "How are you doing?"

"Fine." The lie was so palpable he could not look at her. He hurried on, changing the subject. "But something happened at the office today."

"You went to the office? Dylan!"

"It's better to keep busy. And it's a damned good thing I did. I found out Christine fired Rich yesterday."

"My God," Heather said, turning to stare at him.

"Pretty, isn't it?"

"What was her reason?"

"Rich said she told him his position was redundant and there wasn't another role for him at the firm."

"That's harsh. Do you believe it?"

Dylan said nothing as he pulled into his parking space. The bright sun shone through the windows. "Maybe he knew too much."

Heather gave him a puzzled look. "What do you mean?"

"Rich told me a strange thing about what's going on in finance."

"Which was?"

Dylan opened his door. "I'll tell you inside."

In the living room, Dylan fixed a vodka tonic for himself and poured a glass of white wine for Heather. He'd wanted a drink all day but hadn't had anything, knowing he had to drive.

"Rich said Christine forgot to include the reserve for the acquisition of MobiCelus in our prospectus."

Heather shook her head. "I'm not sure I understand."

"The SEC requires complete transparency, meaning you have to report everything."

"Then why wouldn't they include it?"

"I don't know. I confronted Art about Rich, but decided not to let him know what Rich had told me. And I demanded to have access to the financials."

Heather looked at him. "Do you think Art and Christine will agree to that?"

Dylan took a sip of his drink. "I'm not sure. But I think it's my business to know."

"You know, Art said something odd," she said. Then the doorbell rang. Dylan rose and peeked through the spy hole. "It's Rob," he said, opening the door.

"Hi," said Rob. He looked as if he hadn't slept all night. "Didn't want you to think I'm checking up on you, but—Heather!"

She went to him and put her arms around him. Dylan stepped back and looked at the floor. *So they were speaking again.*

Rob pulled away first, turning his head to wipe the tears from his eyes.

"I'm okay," he said in response to Heather's look. "No, I'm not. I'm a mess. But I can't do anything about it."

Dylan got him a drink and refilled his own. Rob drank quickly and threw himself on the sofa. "God, what a day," he said. "Jesus, Dylan, I'm sorry to intrude, but I have to tell you something."

"Rich?"

"You know?" Rob set his drink on the table.

"I was at the office this morning. Went to see him about something and saw his empty office."

"I found out this afternoon. Christine sent me an e-mail. I knew it would rip you, so I thought I'd better come over and tell you myself."

"Thanks. Maybe you can also tell me the real reason she did it."

Rob shrugged. "There's no hidden reason. You know I thought you were getting him in over his head at MobiCelus. And the water's a lot deeper at Mantric. I take Christine at her word. He couldn't handle the job. But Jesus—"

"They had no right to fire him without consulting you, Dylan," Heather interrupted. "Maybe you can convince Art to take him back when you talk to him again about having access to the financials."

Rob looked from one to the other. "What's going on?" he asked cautiously.

"They're keeping me on the fringes, Rob," said Dylan. "First the road show, now firing Rich behind my back."

"Technically, they have the right now to do that," Rob said.

"I know. They're testing me. If I don't push back, they'll steamroll me and I won't have any power at all."

"So much for the benefits of acquisition," said Heather.

Dylan looked at her and heard anger in her voice, saw fire in her eyes.

Rob drained his drink. "I've gotta go." He rose. Dylan hugged him again and led him to the door.

"Take it easy, Rob."

Rob's eyes met his. He nodded and left.

Dylan went to the bar. "You want another drink?"

"Sure." Heather kicked her shoes off and curled up in the corner of the sofa.

Dylan fixed the drinks and then returned to the living room. He took a healthy gulp. The excessive alcohol had made a significant dent in his misery, but not in the doubts that flooded his mind.

"What were you saying before? Art said something odd?"

Heather nodded. "It was at a meeting in New York last week. He was talking to the project managers, telling them how proud he was of them for the revenues they were generating. He said the New York headquarters was our most important office because it accounted for forty-five percent of our revenues."

"He said that?" It was the first time Dylan had ever heard a breakdown of their revenues by office.

"It's probably nothing, but it just seemed awfully high. Almost half the revenue generated by only one of our ten offices?"

"Yeah." It seemed high to him as well.

"Plus, aren't only about twenty percent of our people based here in New York?"

"Uh-huh. That doesn't add up. There aren't nearly enough people in New York to generate forty-five percent of Mantric's revenues."

"My thoughts exactly."

Dylan rested his head in his hands. "Jesus." He didn't want to show his reaction, but the alcohol had him now, and the doubts that had been lurking behind his misery grew and multiplied: the road show, Rich being fired, and even Rob's reaction to Dylan's anger. For every argument Dylan made, Rob countered. Dylan shook his head to clear his thoughts. Perhaps Rob was right, and Dylan just needed to feel there were more people on his side. But then again. . . .

Heather put her drink down. "We shouldn't be talking about this now. Dylan, we need to talk about Tony, about what's being done."

He nodded. "His father's in town. He thinks the funeral will be on Saturday."

"I know. I spoke with him this morning. But that's not what I meant. I've been so upset since you called. I put it out of my mind while meeting with my client—I had to—but on the flight back, it ate me alive."

"I hear you," said Dylan, draining his drink. "It's a terrible feeling."

Heather nodded and shifted her position on the sofa, moving closer to him. "The thing is—I don't know how to say this, but it just doesn't seem like Tony to have made a stupid mistake that would cost him his life. Have you talked to the police?"

"Yeah."

"And?"

He looked down at the empty glass in his hands. "They said it looked like an accident. The press said it would take about a week to get the final cause of death. That's all I know." He did not like leaving Heather out of the conversation with the police, but for the time being he would.

Heather leaned back against the soft sofa cushions. "Remember that time Tony rigged the office phones to start ringing each other on Sarah's first day with MobiCelus?"

"Yeah," said Dylan with a smile. "That was a good one."

"We all knew and were lounging around watching. But you were just as surprised as Sarah."

"What's your point?"

"Tony didn't tell you because you don't lie very well."

Dylan looked at her, uncomprehending for a moment. Then it hit him. "Why would I lie?"

"About a week ago, I got an e-mail from Tony."

A shiver ran down Dylan's back. "About what?"

"He wanted to ask my advice about something. He said he was in a tricky situation. A question of ethics. He didn't give me any details."

"Christ."

"We exchanged a few e-mails over the weekend. In essence, I advised him to make sure of his facts before he leaped to conclusions, and he agreed. That was it. But I got another e-mail Wednesday."

Dylan sat bolt upright. "When?"

Heather met his eyes. "Does it matter?"

"Yes!"

"He sent it at about three-thirty. I read it later that night in the airport."

"And?"

"He said he'd solved his problem. Said he was e-mailing you about it."

"Fuck!" Dylan sprang up and crossed the room. He knew he should control himself, keep his feelings intact, but the barriers were down, and fear and sorrow overwhelmed him. "Why the hell didn't he call me sooner?"

Heather stood up and moved to his side. "It wasn't an accident, was it?"

Tears welled up in his eyes. "If I'd been there to take his call, he might still be alive."

"Stop it." She took him by the arm and led him back to the sofa. "Tell me what's going on."

"I don't know. But the cops don't think it was an accident." He looked at her face. "Murder."

"I knew it," she whispered.

"The police want to stall for a week or so. They're not mentioning the murder until the medical examiner's report is filed. But they're out there looking for whoever did it. I'm not supposed to say anything. And you can't either."

"I won't."

"It could be anybody. Tony had a lot of friends and did a lot of crazy stuff. But Jesus! What if it has something to do with Mantric? I made him promise he would talk to me if he ever had any problems at the firm, and in his last voice-mail, he said he was keeping his promise. He said he had prepared a file for me and asked me to stop off that night to talk about it."

"Oh, Dylan."

"And now I hear the sort of crap Christine is pulling. I don't know.

I'm seeing ulterior motives behind every word." His words poured out, too rapidly, but he didn't care. "Or maybe he was doing something on the sly. I don't know. All I know is he's dead, and I'm never going to be able to talk to him again, and it's killing me!"

Heather put her arms around him, running her hands up and down his back. He closed his eyes and held her, letting his sadness flow into her, and, by sharing, diminish.

They sat for a long time in silence until, regaining himself a little, Dylan pulled away and took her hand. He felt calmer and clear-headed. He smiled sadly at her. "Thanks."

She touched his face, wiping away a few tears.

"We have to tell the police about your e-mails. I want to read them too."

"I'll forward them to you. Later."

"I'm glad you know. I've been trying to think of what to do, but it's like my brain is short-circuited."

"It'll pass. You've got to take time for yourself."

"Everything seems to be happening so fast." They talked about Dylan's discussion with Detective Baldwin and his attempt to access Tony's computer. "Not that I would be able to get past his security."

"Maybe the police experts can get in."

"I doubt it. It's Tony, remember?"

"Right. How many computers does he have?"

"About ten, last I knew. But that he actually uses? Not counting just for video streaming? Two, I think. The big desktop at his apartment and his laptop."

"What about the one in his office? Maybe you can access that."

"I can try. But what's my excuse for snooping?"

"You don't need one. He called and said he was going to send something to you, and you want it because it's the last message you got from your friend. Are you absolutely sure you have checked all of your accounts?"

Dylan gave her a sidelong look. "Maybe not."

They went to his computer in his home office, and Dylan checked the Gmail account he rarely used but found nothing.

"Well, it was a good idea," he said glumly.

"It's just a start."

"You're terrific," he said, and kissed her on the cheek.

She placed a hand on his shoulder as he started to move away. "How come you've never made a pass at me, Dylan?"

Her face was very close to his, and he looked into her green eyes. "You've been unavailable."

She looked deep into his eyes with a sad, dreamy expression on her face. She swept her long, strawberry-blonde hair to one side, quickly leaned forward and kissed him lightly. "Maybe that was because you were unavailable too," she said through full and slightly parted lips. She exhaled as she moved forward again and pressed a finger to his lips. She pulled his arms around her waist and pressed her body against his, kissing him with more passion.

He smelled her perfume, the scent of her hair. He kissed her deeply.

"I've wanted you for a long time," she said with an intensity he had never heard before.

"Me too," he said, responding to her. He kissed her again, letting his hands slide down to the small of her back.

She stroked the back of his head and kissed the back of his neck. She exhaled and pulled him closer.

Dylan looked at her face; her cheeks flushed, her eyes closed. She looked almost angelic, with her mouth slightly open and just a hint of a smile. He let his desire take charge. He felt the warmth and rose, leading her to his bedroom.

"Heather," he said, gently laying her on the bed, "I want to make love to you."

She stopped and looked up into his eyes. "I want that too." Her black skirt was now bunched up around her waist. Then he slipped his fingers under her panties. She responded instantly, her body writhing, rolling over and onto her back as she reached to pull her panties off. He helped, tugging them down to her knees, and then she kicked them off onto the floor. "I want you in me," she said breathlessly, pulling him against her.

He fumbled undressing as he kissed her again. He paused for just a moment, and then he entered her. He felt her tense up at first, and her eyes seemed to close halfway. Then she grabbed him tightly to her. He moved slowly, rhythmically. She shifted her body a bit. He could hear her quick breaths with every stroke. He was definitely going to explode. He didn't want to. Not yet. He stopped, took her by the waist, and rolled her over.

"Nice move," she said, tossing her hair back with a grin. She was on top now. She leaned forward, kissed him again, and then sat upright. She closed her eyes and started moving again, slowly at first, and then faster and faster. "Now!" she said, as if she could read his mind.

Dylan felt her tense up and shiver, just as he did, for what felt like minutes. Then she collapsed on him.

They lay quietly, and Dylan stroked her hair as his heartbeat began to slow.

Chapter 12

Dylan's eyes jerked open. The morning sunlight dappled the empty pillow beside him; a light breeze blew through the window, moving the sheer curtains. Where. . . ? He lay still, listening. An unbroken emptiness filled every corner of his apartment. The sudden sense of loss smothered the lingering pleasure. He rolled onto his back. What had he done? He'd slept with Heather, and it was wonderful. She had invaded his psyche, and no departure ever made him feel so alone.

Then he remembered.

He rolled out of the bed in an effort to escape the grief that had seeped back into his consciousness. He couldn't let it conquer him—wouldn't allow himself to be defeated by it. He was tough: a self-made man, admired by his friends, envied by his rivals, someone to be depended upon. He rubbed the sleep out of his eyes, padded into the bathroom, and turned on the shower.

The hot water flowed over his body, pulling the tension out of his head and shoulders. The steam cleared his mind, bringing vague memories of Heather's pre-dawn departure, her naked body crossing the room, the strip of light when she opened the bathroom door, the softest of good-bye kisses, not to wake him as she left. In the past, his relationships with women had been shallow, unimportant, and he wondered how last night would change him. He stepped out of the shower, toweled off, and glanced at the clock. Only seven-thirty.

Ten minutes later he sat down at the dining room table, a coffee cup and plate of toast to one side, his laptop open in front of him. He checked his personal e-mail account, and three forwards from Heather leaped out at him. His hand jerked on the track pad as he clicked on the first one.

"Start at the bottom," he read. "Call me."

Call me. Simple words, but the blood in his veins grew hot at the sight of them. Clenching his jaw, he scrolled down to read Tony's original e-mail, in a blue font, ferociously indented.

> "To: Heather Carter
> "Date: April 23
> "Subject: Favor
> "Okay, see I have like five minutes and I've gotta be somewhere unless I can work out the kinks in that transporter! Normally I'd wait till I could see you face 2 face but you travel too much! So can I ask your advice about something? Not personal but sticky—okay maybe personal in that it's always personal when you know you're gonna hurt someone. But anyway it has to be kept secret so tell me first if you'd rather not. Mmmwaa!"

Dylan scrolled up to Heather's reply, in red:

> "To: Tony Caruso
> "Date: April 23
> "Subject: RE: Favor
> "Of course you can talk to me, sweetie, and I'm insulted you would suggest I would tell anyone anything that is none of their business. When have I ever ratted on you???"

Next up was Tony's second e-mail:

> "To: Heather Carter
> "Date: April 23
> "Subject: RE: Favor
> "You are the goddess of ~~circumcision~~ circumspection. [ha ha] But seriously, this information fell into my hands and I don't know what to do. Impossible to ignore, but when it gets out, heads are gonna roll, maybe even mine. The thing is I don't want to be the one to spill the beans. I'm such a coward. What do I do? Bewildered on Beacon Hill."

> "To: Tony Caruso
> "Date: April 23
> "Subject: RE: Favor
> "Dear BBH—Okay, screw that, this does sound serious. But I can't tell you anything you don't already know. Yes you have to spill

the beans. But what do you mean your head may roll too? Did you do something stupid?"

"To: Heather Carter
"Date: April 23
"Subject: RE: Favor
"You mean lately? Yeah, well, maybe. Unintentionally. All I ever wanted to do was to play with computers and make them magical. Yes, I know I have to tell. The question is how?"

"To: Tony Caruso
"Date: April 23
"Subject: RE: Favor
"I don't know, sweetie. You're being very cryptic. If it's business tricky, ask Dylan. He knows about that stuff better than me."

"To: Heather Carter
"Date: April 23
"Subject: RE: Favor
"Maybe. But the thing is I don't want to shock him."

"To: Tony Caruso
"Date: April 23
"Subject: RE: Favor
"WHAT HAVE YOU DONE???"

"To: Heather Carter
"Date: May 2
"Subject: RE: Favor
"Don't worry. I'm not the one who does dumb things. Much. Okay, maybe I'll talk to Dylan. Something else has come up that maybe makes that a good idea. I can trust you to keep quiet until then—right?"

Dylan read them through again. "Tony," he whispered. If only his friend had confided in him sooner. Or told Heather what the hell was going on!

He wandered around the condo, unable to concentrate. He noticed the growing pile of unopened mail on his desk and quickly flipped through the advertisements and bills. A crumpled postal envelope that had become stuffed inside a Best Buy flyer fell out and landed on the carpet near his feet.

Dylan picked up the envelope, and his heart jumped as he recognized the nearly unreadable handwriting as Tony's. He ripped it open, and a flat manila envelope sealed with Scotch tape slid out onto the desk. He stared at it for several moments, unable to pick it up, as if it would dissipate in the air if he touched it.

He took a letter opener from his desk drawer and slit open the envelope. Inside, a single, wrinkled sheet of yellow paper waited to be removed. He pulled out the paper and felt the pit of his stomach lurch as he again recognized Tony's handwriting. He wondered if this could be one of Tony's recent inventions.

His spine tingled. It was Tony's work, all right. The drawing and the few lines of writing beneath were scribbled sideways. Dylan pictured Tony on his computer, with the paper to the right of his keyboard. At first glance, the drawing appeared to be some sort of electrical device. On the left side of the page was a coil, and, on the right, something that looked like the schematic for an electrical circuit.

He stared at the graphic. Honestly, Dylan had to admit, it could have been anything. One thing for certain, it had nothing to do with software; this was a drawing of a physical object. And the simple schematic to the side affirmed that.

His eyes moved down to the writing. He noted it was written at a markedly different angle than the doodles or the sketch. He read the words again, then stared open-mouthed, adrenalin shooting through his veins and energizing him. At the bottom of the page was a word in one corner of the sheet, barely legible: "Prometheus."

Chapter 13

"Dylan?" Sarah stared at him through wide, moist blue eyes.

He gave her a brief hug. "You okay?"

"No," she admitted. "But I'm here. The old gang had a meeting yesterday. We want to do something special for the funeral. I've sent you an e-mail."

Dylan shuddered. "Funeral," he muttered. He tried to put it out of his mind and regain his composure. "Thanks. What else?"

"Matt's been handling the Hyperfōn launch as well as he can, but he could use some help. Oh, and I've got the number for Tony's father." She handed him a Post-It.

"You're the best, Sarah. I've got some loose ends to tie up, and I need you to get in touch with Sandeep Nigam and tell him I need to speak with him. I'll be back in about an hour."

Dylan walked across the building to Tony's office to check Tony's computer for the mysterious message. At the door he hesitated. A wave of nostalgia washed over him. He had always loved visiting Tony's room, which looked more like a junk shop than an office. The tables were littered with computer paraphernalia, and yet Tony always worked on the sofa. Dylan shook his head, shoved down his surging emotions, and entered the office.

Ivan stood behind Tony's computer. A toolkit lay open next to it.

"What are you doing here?" said Dylan, startled.

"My job," Ivan answered without looking up.

Dylan strode forward. Ivan opened the computer, its motherboard, power supply, and other components revealed.

"You're taking out the hard drive?"

"Yes." He detached the cables carefully.

"Jesus Christ! What gives you the fucking right?"

Ivan looked up at last. There was no emotion in his dark eyes; his mouth twisted upwards in an impatient sneer. "Is there something there you don't want me to see?"

Dylan's blood raced; anger screamed through him. "You've got a hell of a nerve. The man is dead, for God's sake."

"Which hardly relieves me of my responsibility to investigate irregularities," Ivan retorted.

"What the hell are you talking about?"

"I don't owe you an explanation. I'm following orders."

"You son of a bitch." Dylan leapt forward, his fists clenched.

Ivan sprang up like a cat, grabbing a screwdriver from his toolkit.

Dylan stopped, breathing hard. The air in the room sizzled.

"Security alert," said Ivan softly.

Dylan blinked and refocused his gaze to the headset on Ivan's ear. "Calling in the cavalry?"

"You leave me no choice," Ivan answered, grinning.

Dylan nodded. "Good. Don't touch anything until they get here."

Ivan's mouth curved into a sardonic smile. "I think you're under a misconception, Mr. Johnson."

"What? You're telling me you weren't planning to walk off with Tony's hard drive?"

"That's exactly what I'm doing. Except it's not Mr. Caruso's. It belongs to Mantric. I'm removing it for security purposes." He replaced the screwdriver in the kit. "Standard procedure."

Dylan felt his face flame. *Idiot!* What had he been thinking? His hands opened and dropped to his sides. His knees began to shake, and he sat on the arm of the sofa. He had to keep it together.

The door burst open, and two blue-clad security guards rushed in. Dylan took a deep breath. Ivan stepped forward. "False alarm," he said curtly. "I thought Mr. Johnson had taken ill—the recent tragedy—but he assures me he is fine. Stand down." The two men relaxed and left, throwing disapproving glances in Dylan's direction.

Ivan turned and looked down at Dylan. "You would have been wise to take some time off, Mr. Johnson. You are obviously overwrought."

"I want to go through the files before you remove them," Dylan demanded.

"Not possible, Mr. Johnson."

"Why not? Unless there's something there you don't want me to see?"

Ivan folded his arms. "Not having seen the contents of the drive, I have no idea. Now, if you don't mind." He glanced at the door.

Dylan knew he had no bargaining chips. Helpless in the face of

Ivan's corporate right to be there, he tried to appeal to his human side, assuming he had one.

"Tony sent me an e-mail, but for some reason I didn't get it. I just want to see what it said, for sentimental reasons. His last words to me—" He stopped, wondering if Ivan would buy that.

"I see. Well, I'll look for it, if I can access the files. And I promise you I shall certainly tell you if I find anything that seems to be for you."

Dylan eyed Ivan suspiciously, but he took the hint. It was time to go before he did any more damage. This wasn't the way to help find Tony's killer. Far from it. He would have to call Baldwin and tell her that if she wanted the hard drive, she would have to get it herself. He forced himself to walk with a firm step toward the door.

"Oh, and Mr. Johnson."

Dylan turned and met Ivan's eyes. "Yes?"

"My condolences."

Chapter 14

May 5, 11:00 a.m. Boston

Dylan sat at his desk and stared at the glossy screen of his computer, looking at his own face staring back at him: a picture of loss, sadness, and anger. He reached for his cell phone.

Call me. Those two words . . . so telling, so inviting. For a moment he lost himself in memories of the previous night. Then he returned to his computer and double-checked his e-mail, looking again for the one from Tony. He checked his spam folder to make sure the filters had not accidentally blocked Tony's e-mail address. He checked his quarantined e-mail on Mantric's system. Nothing.

The missing e-mail would explain what had been bothering Tony and either prove or disprove Dylan's dread that it had something to do with Mantric and Tony's death. But such thoughts opened a flood of questions.

He pulled the folded sheet of paper from his pocket, flattened the schematic on the desk, and stared at it. He opened his web browser and Googled "Prometheus." Six million results. He Googled "Prometheus plus technology plus next-generation." Fifty-eight thousand results. That wasn't going to get him anywhere.

His computer chimed softly: the sound it made when someone on the network wanted to communicate. He opened up the conference window and saw Sandeep's name and avatar bouncing in the dock. He clicked on "accept," and the window filled with Sandeep's olive-toned baby face.

"Dylan," he said. "I got your message. I am extremely sorry about Tony. Everyone in the department is. He will be missed."

"Thanks, Sandeep. I appreciate it. Listen, I wanted to talk with you about a couple of things, tech-related."

"Fire away."

"Let me ask you. Who are the real tech gurus Tony might have been working with on one of his pet projects?"

"Well, there is Miss DaSoto. As you know they were working on the beta release for our client Scyant. And of course there are many others."

"Actually, I mean outside of work."

"Oh." Sandeep paused. "I wouldn't know anything about that, Dylan. But I'm sure whatever Tony did outside of his work here was just for fun."

"Do you know if he was doing anything in New Jersey?"

"I really have no idea, Dylan. I'm sorry." His answer was sharp.

"Don't worry about it." Dylan swiveled in his chair and gazed out the window. "Sorry if these questions seem odd. This has hit me hard, I guess. I just feel a need to locate and talk to some of Tony's friends. Maybe get together over a drink and shoot the breeze. Stupid, I guess."

"Not at all, Dylan. I understand completely. To mourn is an important part of life you Americans often neglect. It's good for you to allow yourself to feel."

"Right. Well, thanks, Sandeep."

"Take care." Sandeep ended the chat.

Dylan slumped back in his chair and stared again at the face in the monitor. He resumed painstakingly looking through every folder in every e-mail account he had to make sure there was nothing from Tony.

This was no good. Never in his adult life had he shied away from the job at hand. Tony's laughing voice came unbidden into his thoughts: "Hey, man! Geniuses can't turn it off and on with a switch. You gotta be in the mood to be brilliant." Dylan grabbed his jacket and headed out.

• • •

May 5, 3:45 p.m. Boston

Dylan picked up his cell phone, dialed the number for the Liberty Hotel, and asked for Dominic Caruso's room.

"Mr. Caruso? It's Dylan."

"Ah, Dylan. Where are you?"

"At a coffee shop. I just needed to be alone."

"I understand."

"Are you okay? I mean, do you have everything you need?"

"Yes. The company has been very generous. I have everything. Well—" His breath caught in his throat.

"I know. I can't believe it either."

"Detective Baldwin—she says they're not sure how he died. They're

93

investigating. She said I could talk about it with you but no one else 'til they know more."

"I know. I think it's best. They're working hard." He spoke the last sentence more for comfort than belief.

"Who would do this to Tony? Everybody loved him. From the time he was a baby." Dominic Caruso's voice broke with emotion.

"I know." Dylan choked on his words.

"It's because he was too smart. When he was ten years old, his school came to us and said he was too smart for them. That he should go to a special school. For mathematics. His mother and I were very proud. But he didn't want to go. Math camp in summer, okay. But the rest of the time he wanted to be with his friends and play baseball. When he was eleven, he built a robot to let the dog out. Eleven!"

"I know."

"You were a good friend to him. He always told me how you took care of him, how you carried him on your coattails. Made it easy for him to do what he loved."

"He carried me, Mr. Caruso. He carried me." Tears welled in his eyes.

"Look Dylan. I want you to give the eulogy."

"Mr. Caruso, really, I'm not the one—"

"You are, Dylan. You were his best friend. It's what he would have wanted. Okay? I won't take no for an answer."

"Okay," Dylan whispered. How could he say no? Just because, somewhere buried in his heart, he feared maybe he had caused Tony's death by bringing them all into Mantric?

"And I want to get together with you and Heather and Rob. Maybe after the funeral."

"Of course. We'll drink a toast."

"That Heather. She's something. She's called me three times."

"Was he happy, Mr. Caruso, with the move to Mantric? I mean, did he ever say anything, anything remotely odd, about the new setup or anything else?"

"He was happy, Dylan. There was nothing on his mind. Change is always tough. He said he wasn't completely sure about his new boss, but, like I said, change is always tough. He told me, 'Pop, in six months I'm gonna have achieved amazing things and made enough money to set us both up for life.' That was his dream from when he made that robot. To see his work out in the world, to make people's lives better with his work. That's what was important to him."

"I know, Mr. Caruso, I know. That was Tony."

"Then you'll for sure do the eulogy?" Mr. Caruso asked.

"Of course." They finished the call, and Dylan closed his eyes and stared across the coffeehouse, not seeing anything but Tony's face.

His mind wandered over the events of the past days. He was missing something but was unable to wrap himself around it. So many thoughts raced through his mind. He thought back to his conversation with Tony over that first cryptic message. Cryptic! Suddenly, he bolted upright. He fumbled in his pocket and pulled out the schematic. He placed it on the table in front of him and smoothed it. He bent over, close to the paper, and focused on that single word in the lower corner.

Dylan sat back, stunned. How could he have misread this? Of course his Internet searches turned up nothing of value. The word was not "Prometheus." It was "Prom3th3u5."

Chapter 15

Dylan nosed the rented Ford Fusion out of the Lincoln Tunnel and into the rush-hour-filled maze of concrete roadways. The words "Welcome to New Jersey," emblazoned across the face of a large granite bank, greeted him.

The Garden State, mused Dylan as he headed south on the Palisades Parkway. Who thought that one up?

He had spent the previous evening Googling "Prom3th3u5" and had accessed twelve hits. Four were in character sets other than English. Five appeared to be random expressions, the sort of thing Internet vampires included in their key words to attract as many hits as possible, no matter how irrelevant.

But the other three had held the key to his search. One was a five-year-old post on an archived listserv. It read "Dream on Fizz It's a polymer you idyot It isn't effected by EMI at that freakwency—Prom3th3u5." That settled the question of whether Prometheus was a person or a thing. He or she was definitely a person. The second was a four-year-old post in the same archive, saying, "Ha ha just wait till Joon u'll c. And down will cum GOOG. Prom3th3u5." GOOG was the trading symbol for Google. And the last, dated the previous January, was on a message board dated just a month earlier, saying, "Crap Did U C who was there? Prom3th3u5 himself!" The message board was for an online unlocked cell phone store called Technochondriacs.

Dylan spent a frustrating two hours tracking down a phone number that was out of service before finally coming up with the address in Bayonne, New Jersey. He took the shuttle to New York, passed the time by working on the eulogy, and booked into the Avalon Hotel on the lower west side.

Technochondriacs was one of the many unlocked phone sales outfits that had sprung up like mushrooms in the past year. Dylan cruised through the back streets of south Bayonne at noon: second sunrise, as Tony had called it—the time when all geeks, having rolled out of bed an hour earlier, thought about breakfast but not much more. The varicolored two-story false fronts dated back to the 1940s. The GPS announced he had arrived at his destination, but he saw nothing that informed him of a technology business—only a grimy sign proclaiming the establishment as Crown Candy Shop: a place that sold newspapers, cigarettes, phone cards, and beer.

Dylan parked a couple of blocks away and emerged from the air-conditioned comfort of the car only to be greeted by the stench of garbage rotting in the warm May air. He locked the car and hoped it would be there when he returned.

The Crown Candy Shop turned out to be predictably cluttered but surprisingly cheery. The storekeeper, an elderly woman sporting an unexpected crew cut, was organizing a shelf of ramen noodles and canned soups. A couple of pre-pubescent girls browsed through a rack of teen magazines. Dylan idled by the counter until the woman finished her task and gave him a glance.

"What can I help you with today?" she asked.

"I think I'm a little lost," he said to her with a self-effacing smile. "I'm looking for a business called Technochondriacs."

The woman turned to the candy rack and pulled out an empty display box. "Hmm. Don't think I've ever heard of that one. Or are you talking about the walk-in clinic on Prospect Avenue? The AIDS test was last Wednesday."

"No, this would be something to do with cell phones or electronics."

The woman shook her head. "There's no store like that around here."

"Gran," said one of the girls, a sassy redhead in a Yankees cap. "He's talking about Darryl."

"Oh!" The woman scratched her spiky hair. "Maybe he is."

Dylan nodded encouragingly.

"I thought that idea was a bust," the woman added. "He doesn't talk about it, and he never gets any mail."

"It's all online now, Gran," the girl said without looking up from her magazine. Her dark purple nails turned each page with care.

"Where do you think I could find Darryl?" asked Dylan.

"He lives upstairs. Just go around through the alley to the red door."

"Thank you."

"Keep ringing," said the woman. "Sometimes he's a little, uh, pre-occupied."

"I understand," said Dylan, with a wry grin.

He hurried out the door and around the corner, where he found the back door and rang the bell. Then he rang it again, and again. He had turned back toward the Candy Shop to ask Gran for Darryl's phone number when he heard the thud of feet on a wooden staircase behind the door.

The door opened and a narrow-faced youth in his early twenties appeared. The buds of a headset protruded from his ears. He blinked his large eyes, furrowed his brow, and pursed his lips. "You're not pizza."

"I'm Dylan Johnson, from Mantric."

The kid gave him a blank look. Long enough for the star on the left earpiece of the headset to flash blue twice.

"We're a technology firm," Dylan explained. "I head up the mobile computing division." He handed the kid his business card.

"Oh Jeez," said the kid. He eyeballed the card, then offered a hand. "Darryl Bachman. You're here about the letter Mulroney sent. About the funding."

Dylan opened his mouth to deliver a polite denial then stopped. He had no idea what Darryl was talking about, but it didn't take much imagination to realize the kid had handed him an in, and he might be able to use it to get the information he wanted.

"Is there somewhere we could talk?"

"Yeah, sure. Come on up." Darryl led Dylan up the dark staircase. The scent of stale pizza and dirty carpet wound its way through Dylan's nostrils. He scrunched his nose.

The apartment was not the cluster of unkempt little rooms that Dylan had expected. Instead, it was one high-ceilinged chamber, furnished with minimalist furniture and a scattering of stainless steel computers and flat-panel displays. It was clear the original structure had been modified; the attic was taken out and skylights were installed in the peaked roof. Another youth, built like an apple with legs and arms, barely glanced up from his computer when they entered. Darryl pointed Dylan to a comfortable vinyl chair and offered him a Coke.

Dylan had the whole picture within fifteen minutes. Darryl and his friend Mulroney, the apple-shaped youth, had joined forces after both had graduated from Rutgers the previous year and started up a small, somewhat sketchy unlocked mobile phone business. They had very little overhead, as all orders were taken over the Internet and fulfilled from a warehouse in Elizabeth. This paid the bills and left the boys time to pursue their passion, which turned out to be interactive gaming.

"We do a good trade in selling and reselling unlocked phones. Amazing how many people want them. It's cool because we deal with a bunch of different wholesalers, and our fulfillment house ships the stuff." He laughed and snorted. "Most of it we never even see."

"He knows this, Darryl," rasped Mulroney. "Talk to him about Inventure."

"Sure." Darryl said, oozing excitement. "It's a new technology we have for role-playing gamers. Imagine really fighting the dragons and killing those bastards in a truly 3-D virtual reality environment. This will make Wii seem like a hobby horse."

Dylan nodded—not too encouraging, but listening.

Mulroney rolled over to join them, helping himself to a Coke. "We've got a lot of bugs to work out, which is why we're looking for sponsorship."

"I see." Of course they were. "Let me ask you—why don't you incorporate and manage it yourself?"

"We're not business types," Darryl said with a shrug. "We just want to take a fat cut in perpetuity, which will be a hell of a lot more if an established company does the marketing for us. Right?"

"Could be." Dylan marveled silently at their naiveté, but this wasn't the time for a lecture on the cold realities of the corporate world. "What's your competition doing while you're looking for corporate sponsorship?"

"The same as us, probably," said Darryl with a smile.

His cheerfulness annoyed Dylan. "Well, that's not in your favor."

"Hence the 'sell-it-now' idea," said Mulroney, wriggling his eyebrows.

Dylan took a swig of his Coke. "In my day, it was easier to keep ahead of the curve because everything was new. You could make a killing and then move on before the floor fell out."

"You were there at the beginning, weren't you?" Darryl asked, in awe. "That must have been some fun."

Dylan looked around the loft. Was it so different, after all, from how he and Tony and Rob and Heather had gotten their start five years earlier? Had they been smarter, or just lucky? In fact, wasn't Darryl a tiny bit like the Tony he had first met at MIT?

"Yeah. It was." He drew a hand across his eyes. "But it's a lot different now. You've really got to come up with something different. You guys heard of Prometheus?"

Darryl and Mulroney exchanged glances. "Yeah."

"He's the kind of guy who could make something like what you're talking about a reality, don't you think?"

Darryl shrugged, suddenly impatient. "I think we're the kind of people who can do this."

"Maybe. If you're serious."

"What's your point?" asked Mulroney, suddenly wary. "That it's all about the fame, not the fun? I guess you made it big, and you think everyone who didn't is a jerk—right? Big deal. We're not egomaniacs."

"I'm not—" Dylan stopped, suddenly confused. "I'm not questioning your motives. I didn't bring up Prometheus to show you up. Actually, I wondered if there was any chance you could bring him on board your project. Do you know him?"

"Sort of," said Darryl.

"Wait a minute," said Mulroney, shoving back his chair. "Who are you with?"

Darryl handed the round young man the business card.

Mulroney scowled. "I didn't send the letter to Mantric."

"I know. I heard about you through other channels."

"From who?"

"I'd rather not say. But—"

"Man, I don't believe you guys!" said Mulroney, springing to his feet. "You're not interested in us! You just want Prometheus!"

"Sorry." Dylan held up a hand. "Look, it's not like that—"

"I think you'd better leave," Darryl said unapologetically.

Dylan rose and walked to the door, where he turned and gave it one more shot before leaving. "Listen, it's true I came here looking for Prometheus, but it's not like you think. In fact it has nothing to do with business at all."

"Oh that's reassuring," said Mulroney. He flipped open his phone and punched in three numbers with his thumb.

Dylan nodded. "Okay, I'm going." He still stood with his back to the door. "Look, my best friend died this week. We were like you guys once. He was a friend of Prometheus. I'm just trying to get in touch with him."

Darryl looked sympathetic, but Mulroney smirked. "Right. Are you going?"

"Just tell him I'm looking for him. Please."

"I bet," Darryl said. "Get out."

"Just tell him it's about what happened to Tony."

Dylan opened the door and rushed down the stairs, cursing himself. What good was he if he couldn't handle a couple of wet-behind-the-ears wannabes!

Chapter 16

Dylan arrived back in New York at two o'clock, depressed and disillusioned.

"Dylan?" Rachel, his New York secretary, looked up anxiously as he entered his outer office. "Matt Smith has been looking for you. He's frantic."

Dylan gritted his teeth. Matt was the most competent, and composed, senior consultant at MobiCelus. He only called Dylan during a crisis.

"I'll call him right away."

He went into his office and closed the door, then settled in at his desk and punched up Matt's number. Matt answered on the first ring.

"Dylan! Where've you been?"

"Chasing some ghosts." No point in advertising his extracurricular activities. "What's up?"

"Haven't you checked your e-mail, for God's sake?"

"No, sorry, I didn't."

"Well, we have a problem with Hyperfōn."

Shit. He hadn't paid much attention to Hyperfōn since Tony's death. "What kind of problem?" he asked.

"LC is about to announce the launch of Gazi. My contact tells me their website is ready and they will be taking orders as soon as their national advertising campaign rolls out next week." Matt paused for a moment. And then he added, "Dylan, Gazi is an exact replica of Hyperfōn, and they've beaten them to the punch. Hyperfōn's screwed."

Dylan opened his browser and read the press release. LC was one of the largest technology conglomerates in the world. Dylan and his consultants knew LC's businesses backwards and forwards. There was no way LC could develop a competing business like Gazi this fast.

"Matt, how the hell can that be?"

"I don't know. I mean, once we launched Hyperfōn, it should have taken any competitor at least a year to launch a competing business from scratch. Nine months at a minimum. They'd have to reverse-engineer the technology, get around the patent protections, develop the software—"

"Exactly. And Hyperfōn's only been up and running for—what? A month?" Dylan's mind raced through the ad campaign and the launch over the past month, unable to determine how LC could have developed their product and gotten it rolled out so quickly.

"I know. It doesn't make any sense. It must be a coincidence. LC must have had this new business in development for the last year. We must have missed it when we did our research."

"Do you really believe that?"

"No, but what else could it be? We worked our asses off and studied every possible competitor. And we looked hard at LC. Things were crazy during the buyout, but we did our homework, Dylan."

"I know you did." This was bad, very bad. They had promised Joe that Hyperfōn was going to be one of a kind, with at least a year's head start on the competition.

"Dylan, I'm up here doing everything I can to try and hold this together. Ferrano is furious, and the venture capitalists are all over him."

Dylan's concerns over Prom3th3u5, and Tony's death, so omnipresent for the past three days, were pushed back by this new disaster. "Listen, Matt, tell Joe right now that I'm taking the next shuttle up to see him in person."

"Okay, I will. What are you going to do when you get here?"

"We'll think of something. Our work was solid; I know it was. I want Joe to know that we stand behind our work, and I am personally going to help his company through this. I should be there in less than two hours. In the meantime, do the best you can. And get the team to dig around. See what you can find out about LC and how they did this. Hang in there—okay?"

"Okay. Thanks. Call me when you get here."

Dylan hung up the phone and ran out of his office and stopped at Rachel's desk.

"Listen, Rachel, something's come up. I have to go to Boston."

"I know."

Dylan was confused. "Did Matt tell you?"

"Tell me what?"

"About Hyperfōn?"

"No. Michelle called," she said, referring to Art's assistant. "Art's in Boston getting ready for the funeral. He wants to meet with you this evening for drinks at Radius. I told her I would check with you and get back to her."

Dylan frowned and looked at his watch. "Fine. Call Michelle back and have her tell Art that'll work, since I have to go to Hyperfōn for an emergency meeting."

"Okay."

Dylan paused, biting his lip. Did he really want to draw Art's attention to Hyperfōn right now? "You know what? Don't tell Art that. Just tell him I'll meet him at seven." He rushed out of the office. What the hell could be so important that Art wanted a private meeting?

• • •

May 6, 3:30 p.m. Boston

Dylan jumped into a taxi at Logan Airport, and within twenty minutes he arrived at the Hyperfōn offices. He pulled out his cell phone and hit the speed-dial number for Matt Smith.

"Hello, this is Matt."

"Matt, it's Dylan."

"Where are you?"

"Three stories below you. Can you meet me in the lobby? We should probably talk privately for a few minutes before I come up."

"I'll be right down."

Dylan walked into the lobby of the building and took a seat in one of the chairs. Moments later, Matt appeared and took the chair next to him.

"Christ, am I glad you're here." The normally cool Matt looked paralyzed with fear.

"How bad is it?"

"Real bad. After I told Joe you were flying up to see him, he abruptly ended our meeting. Our team is holed up in the workroom. They're scouring the Internet and making some calls to try and figure out how LC could have possibly pulled this off. It's like they knew everything we were doing for Hyperfōn all along."

"Any ideas?"

"No. None. We're all stumped."

"Does Rob know?" Dylan asked.

"Yeah, I told him as soon as I saw the news. He's been in constant contact with me. He's doing some research from his end. Wants you to call him when we're finished here."

Dylan ran his fingers through his hair and let out a sigh. "Well, I guess it's time to face the music. Any advice for me before I meet with Joe?"

Matt stood up, looked at him and shrugged. "Bring a heat shield?"

Dylan smiled. Matt was very talented, and this wasn't his fault. "Okay. Let me see what I can do. In the meantime, start thinking about how Hyperfōn can respond. Maybe there's a way to turn this situation around to their advantage."

"I'm already on it," said Matt, but he didn't sound confident.

They went up to Hyperfōn's office, and as they emerged from the elevator, Matt turned right and returned to the workroom, while Dylan turned left, hurrying toward Joe's office. Joe's secretary was expecting him and showed him in.

Joe's usual warm and friendly demeanor was absent. He was grim. "I'd offer you a drink," he said, "but this isn't going to take long."

Not a good start, thought Dylan. "Listen, Joe—"

"It's over, Dylan," he interrupted. "It's a hard decision because I consider you a friend. But I can't afford to be sentimental. My board is furious, and they want blood. Your blood. They're demanding we terminate our contract with you. And, if we don't, the venture capitalists say they'll pull our funding." Joe wiped his face. "And frankly, I agree. How the hell did your team miss the Gazi project?"

"Honestly, Joe, I have no idea. We did exhaustive research on LC. It doesn't make any sense. But I have the team looking into it right now. We'll figure this out."

Joe shook his head. "Don't waste your time. It doesn't matter anymore. With their resources, LC is going to crush us."

"We don't know it's over yet, Joe. Hell, there may be a way to use LC's move to our advantage."

Joe regarded him thoughtfully. "Listen to me carefully, Dylan. You're good with people. You could talk a teetotaler into having a drink with you. But it only works when you've got the goods. This is a goddamn catastrophe for an outfit the size of Hyperfōn. We could be out of business within three months. I have to let you go."

Dylan thought quickly. There had to be a way to recover this. "Joe, give us two weeks. I promise you we'll come back with a new strategy for your company."

"Sorry, Dylan. I can't do that. And I hate to do this to you, but I can't pay you what we already owe you. As far as we're concerned, you didn't deliver what you promised."

"But Joe—"

Joe stood up. "It's over, Dylan."

"It's not over, damn it! Look, Joe, we did our job right. We made sure the market was wide-open for you. Somebody's fucking with us."

Joe shook his head. "I'm sorry, Dylan. I hate to say I told you so, but I saw this coming. This is the sort of thing that happens when you sell your company but think you're still in control. I warned you, but you could only smell the dollars you'd get if you went with Mantric. You were smart kids once, and MobiCelus was a great company. You killed it when you went with Mantric. I sincerely hope you get the message."

"Listen to me, Joe. You have to give me a little time. I'll figure it out." Dylan's mind went into overdrive, thinking back to the very beginning with Joe and Hyperfōn.

Joe shook his head. He walked over to the door and opened it. "You've got other things to do, Dylan. I'm sorry about Tony. Go bury your friend. Under the circumstances, I think it's better if I don't go to the funeral."

Dylan walked down the hall to the workroom, where he motioned for Matt to come out into the hallway.

Matt took one look at Dylan. "It's over, isn't it? I might as well pack my bags now."

"It's not over," Dylan said, his eyes flashing with anger. "Not yet."

"So what do I tell them?" Matt said, nodding towards the team.

Dylan paused for a moment. He didn't want his people making a scene at the client site. "Wrap it up and get everyone back to the office. Then I want you and the team to find out what the hell happened. That's your one and only priority."

"How?"

"I don't know, Matt," Dylan said sharply, "But the last time I checked, this was your damn project. Why don't you figure it out?"

Matt blanched. Dylan had never spoken to him like that before.

Dylan looked at his watch. It was almost five o'clock. "Shit! I've got to go. Look, I'm sorry, but call me the minute you find anything, no matter how small, no matter what time."

"Okay. I'll do my best, Dylan."

Dylan said nothing. He turned and walked back to the elevator.

• • •

Dylan raced home, took a quick shower, and changed clothes for his meeting with Art. It was six-thirty when he left his house for the drive to Radius. He would be a few minutes late, but he decided not to call Art. He checked his voice-mail. Nothing.

Damn LC! How was it possible all these things were happening to him? He felt pressured from all sides. Tony's death. Hyperfōn. What was next? He seemed cursed with bad luck.

Dylan frowned. Bad luck? What if it wasn't luck at all? What if this latest disaster was just one more link in the chain of problems forged since they had come to Mantric? What if someone was driving these things?

Radius was the hottest bar and restaurant in the neighborhood for business executives who could afford its prices. Dylan looked over the sea of suits and saw Art seated alone at a corner table near the back of the bar. Art waved him over.

As he sat down, Dylan saw that he was already finishing off a glass of red wine. He wondered how many glasses Art had finished by this time.

"Hello, Dylan. Thanks for meeting with me. Do you want something to drink?"

"Sure, I'll have whatever you're drinking."

Art caught the attention of the waiter. "Bring my friend here a glass of the 1989 Chateau Palmer Bordeaux. And another for me." The waiter nodded and disappeared. "It's an excellent vintage," Art said, raising the nearly empty glass and gently spinning the stem between his thumb and index finger.

He certainly did seem to know his wine. "Thanks," Dylan replied. "So, Art," he said tentatively. "How are the plans for the funeral?"

"Everything's set. We've got a charter bringing up whoever wants to come from New York. It'll be a big turnout, I think. Tony was well liked. I understand you're doing the eulogy?"

"Yeah. Mr. Caruso asked me."

Art nodded.

"How are you doing, Art?"

"Aside from Tony's death, I'm good. Why wouldn't I be? Our numbers are great, the market is great, and our stock is kicking ass. How could I be anything but great right now?"

Dylan noted a slight slur in Art's words. "That's good to hear."

The waiter reappeared with their two glasses of wine.

Art raised his glass and said, "Here's to the greatest stock ride ever."

Dylan and Art clinked glasses. "Amen to that," Dylan said before they both took a sip. Dylan put his glass down. "So what did you want to talk about?"

Art set his glass down in front of him. A blank look wandered across his face, and for a moment he said nothing. He took another sip of his wine. "Actually, I wanted to talk to you about Hyperfōn."

Dylan stared back at him. *How the hell had Art found out?* he wondered. "What about them?" Dylan said, cautiously.

"I know this is a bad time for both of us." Art's eyes narrowed, and he glared at Dylan. He put his glass down and gripped the stem. "But I want to know what happened and how you're going to get us the fucking money they owe us."

Dylan felt his heart pounding. How had Art heard about this? And how did he know about the money? "How did you find out? I just found out about it myself."

Art's demeanor changed. "That's a bunch of crap coming from the boy wonder who demands to have access to board information and company financial records." Art's tone darkened with a mixture of wine and anger. "Tell me something, Dylan," he continued, his voice dripping sarcasm. "How is it you only found out about it today? What the hell was Matt Smith doing?" His voice rose slightly.

Dylan moved forward, looking around the room, trying to control the conversation. "Art, no one on the team saw this coming. We studied LC a year ago when we first took on Hyperfōn at MobiCelus. We didn't find any evidence that they, or anyone else, were going to launch a business like this."

"Is that supposed to make me feel better?"

"No. I'm just answering your question."

"You're not answering it very well. I bought your company because you were supposed to be the best mobile computing consulting firm out there, and your clients made the deal attractive. I even gave you and your buddies the roles you wanted and 100,000 extra shares of stock. Do you have any idea what will happen to us if your division falters?"

"Art, I guarantee you it won't. Even if we lose Hyperfōn—"

"Jesus, Dylan," Art said loudly, ignoring the turned heads of the people nearby. "How do you think the market will react when they hear about this?"

"Probably not well," Dylan admitted.

"Not well? Christ, they'll *crucify* us. They'll say we fumbled the ball, that we bought a mobile computing firm to expand into a hot sector and the firm turned out to be a fucking disaster. And now, here we are, a public company with people scrutinizing our performance." His anger boiled over. "I understand Hyperfōn owes us close to one million dollars. Is that right?"

Dylan took a big gulp of his wine and grimaced. "Yeah, that's about right."

"For your sake and the firm's, you better recover those fees."

"That could be difficult," he said, staring at the table.

"What do you mean, 'difficult'?" Art demanded.

"I met with Joe Ferrano this afternoon. He told me he and his board have decided not to pay us." Dylan looked up at Art. "His venture capitalists are all up in arms, Art. I tried my best, but he wouldn't budge."

Art bit his lip and shook his head slowly. "Dylan, you know you've put this firm at risk, don't you?"

Dylan was startled. It was bad, but not that bad. "I'm sorry you feel that way, but—"

"I'm afraid 'sorry' is not good enough. You know what you have to do. Just fix it."

His words hit like a blow to the face. "I'm taking this one step at a time, Art. I've got the whole team looking into it. I don't believe we were at fault. We're going to find out what happened."

"You do that. And you should consider this conversation to be an official warning. Do you understand? This is business; I can't give you any breaks just because this is a tough time for you. You're slipping, Dylan. Not getting the job done. I am not happy with your performance. And we'd better not lose any more mobile computing clients."

Christ, Dylan thought, *he's threatening me?* "Art, I'm doing my job. And my division is in fine shape."

"Now, maybe, but—"

"I promise you this won't happen again."

"Okay. You've been warned, then. That's it. This conversation is over. We won't discuss this again."

Art sat back and said nothing more, silent, staring at Dylan. Dylan nodded, stood up, and walked out of the restaurant.

May 6, 9:00 p.m. Boston

Dylan walked slowly down High Street and then turned west on Summer Street. The sky dimmed as the sun set. He looked up at the thick clouds that overran downtown Boston. He had no idea where he was going. He just needed to walk.

Art's fury about the loss of Hyperfōn and the money could be understandable, except that he didn't take into account the fact that Mantric's revenues were way over plan or that the company's stock was higher than anyone had expected and its market value now approached two billion dollars. Dylan was baffled by Art's behavior over one account. He turned these items over and over in his mind, now confronted with a mixture of emotions, in particular confusion and fear.

Dylan turned the corner at Arch Street and walked north. He was oblivious to everything around him as he went over what had just happened. Why had Art wanted to meet over a drink? Why had he started the meeting talking about the funeral, only to berate and threaten him? And how the hell did he know about Hyperfōn?

The sense of helplessness that had been growing within him since Tony's death continued to plague him. A chill ran through his body, and he instinctively looked back to see if anyone was following him. He felt scared and alone. Tony gone. Rich gone. Would he be next?

He shook off his fear and forced himself to focus. His thoughts turned to figuring out how LC had been able to pull it off. He would meet with Matt and the team first thing tomorrow. His mind raced. They would do the postmortem, dig around, and try to figure out what went wrong. He would call for an immediate review of all their other clients and their potential competitors. There might be another LC lurking out there, just waiting to pounce.

Ideas and thoughts darted through his mind—and then he remembered. Tomorrow was Tony's funeral. Jesus, how could he forget? He bowed his head.

As he approached the Old South Meeting House, Dylan pulled out his cell phone and hit his speed-dial number.

"Hey," came Rob's voice.

"Can you talk?"

"Yeah. We just took a break." Dylan heard the sound of a door closing in the background. "So how'd it go with Joe?"

"Not good. He fired us."

"What? You're kidding."

"No, I'm not."

"Jesus Christ! Didn't you try to talk him out of it?"

"Of course I did. But, Rob, you wouldn't believe how angry he was. He's even refusing to pay us the million he owes."

"Holy shit! I can't believe this!"

Dylan breathed deeply. "We'll just have to find out how it happened."

"What do you mean?"

"Well, our team sure as hell didn't miss this! I think somebody somewhere sold us out."

"Oh, man. Are you serious? So does the team have any clue yet about what happened?"

"No. We'll meet Monday here in Boston. I know you're very busy, but can you join us?"

"Of course. I have things in hand here now. Don't worry. We'll get to the bottom of this."

He wondered if Rob really had any faith they could get to the bottom of it, or if he was just telling Dylan what he wanted to hear. "Thanks. Maybe we can find a minute to talk about it tomorrow."

Something remained unanswered in Dylan's mind. Nothing made sense to him: Rich's comments about Christine and the reserve, the severance package they gave Rich, Heather's point about the profits of the New York office. And what about Art not allowing Dylan to go on the road show or even look at their financials? Things just didn't add up; something was very, very wrong. But what? His mind flashed back to Tony. What had Tony known?

Chapter 17

May 7, 11:00 a.m. Boston

The scent of carnations and roses filled the church. As Dylan walked to the altar, he heard the echoing crash of kneelers inadvertently kicked by the mourners, the snap of purse latches as women removed their handkerchiefs, the muffled coughs.

In the pulpit, Dylan stood high above Tony's many friends and took a deep breath. His nerves tingled until the moment he began to speak, and then peace enveloped him as he recounted stories of Tony's brilliance, his unending generosity, and his lovable irreverence. As he spoke of Tony's integrity, his eyes locked with Art's, who looked away.

When he stepped down from the pulpit, the sound of sobs scattered throughout the congregation, and yet Dylan felt strangely tranquil as he walked over to the casket, touched it, and then returned to his seat in the pew between Mr. Caruso and Rob. Heather sat on the other side of Mr. Caruso; tears stained her cheeks.

Dylan knew Tony had many friends, but he hadn't expected the crowd of people who attended the mass. He estimated several hundred people crowded into the small church, many standing or leaning against walls.

In addition to Art, Christine, and Stephanie, many others from the firm had come up from New York to express their condolences. Even Ivan appeared, sitting motionless through the service, his eyes roaming the room as if looking for something or someone. The entire Boston office sat close together, and Dylan saw some faces from their MIT days, yet there were many more he didn't recognize. Dylan realized that, although he considered Tony to be his best friend, there was another side to him. He scanned the many unknown faces in the crowd, suddenly aware of how fleeting life could be.

The sun warmed the dry air as the funeral procession wound its way through Mount Auburn Cemetery in Cambridge. Founded before the Civil War, it was one of the most famous burial grounds in the country and the final resting place for such luminaries as Henry Wadsworth Longfellow, Oliver Wendell Holmes, B.F. Skinner, and Winslow Homer.

As he followed the black limousine, Dylan smiled, recalling the times during college when he and Tony had walked through these grounds and shared stories about their dreams for the future. How ironic, Dylan thought, that he was now there to bury his friend. It was only when Tony's mother had died that Dylan learned that the Carusos owned one of the precious few open plots at the cemetery. Now here he was again—this time to see his best friend laid to rest next to his mother.

Dylan drove to the top of a small hill and parked his car. The burial site was covered with a dark green awning. Rob and Heather drove up and parked behind him. Heather went up the hill alone, but Rob and Dylan joined Tony's father and the other pallbearers as the casket was slid out of the hearse. They lifted it and carried it up to the gravesite, followed by a sea of mourners clad in black.

After they placed the casket on the straps over the perfect rectangular hole in the ground, Dylan stepped back and looked at the faces around him. Art and Christine stood together across from him, staring at the ground and fidgeting. Stephanie was behind them. Poor Rich, looking lost and yet a little defiant. Matt, Sarah—they were all there. All the old MobiCelus gang, as well as the staff of the entire Boston office. Everyone was there who should have been there, thought Dylan with some satisfaction.

Except—he looked around Art's group—no Sandeep. Surely Sandeep should be there. Good God, Tony had been his second in command. Dylan stood up and circled around the back of the gathering. But there was no sight of Sandeep's slight figure.

Suspicion, fueled by an icy anger, bubbled in Dylan's mind. Why wouldn't he come? Of course, he had been in L.A., but surely he could have arranged his schedule to get back for the funeral. No, there had to be a reason. Jealousy? Or guilt? Had his jealousy led him to do the unthinkable? Or had Tony had something Sandeep dearly wanted? Dylan shook off his suspicions. He was beginning to see guilt in every person. *Not now,* he thought. *Not now.*

As the priest began speaking, Dylan glanced at Heather, who stood to his left, holding Mr. Caruso's arm. He watched as a tear wandered down her cheek from behind her sunglasses. He looked to his right, where Rob stood, looking pale and shaken in the bright sunshine. Rob rocked back and forth, a pained expression on his face. Dylan put a hand on his shoulder.

Afterwards, Dylan shook hands with many people who told him how sorry they were and what a wonderful person Tony had been. He thanked them politely, not really knowing what else to say. As the crowd thinned, he spotted Ivan again, standing like a statue on the far side of the grave, his eyes fixed on one spot. Dylan followed his gaze and realized Ivan was staring at Heather. He looked back at Ivan to make sure, but there was no mistake. As Dylan watched, Heather turned and caught Ivan's eye. They stared at one another. Then Ivan turned and walked away.

Dylan was surprised to see a look of cold anger on Heather's face. *What the hell was that about?*

Art had collared Mr. Caruso and was fussing over him as the long line of sympathy-wishers paraded past to shake his hand. Rich appeared in his turn, saying words of condolence to Mr. Caruso. Art reached out and took Rich's hand, muttering a few apologetic words.

"Well isn't that interesting," said Heather, nudging Dylan as she watched the scene. "He actually shook Rich's hand."

"It's a time of forgiveness," said Rob. "Art probably still feels bad about firing him."

Heather cast a scornful look at Rob over her sunglasses. She turned away and looked casually at the crowd that milled around the grave and was slowly dispersing.

"Who's that?" Heather whispered to Dylan. "That guy over there?"

Dylan followed the direction of her glance, and his gaze settled on a middle-aged man in a brown sport coat and jeans, standing close enough to the crowd to be identified as a mourner, but far enough away to avoid any direct contact with friends or family. He fiddled with a red vase of yellow tulips on the ground next to the gravesite, trying to make sure it would stand upright among the other tributes. Dylan didn't recognize him, but his clothing and unkempt hair suggested he was a techie, maybe a professor from MIT.

"I don't know."

"Me either," said Rob. "Why do you ask?"

"I saw him at the church. He came in alone and sat in the back. Never spoke to anyone."

"Just shy," said Rob.

"He looked out of place," muttered Heather. "He kept glancing around the church, but not as if he was looking for someone he knew. He seemed to be on edge, as if he were frightened."

Dylan walked toward him and watched the stranger slip away

114

through the crowd. When the vase of tulips began to list into a bowl of carnations at its side, Dylan stepped over to snatch the vase and prevent it from falling. A small card tucked into the arrangement caught his eye. He discreetly removed the card to see a picture of a yellow flame rising from a copper torch. The words inside read: "Too smart, too good, too young."

There was no signature.

"Somebody got it right," said a voice at his side.

Dylan turned to see Mr. Caruso, his grey hair fluttering in the warm breeze.

Dylan returned the card to the bouquet. "Yeah."

"Heather says she'd take me to my hotel. I need to get some rest before dinner."

"Good. Where are we meeting?"

"At that restaurant called Clink in the Liberty Hotel where I'm staying. Tony liked it."

"Sounds good." Dylan turned to Rob. "Are we off then?"

"I'm catching a ride with Rich," said Rob. "We haven't had a chance to talk."

"Okay," said Dylan. He walked a few steps with Rob. "You didn't happen to talk to Sandeep today, did you?"

"Nope. Why?"

"Wondered why he isn't here."

"He's in L.A. 'til tomorrow, I believe."

Dylan bit his lip to hide his disgust. "What's his story, anyway?"

"Sandeep? Typical geek. Too polite for his own good, though."

"What does that mean?"

"Christine got him for a song. And, unlike the others, his shares don't vest as fast. He could have done a lot better, but he doesn't know how to negotiate a contract."

Heather wandered over and lifted the card from among the tulips. A smile played across her lips.

"What?" asked Rob.

"Just admiring the artistic symmetry. The flowers represent the torch on the card. It's an old symbol of knowledge."

Mr. Caruso took her arm and patted her hand. They were about to walk down the hill, and Rob turned to find Rich. But Dylan stood frozen in place. He looked at the bright tulips and snatched at the card. Symbol of knowledge? Yes! Fire represented knowledge. He had just read all about it. The god who had given fire to humankind had been punished by his fellow Titans for daring to share a wisdom that would make the mortals too powerful. And the symbol of that god, replicated a thousand times in the art of the world for a thousand years, was the flaming torch.

"Prometheus," he said, louder than he'd meant to. He spun around, scanning through the crowd. He saw Heather glance at him quizzically. There was no sign of the brown sport coat and its shaggy-haired owner. How much of a head start did he have? Five minutes?

Dylan raced down the hill toward a man in a black suit standing guard by the parking lot.

"Excuse me. I thought I spotted a friend. Man about forty-five in a brown sport coat and stonewashed jeans. Did you see him leave a couple of minutes ago?" Dylan's head turned in several directions as he spoke.

"Yes, sir, I did." He pointed down the road. "He went that way. On foot."

"Thanks."

Dylan raced across the lot and down the road at full speed. He saw no sign of the man until he found himself in front of a gas station two blocks away, where he saw him approaching a taxicab.

Dylan raced up to the man and grabbed his arm as he was halfway into the cab. "Sorry. I just wanted to have a word."

"Yeah? What about?" He wrenched himself free of Dylan's grip.

"You were a friend of Tony's, weren't you?"

"What's it to you?"

"My name is Dylan Johnson, and—"

But at the sound of his name, the man jumped into the cab, locked the door, and told the driver, "Just drive."

"Wait! Please!" Dylan shouted. "I just want to talk about Tony!" But the window rolled up and the cab accelerated into traffic.

Dylan steadied himself and fixed his eyes on the cab. He yanked his phone from his pocket. He could not get a photo of the man, but he got the next best thing—the number of the cab and the license plate.

• • •

May 7, 7:00 p.m. Boston

The Liberty Hotel, once the Charles Street jailhouse, played on its history with clever names for itself and its restaurant and bar. Dylan walked into the Clink Restaurant at seven p.m. The young woman at the door led him to a private room, where he met Dominic Caruso, Heather, Rob, Matt, and Rich.

Dylan looked around. "No Art or Christine or Ivan?" he asked.

Heather said nothing, just shook her head no. Dylan took the hint and did not pursue it.

"Where were you going in such a hurry this afternoon?" Rob asked.

The waitress brought drinks to the table, and asked Dylan what he wanted. "Knob Creek on the rocks." Dylan did not want to answer Rob's question, not just yet, and he was grateful when Dominic cleared his throat to speak.

"We'll wait until Dylan gets his drink, and then I'd like to make a toast."

Everyone nodded, and the small talk started around the table. The waitress returned with Dylan's drink and a refill for Rob.

"I'd like to make a toast to my Tony," Dominic said. "The best son a man could ever want." His eyes glazed, and he quickly downed his glass of wine. He refilled it from the bottle on the table, and each person offered a toast in turn.

The meals were served and small talk resumed. Heather, sitting between Dominic and Dylan, turned to Dylan and whispered, "What happened with you today?"

"What do you mean?" Dylan knew what she meant, but was not sure how close to keep his information. She was the only person he was absolutely sure of. She could not have murdered Tony because she was on the other side of the country. And yet he was not sure of her relationship with Rob. Would she share their conversations with him? He felt the grip of paranoia as he thought about who could be responsible for Tony's death. Surely not Rob, or Matt, or Rich. But what about Art and Christine? His mind wandered over other names. Sandeep and Ivan. But what motives could they possibly have had? More paranoia.

Heather continued. "You rushed away from the gravesite today like you were being chased by a ghost. What was that about?"

"I just thought I saw someone I knew."

"That's a bunch of crap and you know it. It's me you're talking to, Dylan," she whispered.

He made a snap decision. "Not now. I'll explain later." He kept his voice low. Hell, he wasn't even sure what information he had. Just a series of loose ends he was trying to weave together into an answer. "How about dinner tomorrow evening, my place?"

She smiled. "I'll bring the wine."

Chapter 18

May 8, 6:30 p.m. Boston

Dylan tossed the salad of fresh mixed greens, olives, peppers, and thinly sliced Vidalia onions. He topped it with feta cheese, covered it, and put it in the refrigerator just as the doorbell rang. He hurried over and looked through the peephole to see Heather standing before him, waving two bottles of wine.

Dylan jerked the door open and smiled. It was the first time all day he had genuinely felt the urge to smile. From eight until four, he had sat in the conference room huddled with Rob, Matt, and the rest of the team, reviewing the Hyperfōn situation. Matt had already gone over every file, note, e-mail, and anything else he could think of to see if they had missed something. But they had not. They had originally checked LC as a possible competitor to Hyperfōn; they had copies of LC's SEC filings, annual reports, and quarterly earnings statements, and still they found nothing. They brainstormed for several hours; then Matt and his gang retired to conduct their research again, this time focusing exclusively on Hyperfōn. By the end of the day, they had found nothing.

Dylan felt a surge of relief when Heather entered and kissed him lightly on the cheek. "How was your day?"

Dylan explained about Hyperfōn and the unsuccessful day of research his team had endured.

She remained silent while Dylan opened a bottle of Pinot Noir. Then she said, "Do you think you'll ever figure out what happened with the account?"

"I have no idea. Rob and Matt have looked at every file at least three times and considered every possible scenario, and still we've found nothing."

He walked into the kitchen and Heather followed. "Mmm, smells really good in here. Nice-looking steaks." She pointed to the T-bones sitting on the grill as Dylan turned them. "You know, you're working on two things at once."

Dylan turned and looked at her. "What do you mean?" he asked.

"This Hyperfōn situation on the one hand and Tony's death on the other. Don't you think you should focus? Either solve the business problem and let the police handle Tony's death, or figure out who killed Tony and let Rob and Matt take care of Hyperfōn."

Dylan stopped for a minute to consider her comments. He said nothing, just nodded to acknowledge them. He removed the salad from the refrigerator and gave Heather two salad bowls to fill. He removed the steaks from the grill and two baked potatoes from the oven, placing them on dinner plates.

"Time to eat," was all he said. They sat in uncomfortable silence for several minutes before he spoke again. "You know, Heather, you may be right. I've been very frustrated these past few days between Tony's death and now this Hyperfōn mess."

"So which are you going to follow?" she asked, buttering her baked potato.

He looked at her and a sad smile crept over his face. "I don't really know what the police are doing about Tony. They don't keep me informed. But I can't get him out of my mind. I trust Matt and Rob to get to the bottom of Hyperfōn and keep me informed. So the answer to your question is: to help the police whether they want my help or not. I'm not any kind of detective—I know that—but I also know that if I don't learn the truth, either from the police or on my own, I will never get beyond this thing. It will haunt me for the rest of my life."

"Okay. I'm there with you." Heather put a hand on Dylan's arm. "Bring me up to date. Two heads are better than one."

A renewed energy raced through him. "Well, for starters, you're the only person I trust at this point. I know where you were when the crime occurred."

Heather backed off for a split second, then nodded and smiled. "So I'm not a suspect. That's a good place to start." She cut a piece of steak and devoured it. "What else?"

"You already know about the e-mail Tony sent me, and I looked at the ones you forwarded to me, the ones between the two of you. His messages were so cryptic—it was as if he was afraid someone was viewing them besides you."

"You're right about the mystery of his messages. They made no sense to me at all. But why do you think he was so paranoid?"

"I was thinking about something he said to me a while back. We had gone into his office, which by the way was a huge mess, and yet he felt as if something was out of place. I think that's where his paranoia started. I couldn't see anything, but, then again, it was his office."

Heather smiled. "Yes, I remember how cluttered it was. But what else?"

Dylan told her about the schematic and his trip to New Jersey. "That brings me up to yesterday at Tony's funeral. You asked me about why I rushed away from the grave so quickly. Actually, you're the one who threw that clue at me."

She put her fork down; a quizzical look crossed her face. "Me? What did I do?"

"Remember when you looked at that card, the one with the torch on it? Well, it was then I made the connection between the card and Prometheus."

"Prometheus! That's what you said as I was walking away. I wondered what that was about."

"I realized the guy who stood away from the crowd must have been him. He's the key to the whole thing—it's a long story, but he's the guy I've been trying to find."

"Did you catch up with him?"

"Yes, but only for a moment. He was jumping into a cab, and when I approached him and told him my name, he pulled away from me, slammed the door, and the cab sped away."

"Now we'll never find him."

Dylan pulled the cell phone out of his pocket. "Well, I did get this information." He showed her the picture. "I'm not entirely sure how to pursue this, but—"

Heather stopped him mid-sentence. "I think I have an idea. Do you have any heavy stock paper here?"

Chapter 19

Tuesday morning rolled in foggy. A front had wandered through Boston the previous night, bringing with it heavy rain that dissolved into a dreary mist.

Dylan rolled over and looked at Heather. Her lips turned up into an enigmatic smile, and he wondered what she was dreaming of, where her thoughts were taking her. He slowly turned to the side of the bed and started to get up, when she awoke.

"Hi," she said, stretching. "Thanks again for dinner." She pulled him back into the warmth of the bed and wrapped her arms around him.

"Hi," he returned. "You're most welcome. Thanks for staying."

Her eyes still closed, her smile widened and she nodded. She kissed him—a soft, gentle kiss that grew into passion. Dylan engulfed her in his arms and returned the kiss. They remained entangled in the light blanket for several minutes, when Heather suddenly opened her eyes wide.

"Oh my gosh! We've got work to do." She rolled over, searched through the jacket she had thrown on the floor the previous evening, and retrieved her cell phone. She speed-dialed her assistant's number. "Hello, Gloria—it's Heather. Look, I'm not going to come in for a few days. This entire situation with Tony's funeral has me really down. There isn't anything pressing on my calendar, and if you need me, I can be reached on my cell. I'll get back to you later. Let me know if anything comes up." She rolled back toward Dylan. "You'd better do the same thing. We don't want the office staff worrying about where we are!"

Dylan smiled. "You are very smart." He retrieved his phone from his nightstand and made a similar call to Sarah's voice-mail.

"Now, we have to make me an ID!"

Heather sprang out of bed. Dylan admired her slender body as she hurried into the bathroom. He dressed, went to the kitchen and made coffee, and smiled when she came into the kitchen dressed in his over-sized robe, her hair wrapped in a towel.

He handed her a cup of coffee. "Want a bagel?" he asked.

"Nope, the coffee is fine. Let's get this ID made."

"I'm not sure what exactly it is you want to do."

He followed her into the second bedroom—his office—where she sat down at his computer. He watched over her shoulder as she found software for creating business cards and began to type.

"I'm going to be a police officer for the day."

"Heather, impersonating a police officer is not a good idea. It's against the law."

"Mm-hmm," she said and continued to type.

Dylan read as she typed her name and gave herself the title of sergeant. Not too high up, but important enough to cause someone to answer questions without asking any. She lifted a logo from the police website and pasted it in a corner of the card. "Do you have a picture of me somewhere in here?" she asked.

He sat next to her, opened a photo program, and began to sort through a collection of pictures of his friends.

"Stop! That one. That looks very professional. I'm not smiling, but I'm not snarling either." She cropped and copied the photo and pasted it into the right spot. "Now, where is your paper stock?"

Dylan retrieved a sheet and placed it in the printer, and Heather proceeded to print out her newly created police ID.

"Heather," he said, worry creeping into his voice. "Where are you going with this?"

"I'm going to the cab company. Don't worry. I'll just talk to the local supervisor. If something goes wrong, we'll deal with it then. In the meantime, we need to find someplace where we can laminate this thing."

Dylan reached into the bottom drawer of his desk and removed an old, dusty device. "Jeez, I haven't used this since my early college days. And you don't want to know what that was all about!"

"Good. You laminate a few of these things for me, and I'll go change." She disappeared back into the bedroom before Dylan could once again object. She called over her shoulder, "And then you'll tell me all about this Prometheus character."

May 9, 11:45 a.m. Boston

Heather, dressed in a business suit, her hair pulled back into a tight bun, walked into the Boston Cab Company at noon. She planned her visit to be close to lunchtime, with as few people as possible in the office. She kept her head down and approached a petite woman behind the counter. Fifteen minutes later she walked out of the office, closed her notebook, and put it in her purse.

Dylan leaned over and opened the passenger door. "Well?" he asked, unable to hide his excitement. "No problems?" He wasn't sure if it was the thrill of the hunt, doing something illegal, or getting more information to help their search, but he felt the adrenaline pumping.

"Nope. I talked to an assistant supervisor and showed her my ID. She didn't ask to see a badge. I told her I was looking for someone who was wanted for questioning in a robbery and a witness had seen someone fitting his description jumping into a cab."

"And she believed you?" he asked in amazement.

"I tried to look stern and sound demanding. I told her I could get a warrant if they needed it, but she said they were pleased to be able to help the police. I gave her the cab number and time of day and location, and she pulled up the information. The guy was dropped at the Radisson Hotel."

"Well, shit, let's go."

They arrived at the Radisson twenty minutes later. Heather fixed her hair and makeup, looked at Dylan, and crossed her fingers.

"Let's hope this is just as easy." Thirty minutes later she returned to the car. "Not such good luck."

"What took so long? Did they refuse to help? I was beginning to panic."

"I'm afraid I didn't get much. He had stayed there Saturday and Sunday night, but he checked out early Tuesday."

"Did he use a credit card?"

"That's the curious thing. The hotel confirmed it when he checked in, but when he left he used the auto checkout on the TV in his room. By the time he was gone, they discovered the card was cancelled. They checked the phone number and it wasn't in service, and the address was assigned to some company that never heard of him. They insisted I make a police report. That's what took so long." She started to laugh. "I'm sorry, but I really hated taking all this information knowing it would lead nowhere."

"This guy's good." Dylan stared through the windshield. So much had happened in such a short time, and now he felt Prometheus was slipping away—and with him the solution to Tony's death.

They returned to Dylan's place, where they sat side-by-side at the computer as he typed in the credit card information Heather had picked up from the hotel. "What name did this guy give?"

"Brandon Wist."

Dylan remembered that Tony had mentioned a Brandon. He Googled the name. "Look at this," he said, pointing to the information that appeared on the screen. Dylan reached across his desk and picked up his phone. He dialed information and got the number for Technochondriacs in New Jersey. He waited while the number rang several times until it went to voice-mail.

"This is Dylan Johnson from Mantric. I met you several days ago and I need your help. I need to find Brandon Wist. I know you don't want to help me, but if you do, I'll return the favor ten times over. I have the contacts you need for your venture *and* I will also see to it that they help you. So how important is your future? I'm trying to find out who murdered my friend, Tony Caruso. The police are also working toward that end. So call me and let me know how much help you want to give me, or if I should just let the police contact you. You have my card."

Dylan hung up and looked at Heather. "Guess we'll wait and see if we get an answer."

"Are you really going to turn this information over to the police if you don't hear from them?" Her eyes flashed in a moment of panic.

"I haven't thought it out that far. Let's wait and see what happens. If I do, it will be anonymous."

Chapter 20

May 11, 7:45 p.m. New Jersey

The drive to Westwood, New Jersey, took the better part of the day, and Dylan wondered if this wild goose chase would lead anywhere. But he was no fool, either. He knew it might be a dangerous exercise.

He sat in his car across the street from the little motel in Westwood, which proved to be like a million of its kind: salmon-colored, poorly lit, and close to the train station. The rain started at about seven. Dylan sat, watching room number four and waiting for any sign of activity.

At seven forty-five he saw the short, pudgy figure—wearing the same stone-washed jeans and brown tweed jacket he had worn at the funeral—hurrying through the rain, clutching a laptop case in one arm and a paper bag in the other. The man kept his head down. The rain and wind drowned out the surrounding noise, and he never noticed Dylan exit his car and sprint toward him. The man turned the key and slipped inside just as Dylan arrived and placed his hand on the door.

"Hey, Brandon."

The man jumped and stumbled backwards. Recognition flooded his face. Dylan stepped inside and closed the door.

"You're hard to find." The room was typical: twin beds with hideous orange bed covers, plain side-tables, and well-worn lamps. The musty smell of dirt and decaying food caught in Dylan's nose, and he coughed. He indicated a chair at a little table in the corner. "Why don't you have a seat?"

The man snorted and fell backward onto the chair, his laptop case on his lap.

Dylan stayed close to the door, not wanting to frighten the man. "I just want to talk—okay?"

"Yeah? Too bad I can't believe you. I know who you are."

"You have no idea who I am. The issue is, were you really a friend of Tony's or not? If not, then fine. Shut up, run, or call the cops, and then I'll know. But if you were his friend, you'll talk to me because I was his friend too. All I'm trying to do is find out what he was working on when he died. To make sure he gets credit for his work and not somebody else. I want my friend to go down in history for his innovations." Dylan wondered if Brandon would accept that excuse or not. He waited.

Brandon kept his eyes glued on Dylan. "Fine. Prove you were Tony's friend."

"Jesus Christ! I went to MIT with him. He and I started our company together. MobiCelus!"

"Your card says Mantric."

"We sold the company to them three months ago. Two effing minutes on the Internet will confirm it."

"Oh." Brandon shrank into himself. "Any other proof?"

Dylan had just about had it with this fat, unkempt little man. "Yeah, he grew up in Watertown and was just buried at Mount Auburn Cemetery. But you already know that. You were there."

Brandon stared at him for a moment and then just nodded.

"My turn." Dylan folded his arms. "How the hell didn't you know about MobiCelus being bought by Mantric? Aren't you a technology genius? Don't you do your homework?"

Brandon looked away uneasily. "I don't want to know what the suits do. And anyway, I only used encrypted texts to communicate with Tony. I don't—I have to take precautions."

"Because Microsoft bought you out and burned you."

"You heard about that?"

"Tony told me. Said you took a shitload of money and in return signed a release with Microsoft saying you would never hire on with another company as a developer."

"Right." Brandon relaxed a little. "Well, mostly right. Let's just say I still like to dabble a bit on my own. Okay, so then you know why I make with the cloak and dagger. I got screwed once in my life, and that was enough."

"How long did you know Tony? How did you meet?"

"A mutual friend hooked us up. Five years ago. I liked talking shop with the kids. And Tony was one of the few who gets it. He had a feel for complex software. We'd get together every few months when he wanted to run something by me. Very advanced stuff."

"I know. A smartphone that converts into a virtual laptop."

Brandon laughed. "Yeah. And other things."

"Like what?"

Brandon shrugged.

"Look. I need to know what you helped him with before he died."

"Who said I was helping him with anything?"

"This drawing he sent to me." He pulled a copy of Tony's schematic from his jacket and handed it to Brandon. "Notice your name at the bottom?"

"Oh shit. Who else saw this? Just you—right? Jesus, I risked my life to go to that funeral, for a friend! And look what it gets me!" He grabbed a bottle of Scotch whisky from the bag, opened it, and took a long swig.

"I doubt anyone else noticed you were there."

"Are you kidding?" He leaped up and staggered to the window. "You did! Are the cops looking for me?"

Dylan found himself staring into the face of paranoia. "Not that I know of. They don't exactly confide in me." He took a deep breath. "I have to tell you something. But you really can't tell anyone else."

A slow grin broke out over Brandon's face. "You're asking me if I can keep a secret?"

"Well, yeah. Just for a while. Until—just for a while."

"Uh-huh. And if I don't agree, you'll rat me out to the IRS—right?"

Dylan raised his chin. This was Tony's friend. Tony's mentor. Paranoia personified, if Dylan was any judge of character. He shook his head. "Nope."

"But you could," insisted Brandon peevishly.

"Jesus." Dylan looked at him in disgust. "Tony was right. You are kinda crazy." He waited for a moment, then continued. "Tony was murdered."

Brandon stopped and stared at him. "What? Man!" His mouth dropped open, and he sat down again. "Murder? As in homicide?"

"Yeah."

"I got nothing to do with this!" He jumped up and paced back and forth, staring at the floor, running his fingers through his messy hair.

"I know that." Or probably knew it now, anyway. "But you know what Tony was working on—right? And maybe you know who was involved and who would have been negatively affected by his success."

"'Negatively affected.' I love the way you suits talk." He took another swig from the bottle. "You mean fucking jealous enough to want to kill him—right?"

"Yeah."

"Man. Ain't this a trip down memory lane for yours truly." He turned and took a few steps toward the bathroom, then turned back. "You ever received a death threat?"

127

"No."

"It's not fun. It makes you feel—small. I'm talking mouse small. It makes you decide you'll do anything you have to do so that you don't ever get a death threat again. And the funny thing is? Even when you pay the piper, his tune never really changes. You're always hearing it, always looking under the bed." He opened the laptop case and reached inside. "Checking the closet, the liquor cabinet, the—oh! Look what I found!"

Dylan found himself staring down the muzzle of a squat black gun. "Shit," he whispered. His heart raced, shooting adrenaline through his veins. He backed up, his mind racing for a plausible exit.

"Yeah. I carry it with me wherever I go. Just for you. You bastards chewed me up and spit me out, but even so, I'm kinda attached to what's left of my life." His eyes turned dark, his glance darted around the room. He licked his lips and started pacing.

"Ditto," Dylan whispered. Was there a way out of this? The door was five yards away. His phone was closer.

"I bet." Brandon staggered, then regained his balance.

"Brandon, you don't want to do this."

"I know I don't. But I will if I have to."

"I left a message telling the cops I'm here. If you kill me, they'll nail you for sure. They'll nail you for homicide. Tony's *and* mine!"

"Me?" His bleary eyes bugged out. "They think it was me that killed Tony?"

Dylan frowned. "Wasn't it?"

"No! Jesus, what do you take me for?"

"So you didn't do it?"

"No!"

"Then what the fuck are you pointing a gun at me for!"

"Because I thought it was you! Oh." Brandon put a hand over his mouth, then looked at the gun. "What the hell am I doing?"

"I have no idea."

"Sorry." He dropped the gun back in the laptop case and fell into the chair. "I get a little crazy when people talk about technology in the same sentence as death."

Dylan had no idea what Brandon was talking about and considered it better to just slump into a chair. He picked up a napkin and wiped the sweat from the back of his neck. "Sorry," he said.

"Me too."

For a moment, Brandon smiled sweetly, reminding Dylan for the first time of Tony. They sat for a while in silence, while the clock on the nightstand ticked. Dylan pondered what to do next. "If I can find out anything that will help the police, I want to do that. They don't seem to have much of an appreciation for the kind of life Tony led. Or what his work was about."

"Any leads?"

Dylan smiled and rested his head on the back of the chair. "Look, I've had a long day—"

"Hey, if you want to know, I was in Arizona at the time, communing with the Anasazi." He pulled a wad of receipts and ticket stubs from the outer pocket of his laptop case and spread them on the coffee table.

Dylan glanced through them. Hotel receipts in the name of Dunlop Prince, an airline ticket from Newark to Tempe, receipts for purchases from the Sonora Trading Post.

"Okay. You're off the hook."

"Nice to know, but I want more than that. You say Tony was a friend of yours. Well, he was a friend of mine too. How can I help? Fill me in. Who do you suspect?"

Dylan eyed Brandon. As crazy as he had seemed five minutes before, now he seemed terribly, terribly sane. "I don't have a good list. What I need is a solid motive."

"And how are you going to get that?"

"I don't know. I'm just going to keep peeling things back until I find it. But I think Tony discovered something very serious. I got a voice-mail from him saying he was sending me a file, but I never got it."

"Really?"

"Of course, that would mean it's on one of his computers. But the police haven't been able to find anything on Tony's home computer, and Ivan, our chief of security—"

"No one ever will crack it."

Dylan tightened his lips, overwhelmed with disappointment.

"You said you don't believe I killed Tony. So what do you want me to do?"

"How about hacking into the hard drive of his computer at the office?"

Brandon leaned forward. "I'm sure anything that came or went to his hard drive is already in the hands of your chief of security."

"I doubt that. Tony would—"

"Tony would never have been stupid enough to put anything important on his office computer. He would have known everything that moves on the LAN is subject to company surveillance." Brandon smiled like a cynical cherub. "Every e-mail you type, every website you visit, every phone call you make, every file you download, share, or even store—hell, every friggin' keystroke is accessible by the powers that be." He looked away and started humming "Every Breath You Take."

Brandon was right, of course. What if everything he had said to Tony, to Rob, to Heather, had been observed? Was this what Tony had sensed that day in his office when he knew something was not right? "Then we're fucked," he said.

"Not necessarily. Lateral thinking, Mr. Johnson. It's true you'll never crack Tony's hard drive, but let's take another approach. Where did Tony get the files you are looking for?"

"How can I tell unless I've seen them?"

"Oh come on. He got them from Mantric, didn't he?"

"Maybe." Dylan frowned. "I hadn't thought about it."

"Obviously not. But, in fact, what you're probably talking about are records of some sort that Tony accessed and copied from some server or other at Mantric—right?"

"Yeah, probably." Dylan looked up. His mind became active again.

"Almost certainly." Brandon treated Dylan to a smug smirk. "So the only question remains: can you get access to the root directory of Mantric's administrative server?"

"What do you mean?"

"And you consider yourself a technologist?" Brandon cackled. "The root directory is like the root of a tree, and all branches stem from it. Get into it, and you can get into anything."

Dylan felt embarrassed. "Actually, I depended on Tony to do the deep technology stuff. I primarily handle the client accounts."

"That explains it. A suit!"

Dylan ignored the insult as thoughts began to trip over themselves in his mind. Could he get into the administrative server without being discovered? That would certainly be easier than hacking into Tony's computer. "Say I can hack in," said Dylan. "What good does it do me, other than instantly getting me fired—or worse—the second I'm discovered? Which I will be, because, as you know, all of those directories are constantly monitored to make sure whoever is accessing them has the correct privileges."

"That's a piece of cake."

"For you, maybe." Dylan eyed him. "If you're willing to come to Mantric and hack into—"

Brandon laughed. "Oh, no—but I can give you a script to run that will allow you to hack in without being identified, and without being observed."

Excitement surged through Dylan. This guy was good—and could probably do anything. He might even be able to let Dylan have his way with the files for an hour or so. Dylan leaned back in his chair. Could this really work? Could he dig into Mantric and find incriminating evidence? Would he be caught? "I don't know, Brandon."

"I understand. But I'm going to send you a file—very anonymously, of course—with instructions on how to use it. If you want to, you can."

"Prometheus giving fire to humanity again? Aren't you afraid of the eagle?"

"Pfft. This is nothing, Mr. Johnson. Anyone with a proper understanding of root directories and sophisticated scripts who thought about it for an hour or two could come up with it."

Dylan eyed him carefully. Brandon sat wrapped in his stained tweed jacket, his shaggy hair sticking out in all directions. In no way did he look like Dylan had envisioned. He was neither a mythological creature nor a multi-millionaire. And that, Dylan suddenly realized, was the point. This was a man who buried his true identity deep.

"One more thing. I need you to tell me what Tony was working on." Dylan nodded toward the schematic on the table.

Brandon blinked at him. "Isn't it obvious? It's magical and wonderful at the same time. And it would have changed the world. It's a design for wireless electricity. Imagine a world where you could have all of your electronic devices constantly powered without being plugged in."

"Jesus! How do you know that?"

"Hah! I double-majored in computer science and electrical engineering in college. It wasn't all about the ones and zeros, you know! Anyway, this baby would sure shake up the mobile computing world, among other things. The ramifications are huge, not just for technology, but for everything in everyday life!" Brandon grabbed the sketch. "See this coil? It has a capacitor that resonates and pulses at alternating currencies. If you bring another device close enough to it, you can get them to couple and transfer magnetic energy between them. So it goes from electricity to magnetic fields and back to electricity."

"Sounds dangerous."

"That's what everyone says. But it's not a radiative technology. It's just a magnetic field that's basically the same as the earth's magnetic field. And it's converted back into electricity only by the devices, nothing else."

"Oh my God! So maybe someone did kill Tony for this!"

"Do you really think so, Dylan?" Brandon said with a smirk. "You may find out if you follow my script."

Dylan's mind was like a beehive of thoughts. What did all of this have to do with the file Tony sent him? Was it about this or Mantric? "I don't know," he muttered.

"If they murdered Tony for this, why would they have left the sketch behind?"

"That's just it. They didn't leave it behind. Tony mailed it to me."

"Very interesting indeed," Brandon said, eyeing the sketch. "Give me a day to cover my tracks, and I'll send you the script. To your private e-mail addy. We don't want security stumbling across it."

"You don't know my private e-mail."

Brandon smiled a secret, ironic smile.

Chapter 21

A warm, dry breeze floated through the open window of Dylan's bedroom. He rolled onto his back and stretched. He had enjoyed a deep, restful sleep, one he had not experienced in several weeks. His arrival home the evening before had been later than he expected, and he did not call Heather. Now he turned his head and squinted at the alarm clock on the nightstand. Seven o'clock. He stretched again and sat up, throwing his legs over the side of the bed onto the floor.

He wandered to the window and looked out. The day began warm, but not hot. A nice spring morning, he thought. He hoped it was a sign of things changing. His mind reviewed the many things he had learned, and he felt he had taken a step forward toward determining what had happened to Tony, and why. But *who* was still the bigger mystery.

Thirty minutes later he stood in the kitchen over a hot griddle, fixing a tangy Mexican omelet while the whole wheat bread sat in the toaster turning a light brown.

He heard the sound of a quiet chime from his laptop. He spun it around on the counter to see the screen and found himself looking in his Gmail inbox at a return address from one epimetheus@gmail.com. There was an attachment, and as Dylan scrolled down, he read Brandon's brief instructions explaining how to download and save it as an executable file. Out of curiosity, he hit "reply" and was not in the least surprised when his attempt bounced back.

The phone rang, and Heather's number appeared on the caller ID screen. He smiled. He knew she would not be able to wait any longer to hear about the trip to Westwood.

"Good morning!" He couched the handset between his left shoulder and ear while he poured himself a cup of coffee.

"Indeed, it is. I thought I'd hear from you last night, but when I didn't hear by eleven, I figured you were late getting home. How did it go?"

He smiled as he heard the excitement in her question. "Well, there was one really tense moment, but I'll explain that to you later. This guy is a cross between brilliant and creepy, yet I can see why Tony liked him. He's really paranoid, but from everything Tony told me about him and listening to his story, I can understand why."

"Anything positive come from the meeting?"

"Yes, and he gave me some information on that sketch Tony sent me. It's a draft design of a device for wireless electricity. It isn't complete, but it looks like Tony was on to something big."

"Are you sure?"

"Yes. And in the right hands it could be revolutionary!"

"Do you think someone found out about it? Could it be important enough to kill him over?"

"You mean someone at Mantric? Heather, I'm not the technology brain Tony was, but I've got to believe that something like this—hell— if someone could make this actually work, electric power companies would kill for it." He stopped and realized what he had just said.

Heather took a deep breath. "Well, that could certainly provide a motive. Do you think Tony told someone at the company about this and they realized its potential?"

"I don't know. It doesn't fit with what's been happening at the firm. First Rich is canned, then Tony is murdered, and now Matt is clinging to his job by a hair. And I'm under attack from Art. But I just received a script from Brandon that will allow me to hack into the company's root directories."

Heather let out a small chuckle. "You? You're going to hack into the company's root directories? Dylan, you may be ultra-smart about business, and you have a good understanding of technology, but I don't think hacking is your strong point. I'm coming over. Make sure the coffee is fresh."

Before he could protest, Heather disconnected the call. Dylan thought about her question. Did this schematic have anything to do with Tony's death? And, if it did, what could he do about it?

His mind flitted over many topics. It gnawed at him that he had been unable to find Tony's final message. That was his job, finding that message. Or rather, finding evidence that would confirm a motive for Tony's death. Should he use Prometheus's script that would allow him access to the root directory of the network? He paced the floor, anxious to share the script with Heather. She was the only one he could talk to who knew Tony had been murdered. He needed her input, her eyes, and her help.

His footsteps echoed on the tile floor as he walked across the kitchen to the fridge. It was a lonely sound—a frightening sound. The desire to call Tony and get his advice on how to handle the situation overwhelmed him, and the knowledge that he would never talk to his friend again brought him to the edge of despondency. He had to shake it off. He had to concentrate. He grabbed the orange juice from the fridge and sat at the table in the breakfast nook. He knew Heather was at least another ten minutes away, and his nerves prickled his skin. He reached into his pocket for his cell phone and speed-dialed Rob.

"Hey," Rob said. "What's going on?"

"I'm sitting in the kitchen with juice and an omelet. Where are you?"

"Actually, I'm at my folks' house. What's up?"

"Not much. You find anything out at your end about Hyperfōn?"

"Yeah. I found out a classmate of mine works at LC. He said the creation and launch of Gazi there seemed to come out of the blue. No one he knew had ever heard anything about it in advance. I'm thinking the problem may have been at Joe's end."

"I don't see how. We registered the site and set it up ourselves. We managed it. Joe's people had no access to the back end of the operation."

"But Dylan, for LC to develop this on its own would have taken at least a year, and folks there would have known about it. I think they could have had a source inside Hyperfōn."

Dylan thought for a moment. It was certainly a possibility. "That's true, Rob. That certainly could explain it. But we need to finish looking at all of the possibilities."

"OK. Listen, I'm sorry, but I gotta go."

"No problem. See you tomorrow." Dylan clicked off his phone. He admired Rob for his ability to concentrate and try and figure out any angle to explain the Hyperfōn situation. Dylan, on the other hand, lacked concentration; he kept seeing ghosts everywhere he looked.

The doorbell startled him out of his thoughts, and he hurried to the door. Heather held a big bag from Finagle-A-Bagel. In the kitchen, she removed a half-dozen assorted bagels and cream cheese, then poured herself a cup of coffee.

"Okay. So tell me about this script and your meeting with Mr. Wist." She plopped two bagels on a plate. She eyed the dirty egg dish, looked at Dylan, and smiled.

Dylan set the laptop on the table and showed her Brandon's e-mail and script. He watched her as she leaned in close to the screen. She read the first ten lines and turned to Dylan.

"I think we can do this."

"We?" he asked.

"Well, you're not fast enough on the computer, and your mind is very compartmentalized. You study things before you take any steps. No offense, but you tend to analyze things for too long. I operate more intuitively, and besides, let's not get you fired. If I get fired, I'll land on my feet quicker than you will. Potential employers will think you carry extra baggage, plus Art would probably be harder on you than on me."

They finished breakfast with small talk, each deeper in thought about how to move forward. Then Dylan's computer beeped at him, and Christine's ID bounced on the screen. Dylan looked at Heather, who wiggled her eyebrows and moved behind the computer out of camera view.

"Good morning," Dylan said coolly.

Christine looked peeved. "Dylan, I just received a call from a Detective Baldwin from the BPD."

"Really?" He offered nothing additional.

"She said they are just following a few leads before closing the file on Tony's death."

"Well, I guess they know their business. So Christine, what can I do for you?"

"Did you know anything about this? Did they talk to you?"

"They interviewed me extensively after I found Tony's body, of course."

"They didn't ever give you the impression that his death wasn't an accident, did they?"

"Seriously? No." He met Christine's digital gaze calmly. "Why? What did she say?"

"She *says* she's just checking to make sure there were no problems with Tony at work."

"Well, that's her job, I suppose."

"She wants to see Tony's computer. She said she'd get a court order if we didn't hand it over."

"I assume you gave it to her?"

"Of course. I told her we would cooperate in every way."

"Good. Was there anything else?" He anticipated there was more to her call than an update on Detective Baldwin's progress.

"There is something," she began.

Dylan glanced toward Heather.

"It's important that you tell your people to cooperate fully with the police. They knew Tony much better than the rest of us, and I'm sure the police will want to interrogate them thoroughly."

Dylan regarded her pinched face. Her use of the word "interrogate" did not slip past him. Her expression was icy, veiled, almost threatening.

"Of course," he said lightly. "I'll make sure they understand."

As Christine reached forward to cut the connection, Dylan saw a reflection in the window behind her head and to one side: Ivan.

He closed the laptop and looked up at Heather. "It's time to get back to New York," he suggested. "Christine was not alone in her office."

"How do you know that?"

"Reflections."

Chapter 22

Dylan walked into Docks, an always-crowded upscale bar in midtown Manhattan. Suits and skirts packed the bar. Men lingered over Crown Royal on the rocks, being careful not to spill it on their thousand-dollar suits. The women in the bar fell into one of two categories—the successful, and the other. The successful women did not dress off the rack. Their appearance, from five-inch spiked heels to uptown haircuts and make-up, spoke volumes about their success and their choices in both fashion and men. The other women, easier targets, prowled around the men, accepting their offers of a drink—almost always choosing a martini.

Dylan worked his way through the crowd, looking for Heather. He went around one side of the bar, but she wasn't there. Maybe he'd arrived first. Then he looked across the bar to the other side. Four men were huddled around a woman, talking animatedly. He moved to get a view of the woman and then spotted her strawberry-blonde hair.

He made his way through the crowd and around the bar. "Hi, Heather.

"Hey, Dylan," she said with a broad smile and gave him a light kiss. She turned to introduce him to the others, but they quickly glanced at each other and muttered "Nice to have met you." Then they disappeared.

"You made quite the fan club." He noticed a tinge of jealousy in his tone.

"Just a bunch of investment bankers trying to impress me."

"Oh I'm sure," he said lightly.

"Actually I was doing a little bit of free market research."

"Market research?"

"Yeah. I asked them if they'd ever heard of Mantric."

"And?"

"Not only had they heard of us, but the two that cover the technology

138

sector knew everything. They said we had great 'buzz' and they couldn't believe how well our stock was doing."

The hostess greeted them at the dining room and showed them to their table. Dylan pulled a twenty-dollar bill from his clip and asked for a table in the back, far from the noisy bar.

Heather opened her menu. "The seafood here is excellent."

Dylan scanned the menu but had difficulty concentrating. The events of the past few days kept running through his mind like a tape being played over and over.

The waitress appeared and poured water for both of them while reciting the specials of the day. Heather ordered swordfish, and Dylan ordered salmon.

The waitress disappeared, and, just as Dylan was about to speak, his cell phone beeped. He answered, but said nothing. He kept his eyes on Heather as he nodded his head up and down in agreement with whatever his caller said. The call lasted only a moment.

"What was that all about?"

"That was Detective Baldwin. She said they now have Tony's computer." He stared beyond her, deep in thought, then added, "But it's meaningless."

"Why?"

"We already know Ivan got in and probably deleted everything, or at least anything they would consider damning evidence. I saw that in Christine's eyes when she told me the police wanted Tony's computer. Baldwin and her folks won't find anything on it. And if the e-mail Tony sent me was on it, neither will I."

Heather's eyes hardened. "Ivan. That pig," she said, fairly seething.

Dylan's attention wavered. "What is it with you and Ivan? I saw him staring at you at the funeral."

Her expression darkened, and she looked away. "He made a pass at me, that's all. A very crude, medieval pass."

"What? When?" Her admission angered Dylan.

"It happened when we first came to Mantric. I remember he asked if I was having a relationship with anyone at MobiCelus, other than friendship. I told him it was none of his business." Her eyes narrowed. "Believe me, I can handle that sort of crap." Her anger startled Dylan. "But Ivan won't forget my rejection. I see it in his eyes every time he looks at me. Like he's obsessed or something." She shook her head, then smiled. "So now you know. Let's get back to the issue at hand. How are you going to find Tony's e-mail?"

"If Tony sent it from his computer at the Boston office, Ivan has it now. In fact, he probably intercepted it, which is why I didn't get it in the first place. Brandon brought it to my attention that if Tony was sending me proof Mantric was up to something, like they discovered what he was working on and were going to try to steal it from him, then he must have gotten proof from somewhere. And the most likely place to find it is on the protected servers here in the New York office."

"Okay. I buy that. And by now they're probably destroyed."

"Maybe, maybe not. If they're the sort of files I think they are, they wouldn't be destroyed except on the way out the door."

"Why not?"

"If you're playing around with the financials or doing something else criminal, you still need to keep track of the figures just as carefully as you do when you're on the straight and narrow. You just bury it where you think no one will find it. In my gut, I think Tony found something, and that was the file he wanted me to see. And for that, I need to hack into Mantric's secure servers."

Heather nodded. "That's where I come in. I will be much less conspicuous than you. I'm the perfect person to do this. I'm a senior member of the management team. I can go anywhere I want to in the company. Nobody would ever think I would be hacking into the root directories. I may have a degree in digital media, but I minored in information technology. I can hold my own with the nerd herd anytime."

"I've got Brandon's script, but I'm not comfortable with you being put at risk."

She countered, "That's just it! The script will hide me while I search. I'll run it, and it'll cover my tracks by shifting the IP address of my computer while I work."

"Are you absolutely certain?" he asked. "I can do it."

"We have to do this, Dylan, and you're overwhelmed emotionally by what's been happening. Tony's death, this Prometheus business, the Hyperfōn disaster. Are Matt and Rob learning any more about that?" she asked in a whisper.

"No. When we did our investigation, there was no sign LC was even thinking of getting into this business. It's like they knew all along about the business we were creating and somehow kept it hidden while they built one themselves."

"How could they? We keep all our work confidential."

"Rob thinks it was an inside job at Hyperfōn. He might be right. Then again, now we're part of Mantric, and someone somewhere in the company could just as easily have leaked information. But why the hell would anyone at Mantric want to hurt our revenues just after we've gone public? They'd only be hurting themselves. It doesn't make any sense."

"No. A lot of things don't make any sense." She averted her eyes.

"Such as?"

She touched her napkin to her lips. "Remember how we all thought Art was an idiot when he wouldn't let you attend his management meetings or go on the road show?"

"Like it was yesterday."

"What was his reason?"

"He said he didn't want me distracted from the business."

"No, when you pressed him, what was the real reason?"

Dylan thought for a moment. "That the board didn't want anyone else to see the detailed financials."

"Bingo," she said as she picked up her wine glass and took a sip.

"I'm sorry, Heather. I'm not following you."

She set the glass down. "Didn't Rich tell you he thought Christine was incompetent at running finance?"

"Yes, that's right," Dylan agreed.

"And she forgot to include a reserve for the acquisition of our firm in our filing with the SEC."

"Yeah, but you guys all thought Rich was in over his head."

"I know. But what if we were wrong? What if they got rid of Rich and gave him a fat severance because he was getting too close to the truth? And what if Art lied to you about the board not wanting you to see our detailed financials?"

"What are you saying?" Dylan said, leaning in closer to hear her whispers. The noise in the restaurant seemed to increase exponentially with the discussion.

"I'm saying, what if Art isn't an idiot? And what if Christine isn't incompetent? What if, in fact, they're both brilliant? I mean, why else would Art bring down the hammer over the loss of one measly client? He's trying to keep you as far away from the real action as possible."

"He's succeeding."

"Dylan," she said, leaning over the table, her face close to his. "There's something I need to tell you."

"Why do I think I'm not going to like this?"

"Remember I told you about Christine saying the New York office accounted for over forty-five percent of our revenues?"

"Yeah."

"Well, I've been doing my homework, too. I looked up last quarter's revenues for the whole firm. They were 105 million dollars. If New York accounted for forty-five percent of that, it would be over forty-seven million dollars."

"Right."

"So then I did an analysis of our New York revenues last quarter."

"How'd you do that?" Dylan said, surprised. "You don't have access to those numbers any more than I do."

She laughed. "You know, you're a brilliant guy, but sometimes you're just too damn logical. It was easy. I just chatted with people working on the projects based out of the New York office. Every team knows what they are billing their own client. They just don't compare notes and add up a whole office's worth. They love to brag about their individual successes. They never questioned why I needed the information. They just gave it to me. So I quietly gathered up that information and then totaled it up myself."

Dylan certainly hoped she'd done it quietly. Having them both in trouble wouldn't help anyone. "What'd you find?"

"My estimate is the New York office only billed thirty-two million dollars last quarter, not forty-five million." Heather tapped a highly polished finger on the tabletop for emphasis.

"Are you sure?"

"Well, I suppose I could be off by a million or two, but not fifteen."

Dylan took a long drink of his water. "Well, it's not exactly hard evidence, but it certainly is suspicious."

"You are the master of the understatement. And if Tony found out. . . ." She let her statement dissipate, unanswered.

Dylan sat back and slowly responded, "I guess anything's possible."

"If Tony found out about this and maybe approached Art or Christine, would that be a big enough reason for murder?"

"It very well could be, and that's a good reason to hack into the secure server. Honestly, Heather, I think we have to—"

"I know." She licked her lips—a reflexive gesture Dylan knew she made whenever her thoughts overwhelmed her. He had seen her do it at the poker table and at the conference table. It had always endeared her to him. "So you really think Tony was killed because he found out something bad about Mantric?"

"Yeah."

"By whom?"

"Ivan, maybe ordered by Art or Christine. The trio seems to have a

142

tight relationship, though Ivan is certainly under the other two's thumbs."

She nodded slowly. "Can't say I'd put it past the bastard."

He watched her face, knowing her creative mind was churning as she looked for flaws in his theory.

"Okay, we need to do this. Here's how it's going to be, no questions." She looked from side to side, ensuring their conversation would not be overheard.

Dylan drew a deep breath. "I don't like this."

"Doesn't matter," she insisted. "I'm better at sifting through obscure directories than you are, which is why I'm going in."

Dylan shook his head. "It's a big risk. What if you get caught?"

"I like risk. Your job is to keep an eye on Ivan while I'm hacking into the server. Because, in the end, I'd rather you were the one keeping Ivan occupied while I deal with the nice friendly server."

Dylan realized he really had no choice. Heather was right about his methodical, detail-oriented mind versus her intuition. "OK, I'll keep him occupied for you," he finally said, grimly.

Their eyes met. Heather raised her glass, and Dylan did the same.

"For Tony."

Chapter 23

The next morning Dylan arrived at Mantric before most of the staff. He sat at his desk and began to prepare a folder, his heart thumping as he considered the multiple ways the plan could go wrong. If they were caught, could they be arrested? He was an officer of the company, but what about Heather? What jeopardy had he placed her in? They had reviewed every minute of their timetable over and over until they could recite it backwards. Dylan shook his head to dispel the questions. It was too late to go back now. He reached out to the keyboard and called the Boston office a few minutes before eight-thirty and spoke with Sarah.

"So I take it you haven't been able to fix the Hyperfōn problem?"

Dylan felt his heart sink. "Sarah, how many people know about that?"

"Pretty much everyone here, I'm afraid. You can't expect the whole team to keep it a secret when they are suddenly yanked out of a client and told to go back home."

It wasn't what Dylan wanted to hear, but it was certainly understandable. "So where are they?"

"In the main conference room. Ready and waiting for your call."

"Organized as always. Thanks, Sarah."

"No problem. Dylan, is there anything else I can do?"

He sighed. "No. But thanks for asking." Dylan linked to the conference room, where he had a view of the entire Hyperfōn project personnel sitting around the long table. The room fell silent as he came online, and everyone's eyes focused on him.

"Good morning," he said, trying to sound calm and relaxed. He looked around the room and saw Rob seated at the far end of the table. "Hi, Rob. Thanks for coming."

"Hey, I want to help as much as possible."

"I appreciate that, especially since you have your own clients to worry about."

"No worries," Rob said with a smile.

"Matt? What have you guys come up with so far?"

Matt glanced around the room at his colleagues. He looked exhausted. "I'm sorry, Dylan, but we really haven't come up with anything that would explain how we missed the LC move."

Dylan frowned. "Nothing? No clues? Not even a theory?"

"No. Not yet." He looked down at his hands.

Dylan sighed. "So tell me what you've done so far."

"Well, yesterday we made a lot of calls to pretty much everyone we could think of. But we didn't come up with any insights."

"What about the original project plan?" Dylan asked. "Did you review it to see if we missed any important steps or maybe weren't thorough enough?"

"Yeah," Matt said. The somber faces around the table nodded in agreement. "We went through every little detail. We followed the plan just the way we always do."

"How about researching the Internet? Did you find anything to indicate LC had ever even mentioned considering starting a business like Hyperfōn?"

Matt shook his head. "We pretty much pulled an all-nighter on that. Didn't find anything."

"Not even rumors of anyone else doing it?"

"No."

"What about the research firms? Did you check with them?"

"Yes. We didn't find anything there, either."

Rob looked at Dylan and shook his head. Dylan could tell he didn't think this was leading anywhere.

"So, no one here has any idea how this could have happened then. Is that right?"

The room went silent for a moment, and then Matt sighed. "No idea at all." He was clearly frustrated.

"So where does this leave us with Hyperfōn?" asked Hailey Parker, one of the young web designers on the team.

"Well, I'm afraid the project is on hold for now," said Dylan. No one said anything, but their faces reflected their opinion that he was sugarcoating the situation. "The truth is," he added, "it's pretty unlikely we will be working with Hyperfōn anymore."

The team exchanged disappointed glances.

"So what happens to us?" Hailey asked.

"Don't worry," Dylan said, trying to reassure the group. "We have plenty of other work for you. The good news is we'll be able to speed up some of that. I expect you all to be assigned to new projects within the next couple of weeks."

He watched Rob and Matt exchange glances. There was other work for the team to do, but they both knew Dylan would need to quickly land another client or two to make up for the financial loss in his own division.

"In the meantime," he continued, "you should keep working on trying to figure out what happened here so we can prevent it from happening again." They all nodded.

"Anything else?" Matt asked.

"Yeah. Until it's official, please don't tell anyone outside this room our work with Hyperfōn is finished. Okay?"

"Okay," they all said.

"All right everyone. Thanks for all of your help. We'll talk again soon." Dylan cut the conference call and sat back in his chair, his mind a blank slate.

For the next five hours, Dylan and Rob video-conferenced with the project managers of every Mantric mobile computing client. Dylan wanted to be absolutely sure this didn't happen again. He informed them Mantric was conducting a normal security review and told them to personally perform thorough project reviews looking for anything out of the ordinary. He and Rob asked a litany of questions; in particular, he wanted them to redouble their research on the competition and make sure their clients wouldn't be blindsided by any of them.

At two-thirty, Dylan put an end to the calls. "That's it for today, Rob. Thanks."

"Don't worry. This thing will blow over."

"I don't think Art's going to forget it."

"He's just rattling your cage, Dylan."

"I know. But that doesn't make me like it any better." He glanced at his watch. Two thirty-five. "Sorry, Rob, I've got to go."

Dylan rushed back to his office and took one more quick look at the folder on his desk. The spring air had warmed the day, and the sun beat through his window. *Too cold for air conditioning, too hot for comfort*, he thought. He rose and walked over to the window, took a handkerchief out of his pocket, and wiped his neck.

"Rachel?" he called.

"Yes, Dylan?" Rachel said, poking her head around the corner.

"I need some help with some financials that I'm trying to work out on this Hyperfōn mess. Could you call your friend Patty Dowes, over in accounting, and see if she could come down here about three o'clock and try to organize this for me?"

"Sure. I know she'll be happy to help."

Rachel returned to her desk and dialed the number. From his office, Dylan heard Rachel's side of the conversation as she confirmed the meeting. He looked at his watch. Two-fifty p.m. Dylan nudged the envelope square in the middle of his desk, locked the drawers, and walked out of the office.

"I just realized I have to conference with Matt again about Hyperfōn. Just tell Patty the folder on the desk has all the data and I've left some instructions. I would prefer she not take anything out of the office—you know—security and all. I'll be back as quickly as I can in case she has any questions."

"Not a problem. Patty is very reliable and very accurate."

The plan was simple. Dylan hurried through the hallway to the elevator. He speed-dialed Heather's number.

"Okay. Patty Dowes's office will be empty as of three o'clock. I've left enough work to keep her busy for about an hour."

"I'm standing outside of accounting. She just passed by me. There aren't very many people here, and Patty's office is somewhat remote from the others. What luck!" Heather responded.

They ended the call, and Dylan went over the next steps in his mind. With Patty out of her office, Heather would go in, input the password, gain access to the network, run the Prometheus script, and hunt down any suspicious files as per Brandon's directions. In the meantime, Dylan would keep an eye on Ivan and make sure he stayed in his office. If he failed, he would ring Heather's cell, set on vibrate, to warn her. Heather would ring Dylan twice, once when she was five minutes from finishing, and again when she was clear. Under no circumstances would she stay more than half an hour.

Dylan placed the phone in his pocket and stopped just outside of Ivan's office. He took a deep breath and approached Ivan's secretary with an air of confidence.

"Hey, Naomi," said Dylan, adopting his most charming smile. "How's it going?"

The always-anxious secretary looked up, apologetic in anticipation of having to deliver unwelcome news. "I'm sorry, Dylan, he's busy with a salesman." She glanced unhappily at Ivan's closed office door.

"He's always busy. I'll just wait here," Dylan said, taking a seat across from her.

"Oh, well, sure, please make yourself comfortable."

• • •

May 13, 3:05 p.m. New York.

Heather slid forward on the leather chair. With each key-tap, she became acutely aware of the fact that she was leaving fingerprints across the keyboard. She would have to remember to wipe it down when she was done. When she gained access to the root directory of the server, she removed Brandon's coded CD from her briefcase and slid it into the drive.

The root hierarchy filled the monitor to her left. The high hum of the machinery and the clicking of the keys seemed to reverberate throughout the room.

She glanced at the four columns of numbers displayed across the monitor. Every secure computer on the LAN was listed with the corresponding IP addresses of every computer that had visited every location in the past hour—a handy tool for any security director and perfectly justified to ensure a network's security. She recognized that this made it possible for an unscrupulous person to use the system in reverse and find a way into the personal computers of Mantric employees. Heather's eyes flickered as she watched the progress of Brandon's script; using a different address every time, she changed directories and was confident her penetration would not be discovered—not unless anyone was looking right at that moment.

She wandered through a dozen hierarchies looking for Ivan's directories and found them fairly quickly. Bypassing the security directories, she uncovered a string of directories labeled ARCH and four numbers. She glanced inside each one. The file names were coded, but the extensions told the tale: .docx, .txt, .pdf, .bmp, .tiff, .jpg. How much personal information was stored here, she wondered? What e-mails, what transcripts of phone calls, what photos? Her fingers itched to know, but that wasn't her mission.

And yet how was she to find Tony's e-mail, the file he referenced, or any other evidence when all the names were coded? She went through every archive directory but spotted nothing that looked like her prey.

Time was ticking by. She backtracked. Maybe she had missed something. She started over, this time looking in directories with any alphanumeric names, when she came across something interesting: a folder labeled SAVE2012. Inside, more columns of files with alphanumeric coded names: .txt, .pdf, .avi.

She stopped. Avi. That was a video extension. What could those be? Her forefinger twitched, then double-clicked on the mouse.

A small window appeared on the screen as the movie player booted and an image appeared—a generic office with green walls and a wooden table disappearing into the bottom of the window. Heather's eyes widened as Christine walked into view and sat at the visible end of the table.

"So Art," said Christine. "How are we doing?"

Art's voice came from off-camera. "Well, we cut things awfully close with the MobiCelus acquisition. We closed that puppy just in the nick of time to play up the mobile computing capabilities in our prospectus. And add in their second quarter revenues."

Christine nodded. "Right. What else?" she asked with cold indifference.

"The SEC was satisfied with Hickman and Ross signing off on our financials and officially stating we followed generally accepted accounting principles," Art said.

"Uh-huh. And what about the investors and brokers?"

"I've taken care of them, too. Everything's set with WMR Capital and their broker friends. They'll know what to do when the time comes. So, Christine, I guess that means I only have to worry about you, then. Do you have everything in order with your buddies at Daley and Hahn?"

"Oh, don't worry about them. It's all set. They've assured me from a legal standpoint everything's in order."

The video ended.

Heather pushed back from the desk, staring at the blank screen. What was that all about? And where had the meeting been? Heather hadn't recognized the room. She looked at the file names again and realized that the last four characters of each name could refer to the date. She saved the .avi, returned to the script, and ran down the column of files till she found the days immediately following Tony's death. Then she hesitated, glancing nervously at the monitor. Her proxy IP address had shown up in the SAVE directory. She knew she would be detected if someone were monitoring the directory at that precise time. But, with Ivan safely preoccupied, what were the chances of that? She clicked the next file.

It was the same green room, the same table, but this time there was no one in the picture.

"So is he gone?" came Christine's voice.

"Shit, Christine," came Art's voice. "Close the door!"

There was the sound of a door closing, and Christine came into view.

"Take a seat. So did you let Rich go?"

"Yeah, I did."

"How'd he react?" Art asked.

"I don't know. Shocked. He shouldn't have been. He brought it on himself."

"Christine, have you ever had an ounce of compassion about anyone in your life?"

"I had a dog once when I was a kid. Got sick. My parents had to put it down. I didn't feel too good about that."

"Sorry I asked. So how exactly did you handle it?"

"I told him we would say his position was eliminated."

"Why bother? It just complicates things further to lie."

"Look, you can't just fire someone without reason. They could sue. Things could get messy. Plus, having him sign a release and letting him go this way makes it much less likely he'll create any problems for us later."

"I suppose," said Art. He didn't sound convinced.

"Anyway, we escorted him out of the office and shut down all of his access to our telephone and computer systems. And I gave him severance in exchange for the release. He didn't even read the document. He just signed it."

"Did you meet with them yet?"

"Who?" asked Christine.

"The finance group. When you thin the herd, it's usually a good idea to explain why you did it to the ones left standing."

"I sent them an e-mail."

"A personal meeting would have been better, don't you think?"

She said nothing.

"So?" Art asked, exasperation in his voice.

"I told them it was purely an isolated performance issue. And, while I didn't like doing it, I had to have him escorted out for security reasons. I think they understood. I don't think any of them are going to miss him, anyway. He was never a part of our team."

"Anyone send you any questions we should be concerned with?"

"Nope. It was pretty straightforward."

"I suppose," Art said. "But you should have told me you were going to give Rich two years' severance. That was way too fucking generous. And it raises too many questions."

"Questions no one will ask," said Christine.

"I just wished you'd told me first, that's all."

"I was planning on telling you tonight. So tell me about your meeting with Dylan."

"Well, that's the real reason I wanted to see you. Dylan told me. Seems he spoke to Rich this afternoon."

"What?" asked Christine, with apprehension. "What did he say?"

"He was pissed. He wanted to know why I didn't tell him first, why we had Rich escorted out of the building. And why we couldn't find him another job here."

"But you handled it—right?" asked Christine. "Now we can get on with our plan?"

Art cleared his throat. "Not quite. I think we may have other problems with Dylan."

"Really? What kind of problems?"

"Founder problems. He used to run his own company. Now he's beginning to feel cut out as a member of our senior management team."

Christine laughed. "I wonder why!"

"Yeah. I handled it. Told him Rich was wrong for the position and we decided he couldn't be trusted."

"So that's that."

"I'm afraid not. Dylan's suddenly taken an interest in getting a closer look at our financials and demanded to see them."

"What are we going to do about that?"

"Like I said over the phone, I told him I'd consider it, but it would be a board decision, that they insisted we keep our financial data held as tightly as possible."

"Did he believe it?" asked Christine.

"I don't know. He clearly wasn't happy about it. First the road show, now this. I think he's getting suspicious."

"Yeah. We should have seen this coming."

"Great. Just great," said Art. "So what are we going to do?"

"Let's keep an eye on him. Maybe it'll pass. But, just in case it doesn't, we need to create something that'll scare him. Something that could put his job and his stock at risk."

"You mean like a performance problem?"

"Yeah. One we can document."

"That could be troublesome. He's doing well against his plan right now," said Art. "But remember, we hold a few cards that can change that in a hurry."

"That's right," said Christine. "We do, don't we?"

Art nodded. *"Let's play the first one."*
The video ended.

. . .

"I thought I was going to be a concert pianist," said Naomi.

Dylan smiled, glad she was finally getting more comfortable chatting with him. "Really?" he said, deliberately sounding surprised. His gaze wandered toward Ivan's closed door. "I used to play the piano myself. When I was a kid, I mean. I liked it, but—well—there's no money in it, of course."

"You never know. It was my parents' dream to see me on stage," Naomi said, a quiet wistfulness creeping into her tone. "When they got sick, I got a job as a secretary to make ends meet. I don't think they ever forgave themselves. . . ."

. . .

Heather's mind whirled. Where had these files come from? Had Tony seen them? And what the hell was Ivan up to, documenting these obviously highly private meetings? Did he have every room in the building bugged? Had Christine and Art known they were being recorded? She doubted it, given the things they had said. And what the hell did Art mean by holding "a few cards"?

She looked at the long list of .avi files. She didn't have time to sit and watch them all. The plan had been to copy Tony's files onto a flash drive, but .avi files are big. She pulled a pendant from around her neck, flipped it open, and plugged it into the USB port. She glanced at the monitor to her right. The script was still working, the IP address shifting every time she clicked on a file. Suddenly she thought to double-check the screen on her right to make sure no one was searching the directory as well. Her gaze scanned back to the route she had taken through the directory.

Nine levels above, she spotted an IP address: 192.191.0.0. And there it was again, beside another directory. And again and again. Following the same path she had taken. Even as she watched, six levels above in the hierarchy of directories, it appeared again: 192.191.0.0. Someone appeared to be following her.

"Uh-oh." Her heart leapt into her throat. "I hope you are keeping an eye on him, Dylan," she said softly.

• • •

"My dad was a no-nonsense guy who wouldn't abide any sissy stuff," said Dylan. "He taught me at an early age that emotions just get in the way. You don't get ahead if you get sidetracked. It was a hard lesson to learn, but it made me strong." He put his hands around the mug of coffee Naomi had made him and stared into its swirling depths.

"Oh," said Naomi softly. "I'm sorry."

Dylan smiled. "You misunderstand. He was a blue-collar guy who wanted better for his son. Because of him, I knew how to get what I wanted. When he died, it was just me and my mom. I couldn't have supported her the way I did—the way I still do—if I'd wasted my time with music or gotten with the wrong crowd. I owe him a lot."

"I'm sure you do. But, Dylan, you need to have balance. We all have our vulnerable side. If you pretend you don't, you get into all sorts of trouble eventually."

Dylan chuckled. "I guess I need to get in touch with my inner *chi*."

Naomi smiled silently.

Suddenly, Dylan's phone vibrated against his hip. Heather. Almost done. Five minutes more and she would be clear. He glanced at the door to Ivan's office. *Got you.*

• • •

"Come on, come on!" Heather whispered, her hands grasping the screen as if to speed it up. The status bar changed colors rhythmically, giving the appearance of three dimensions as it swirled. It had always fascinated her that computers still used so many anachronisms like the barber pole, the sand clock, the trash bin, the floppy disk, the paper folder—all icons, now—incorporeal, shimmering metallic colors on a high-res screen.

The bar disappeared. Heather pulled the flash drive out of the port. She closed it and replaced the slender chain around her neck, relief flooding through her. She put her hands under her long hair, settling it on her shoulders. Time to get the hell out of virtual Dodge. She shut down the browser and emptied the cache. No worries. She glanced at the right-hand screen.

192.191.0.0. had joined her in the SAVE2012 directory.

Damn.

She hit the button on the optical drive. It whirred and spat out the

CD. She hit and held the power button on the tower. *Come on!!!*

The power button went dark.

Fumbling to put the CD into her briefcase, she ran to the door and opened it.

Ivan Venko stood in front of her. Tall and gaunt, his dark hair slicked back, and his bony face morose, he towered over her, blocking any hope for a speedy departure. Ivan reached out and shoved her back into the office.

Chapter 24

May 13, 3:35 p.m. New York

"You know, Naomi, you're probably right," said Dylan, feeling relaxed with Ivan safe inside his office and Heather on her way back to hers. "I should find more balance in my life."

Naomi nodded, touching the copper hoops on her wrist. "You've been under a lot of stress, Dylan. Everybody knows that. When we're upset by something terrible, it dredges up every painful thing that's ever happened to us. It's human nature. I admire you for—"

The telephone on Naomi's desk rang. "Oh, hello Mr. Williams. No, he's not here; he's meeting with a salesman in the conference room."

Dylan tensed. He had assumed Ivan was behind closed doors in his office. Now he had a sinking feeling in the pit of his stomach about Heather's security. He glanced at the clock on the wall. Six minutes since Heather had signaled him.

Dylan bounded out of the chair and rushed to the office and opened the door. To his horror he saw it was empty.

• • •

Ivan's eyes flickered with surprise. "Miss Carter." His deep voice echoed through the room.

Heather flashed a broad smile. She shoved the CD into the pocket of the briefcase and struck a flirtatious pose. "Were you looking for me?"

"Apparently," he said, moving ominously toward her.

"Well then perhaps you'll be able to help me find Sandeep." She kept her tone light, while adrenaline pumped up her heart rate. "Or did he send you to find me?"

Ivan grasped the doorknob and took a step forward, further blocking any possible escape route. Heather quickly considered her options. Either back up, or let him walk into her. Her heartbeat increased as Ivan stepped into the office and closed the door.

"What are you doing?" Heather asked, as a sense of fear scuttled up her spine. She slowly backed up deeper into the office.

"You're asking *me* that? I think the question is better suited to you." He reached a hand toward her briefcase, and she took another step back.

"Give me the CD, please, Miss Carter."

"It's not mine to give," Heather stuttered, her answer caught in a nervous swallow.

"No?"

"No. It was Tony's. I need to find Sandeep to see if he can access its contents. You know Dylan is looking for—"

"Please. Let's not play this game."

Heather heard the sound of her heart pounding as the blood rushed through her inner ears. Should she provoke him to attack? That would give her an excuse to scream or to claim that he had cornered her there. But how could she explain the CD?

"I know where you were—what you were looking at. I'm the chief security officer of Mantric, Miss Carter. I'm not asking you. I'm telling you to give me that CD."

"Why? Why are you so determined to keep Dylan from viewing Tony's files?"

Ivan stepped forward, driving her further back. Heather realized that with each step backwards, she would be closer to the corner between the bank of cabinets and the wall.

She dashed frantically to the left; Ivan parried, pushing her back against the table, his body trapping her, his hands groping for the briefcase she held close to her body.

"You son of a bitch!" Heather cried, shoving his hands away from her body.

She threw up an elbow, whirled, and jammed her fist against his head. Ivan's head snapped back, slamming against the corner of a cabinet and drawing blood from a small but deep gash. He stumbled for only a second before coming at her again, shooting an arm around her neck and moving behind her. His wiry appearance belied his strength and skill in physical combat. She realized she was no competition for him. She pulled the CD out of the briefcase and tried to smash it against the table, but he caught her arm and twisted it, snatching the CD from her. His grasp tightened, and he wrestled her into the middle of the room.

Keeping his left arm around her neck, he patted her down with his right, pressing the thin fabric of her dress close to her skin. Revulsion hit her when he reached into the pocket on her thigh. With a primal cry of anguish, she pushed back against him, kicking at his shins with her three-inch stacked heels.

He didn't let go. His fingers spread as they searched the empty pocket and then moved away. Heather jerked away again, and this time he let her go. She staggered against the computer desk and fell into the chair, shaking.

Ivan's lips curled up into a depraved-looking grin. With an annoyed shake of his head, he went to her briefcase.

As he rummaged through its contents, searching for anything in addition to the CD, Heather's thoughts went to Dylan. Was he all right? Logic told her that he was not, that Ivan had learned of their plan. Fear gripped her. If Ivan were a murderer, would he hesitate to add Dylan to his list?

"So, Miss Carter," he said when he had searched the briefcase to his satisfaction. "I have the CD. So the only other record of what you saw is in your little mind. That won't do."

He took a menacing step toward her, a crooked smile on his face. She had neither breath nor will to scream. She began to fall backward when, through the buzzing in her ears, she heard the sound of the door opening, and in the distance, a voice called, "Leave her alone, you bastard!"

• • •

Dylan met Ivan's gaze. A cool sense of control and calm came over him, and time seemed to slow to a crawl. He was aware of the catch in Heather's hoarse breathing, of the twitch of doubt in Ivan's lips, of the double stream of blood working its way slowly down the side of his face from the gash in his temple.

Dylan stretched to his full six-foot-four-inch stature, towering four inches above Ivan. "Leave her alone," he repeated.

Doubt flickered across Ivan's gaunt face. "I wasn't—" He looked at Heather and then back at Dylan.

"Be careful, Dylan!" Heather called.

Ivan turned toward her and, in that moment, Dylan leapt forward and slammed his fist into Ivan's kidneys, taking the man by surprise. Ivan dropped to his knees.

"I wasn't going to hurt her," he said, slowly rising to his feet, wiping the blood from his forehead. He nodded at Heather. "This woman broke in here to gain access to secure Mantric files. She resisted when I asked her to hand over the CD she used to copy files. I was simply trying to make her explain to me exactly what she saw."

"Tell that to the cops."

"Dylan," whispered Heather, with a warning shake of her head.

"This is an internal matter," said Ivan. "There's no need for the police."

Dylan laughed. "Oh, really? So you think you can murder someone in cold blood and Mantric will take care of it?"

"I told you. I had no intention of harming Miss Carter!"

"I'm not talking about Heather!" Dylan snapped.

Ivan frowned. "You're not?" His eyes flickered back and forth. Then he understood the accusation. "You think I had something to do with Tony's death? But—"

"I don't know. But you're the one threatening Heather. It would not be a leap for the police to believe you could take it to the next step."

Ivan looked at Dylan. "It was murder, wasn't it?" he said, wrapping his mind around the truth. "I knew it," he muttered.

Heather rose and moved cautiously to Dylan's side. "Let's go," she whispered.

"Report me to the police and I'll report your activities to Mr. Williams," said Ivan without looking at them. "I have your CD. I followed your digital adventure. A record exists of exactly where you went and what you saw." Ivan drew a deep breath, regaining a measure of confidence. "Tell me what you saw, Miss Carter, and perhaps I will not mention this event."

"Wait a minute," said Dylan, holding up a warning hand. "You think you can extort our silence with a threat like that? We're taking this story straight to the cops!"

"What story?" sneered Ivan. "That you broke in here to—Yes, I see now. You broke in to find evidence that, that I—" He rolled his hollow eyes. "That I killed your friend. Is that what you were looking for?" He smiled briskly at Heather. "Go ahead, Miss Carter. Tell him all the incriminating evidence you found that I killed your friend. So you can rush off to the police and have me arrested!" He folded his arms, daring her to speak.

Dylan looked questioningly at Heather. She cleared her throat. "Dylan, I didn't find anything to implicate Ivan in Tony's murder, but nothing that clears him, either."

"Are you sure?" asked Dylan.

She nodded slowly. "There were video files. No references that I saw to Tony's death."

Dylan turned to Ivan. "So where were you on May second, when Tony was killed?" he demanded.

Ivan did not answer.

"But it looks like he's been bugging Art and Christine without their knowledge," Heather said, breaking the silence.

Ivan did not respond, but took a handkerchief from his pocket and wiped the blood from his wound.

"You asked me what I saw. I'm telling you," said Heather. "What are you doing, blackmailing them?"

"You don't know what you saw," said Ivan.

"Okay, then *you* tell us what she saw," said Dylan. "Or we'll just ask Art and Christine."

Ivan's expression was as granite. "Those .avi's are Mantric property, made as part of my job."

Dylan put a hand on Heather's elbow. "Let's go."

"Wait!" Ivan took a step forward. "You can't speak of this!"

Heather turned to face him. "Why not? It'll be worth it if it helps us nail who killed Tony."

"I didn't kill him!" Ivan's narrow teeth showed between his drawn lips. "I don't kill people, Miss Carter."

"So why won't you tell us where you were the night he was killed?" Dylan said.

"I was here in New York. I didn't break the law."

"Oh no? You bugged your boss's meetings? I think that would fit the definition of breaking the law. I don't see that being much of a leap to murder. So exactly what were you doing?"

"Protecting myself," Ivan mumbled.

"So it's true. Art didn't know you were making these recordings."

Ivan nodded curtly. "Correct."

"Then perhaps we should inform him!" said Dylan.

Ivan raised an eyebrow. "Frankly, I would prefer you did not." He glanced at Heather. "Of course, I can't stop you, but then again, you can't ask Mr. Williams about these recordings without explaining to him how you came to have this knowledge. Perhaps we are at an impasse on this question. Do you still really want to ask Mr. Williams?"

"Not particularly," said Dylan. This was his chance. It was a complex deal, but he knew he had a strong hand. "But if that's the price of nailing you, I'll just have to pay it. What else have you got?"

"Consider this," Ivan responded. "If my surveillance activities are in any way curtailed, as they surely would be if Mr. Williams found out Miss Carter has seen samples of the videos, he will close ranks with those closest to him, and that will directly affect your ability to find out who killed Tony. And I assure you it wasn't me."

Heather shook her head. "Why should we believe you?"

Ivan's brow furrowed, and he slumped back against the desk. "I had my suspicions. Ever since Tony's death, the situation screamed murder to me, and I began my own investigation, trying to get what you Americans call 'an angle.' Now—" He pointed a hand at them, almost accusingly. "You now confirm my suspicions. If there's a murderer in the company, I want to find him and get him out of here. I want to prove I had nothing to do with this."

Dylan eyed him closely. An hour before, Ivan had been a suspect. Now, he wondered if someone else was the culprit. But who? "It looks like we all want the same thing."

"So what do we do?" asked Heather, not willing to release Ivan as a suspect.

Dylan nodded. "We'll keep quiet. For now."

Ivan's face reeked of contempt, and also of a chilling amusement. "I'll destroy this," he said, picking up the CD and breaking it in half in his hands. "The videos in that archive belong to Mantric, and I can't let you go around hacking into my files. You may have this back." He picked up Heather's briefcase and held it out.

Dylan, sensing Heather's unwillingness to go near Ivan, grabbed it from him. Ivan moved to the door then turned. His face reflected the old unpleasant aloofness for which he was known.

"I'll be in touch," he said, and left. His footsteps echoed down the empty hall.

"You get the files?" whispered Dylan as he watched Ivan disappear in the distance.

Heather put a hand to her pendant. "As much as I had room for."

"Good."

"Dylan."

He looked at her. There was relief in her expression—and anger, too. "What?"

Heather gripped his arm. "You can't trust him!"

Dylan shook his head slowly. "I don't, but I want him to become comfortable, to let down his guard. He pointedly avoided giving me an alibi; he skirted the issue. If he is doing his own investigation, even if he did not kill Tony, he may know who did or have a strong suspicion based on his insights into the people around here. And that may be to our advantage."

Chapter 25

Dylan and Heather rushed back to the twenty-fifth floor, where they encountered nothing out of the ordinary. They remained silent as they reached the bullpen, and Dylan touched Heather lightly on the elbow, steering her toward his office. To his surprise, she gave him a warning glance and pulled back.

"We need to——" he began.

"Dylan!"

He whirled around, heart in mouth, and saw Rachel hurrying toward him. "What's up?" asked Dylan, trying, with little success, to sound casual.

"Matt needs you. He told me to tear the building down if I had to."

Dylan glanced around and spotted Heather's back, moving in the direction of the lounge. He turned back to Rachel. "Okay."

He gathered himself as he walked across the bullpen. Two weeks earlier, the ebb and flow of the office, his relationships with his clients and his staff, had been all-important to him. Clutter frustrated him, and now he felt as if he were walking through an alien landscape.

He sat at his desk and logged onto the LAN. Matt was there, waiting. Dylan acted as if nothing had happened, showing the appropriate response to Matt's comments and questions. His head ached throughout the process.

"Hyperfōn?" Dylan asked. He seemed to see Matt's face at the far end of a dark tunnel.

"Yeah. Everyone's worked like a dog on this—through the weekend and non-stop yesterday. Christ, I think we turned over every stone, pulled in every favor everyone on the team had. They know what's at stake."

Dylan's mind multitasked as it wandered back to Heather and why she had walked away from him. Was she all right? What had happened with Ivan before he had shown up? "And?" he asked Matt.

"And it's paid off." Matt lowered his voice.

Dylan's blood began to pump. He leaned in toward Matt and lowered his voice. "Okay. Good. How?"

"You know how when we write code for our clients, there are embedded comments most people can't read? Stuff for the techies in case there was some kind of a glitch or something?"

"Uh-huh." Dylan waited for more.

"Well, as you know, we always put tags in the source code, tags that make it clear who wrote it and who's licensed to use it. To protect the client. And us."

"And?"

"And," Matt said in a soft voice, "well, I kind of hacked into LC's site."

Dylan shoved back from the desk quickly. "You did what? Jesus, Matt! How exactly did you get your hands on script from LC?"

"Actually a lot of it is sitting right there on their website. All you need to do is fire up your browser and view the source. But the important stuff—" Matt ran a hand across his bristled chin. "Well, I told you the part about calling in favors."

"I see." Indeed he did see. It suddenly dawned on Dylan that he had crossed over to the dark side himself by sending Heather in to hack the Mantric files. Now here he was feigning dismay at how Matt had stolen a competitor's intellectual property. But it was way too late to go back. "So why the hell didn't you look for these tags in the first place?"

"We did. Every piece of code, every page of script. We ran searches for every single tag that would possibly identify Mantric or Hyperfōn."

"So that's how you figured it out?"

"No. We didn't find a thing." Matt's voice broke, and he laughed a little. "Then last night, when I was almost asleep sitting at my desk, it dawned on me. We started working on Hyperfōn long before we ever came to Mantric."

"Jesus," whispered Dylan. He sat back in his chair and realized Matt had gone back to the old MobiCelus tags and tried them instead.

Matt nodded in silent agreement. "Yeah. So I came in early and ran the searches again. And what do you know?" He choked. His hands shook. "Hey, presto! The stupid code on a simple end-user log-in error page was riddled with fragments of MobiCelus tags—tags we wrote to protect Hyperfōn. Man. I should have thought of that sooner." He laughed, then coughed. "They should have, too."

"Take it easy, Matt."

Matt grimaced. "Not possible. You do understand what this means, don't you? Someone from Mantric sold us out to—"

"Hey!" said Dylan sharply. "It doesn't mean that at all. Some hotshot at LC could have stolen the code themselves, or someone at Hyperfŏn could have snatched it."

"That's very reassuring," said Matt sarcastically. "This is a bombshell."

"Just let me think a minute." Bombshell indeed. LC had not magically beaten Hyperfŏn to the punch, and it didn't look like an inside job at Hyperfŏn, either. Someone at Mantric had taken the Hyperfŏn business and given it to LC, probably for a considerable amount of money. But what good did that do? They still could not actually prove Mantric was responsible for the theft. It might even be someone in his own division. "Fuck," he breathed softly.

"Exactly." Matt slumped back in his chair, looking dazed and defeated.

What a time for this to happen! Dylan's mind tore through multiple options. A year ago, he would not have hesitated to bring the staff together, along with Rob and Heather and Tony. They would brainstorm for an hour and come up with the best way to find out whoever had done this, no matter what the cost. But now, what if he made the accusation but couldn't prove it? Wouldn't he simply be giving Art an excuse to fire him? No, he needed hard proof. Otherwise he would be out with nothing but the shirt on his back, and Tony's murderer would never be found.

"Dylan, I think it's probably best if I resign."

"No, you're not going to do that. We're not done yet. And we're not going to mention this to anyone, either."

Matt's eyes widened. "You're kidding?"

"First we need to find out whether it was a sell-out or a theft. Who else knows about this?"

"You and me."

"Okay. Then keep it to yourself. Of course, I'll report it to Art when I absolutely have to, but I want that to be when we know for sure what happened. If this gets out now, it only hurts us. Plus it would make it harder to find out the truth. Okay?"

Matt drew a hand across his mouth as if to wipe away his surprise. "Okay. But what do I do?"

"You need to focus on personal connections between the MobiCelus employees who had access to the Hyperfŏn project and LC. Don't tell anyone what you're doing."

"Except Rob—right?"

"Of course. We need to be sure no one is overlooked. Rob has a lot on his plate and could use the help."

"OK." Matt pulled himself up as if standing at attention.

"Good. Call me if you find out anything. And, Matt, do whatever you have to do, but remember, do it quietly. Good luck."

"Thanks, boss."

"Don't thank me. We still have to figure this out."

Dylan hung up and began reorganizing his thoughts, allowing the memory of Ivan to flow back into his mind like a tide encroaching on an open beach. He had a swift image of Heather standing tall and beautiful, a look of angry triumph on her face and one hand clenched around the flash pendant. He pulled out his cell phone.

"Heather," he said when she answered. "You okay?"

"Sure." Her short, curt answer troubled him.

"I was worried. I was afraid you might be—"

"Listen, Dylan, I'm pretty busy. I'm on my way out the door to catch a shuttle back to Boston, and I really don't want to talk to you. Do you understand?"

"What? But—"

"I said I was fine. Just because we work together doesn't mean you have to check up on me. Okay?"

He hesitated. "Okay."

"Good." She hung up.

Dylan stared at his phone. Call time: twelve seconds. What the hell was going on? Then he had a thought. What an idiot he was! Was there someone in her office? Someone she didn't want to know what they had found or that they were working together? Could someone have been listening to their conversation? Was that why she reacted that way?

He considered racing out the door to fly back to Boston with her, but he needed to be alone for a while to think, to take time to unclutter his mind and put everything in perspective. He picked up a sponge basketball and threw it at a small hoop mounted on the back of his door. He repeated this activity with precision, all the while opening each file in his mind, reorganizing it, and, when satisfied with the process, going on to the next file. He continued to throw the ball at the hoop, but several of the files would not cooperate—the Hyperfōn file, Tony's murder, and his position in Mantric.

His mind refused to be of assistance. He feared discovering that, by joining Mantric, he had become party to a colossal fraud, and he feared he would never find out the truth about Tony. He put the ball away and punched "three" on his keyboard.

Rob answered after four rings, "Hi, Dylan, what's up?"

"I just wanted to alert you I've asked Matt to help you look through the LC-related files."

"Yeah, he's already stopped by."

"Good. Is he there?"

"Hell no. I sent him home for some sleep. He's a wreck."

"Okay. Well, I just wanted you to know. When he comes back in, you and he should double-check each other's work."

"Right. We'll get on it as soon as possible."

"You haven't found anything?"

Rob laughed. "Do you think I'd be sitting here if I had?"

• • •

May 13, 7:05 p.m. Boston

Dylan finally caught the five-thirty shuttle back to Boston, and he arrived home still feeling unsettled and directionless, still trying to figure out what was up with Heather. He slid the knot of his tie down and slipped it over his head. He took off his sweaty shirt, removed his belt, and was kicking off his shoes when the doorbell rang. In another life, he might have let it ring. But this was not another life, so he wandered over to the front door. It might be Matt, with news about the Hyperfōn fiasco. Or it might be. . . .

He yanked open the door. "Heather!"

She gave him a quick kiss that only partly allayed his fears. "Did you just get in?"

"Yeah, about ten minutes ago." He led her into the living room. "I would have called, but—" He sat down on the sofa and shot her a pained look. "You were so—"

"Yeah," she said, easing herself into an armchair. "Sorry if I came off like a bitch. It was all I could think of to say to stop the conversation. I can't believe you called me!"

"You weren't alone? That was all I could think of to explain things."

She raised an eyebrow. "Oh, I was alone. But my God, Dylan. We can't talk on the phone about what happened, about anything that's going on at the office. If Ivan secretly videotaped Art's meetings, then he wouldn't think twice about listening to phone messages or taping other employees."

166

"I know. I'm sorry. I only thought of that after you hung up."

Heather laughed, shaking her head. "Dylan, you should know I'd never talk to you like that without a reason. I figured it wouldn't hurt if anyone who might be listening got the impression we weren't on the best of terms."

Dylan thought about her comment. She was right. "I know. Even Prometheus warned me. No more talking about what we're doing, either in the office or on a Mantric phone."

"Or e-mail," added Heather.

"Well, that takes us right back into the nineteenth century."

"Not quite." She reached into her laptop case and pulled out a couple of cheap flip phones. "This one's for you. I've already put my number in it. If we want to talk, we use these—okay?"

"Excellent." Dylan opened the little phone and pushed a few buttons. "Tracfone, eh?" They were disposable and favored by criminals and terrorists. "Wish I'd thought of that. You did right. It's a good thing, too."

"Maybe the danger of being taped was more obvious to me, given that I'd just spent half an hour watching Ivan's spy videos. My God, who knows what these people are up to or where else they may have placed some bugs?" She leaned her head on her hand and took a deep breath.

He eyed her critically. The strain on her face was clear.

"Okay, we need to pull ourselves together and calm down." He looked at the pendant that hung around her neck. "I think we should watch those vids."

"Right." She slipped the pendant from around her neck, tugged gently on the USB plug, and slipped it into the port on Dylan's laptop.

"Jesus," said Dylan, reviewing the long list of files. "You got a lot."

"This thing has blazing speed. When Tony gave it to me, he told me it could hold twenty-five hours of video. I guess we tested it today. Tony should have patented this baby. It's a monster."

"Where'll we start?"

"Well, obviously, I haven't seen them all yet. But they're in chronological order. Let's start at the top."

Dylan clicked on the first .avi file, dated April 29, and sat back as the media player started up. A still image of Art and Ivan sitting in a green-walled room appeared.

"Do you recognize this room?"

"Not sure. It could be the conference room off his office." He glanced at Heather, then hit the space bar and the video began.

"*Tell anyone who asks we're just checking on our own security before we go public,*" Art said, consulting his notepad.

"*Consider it done, Art.*"

Art stared at Ivan for a moment, then stood up and paced. "*We've worked too hard to let some little screw-up destroy our plans.*" He turned around. "*So you're going to go over every possible scenario of what could go wrong. Got it? The records, Schedule B, my private accounts. I want every single possibility looked at. Is that clear?*"

"*Yes.*"

"*And I swear to God that if somebody in your group screws up this deal, I'm going to cut your balls off myself.*"

"*I understand.*"

"*Good. Whatever's going on, I want it nipped in the bud. And I want it done now.*"

The video ended.

"Any of that mean anything to you?" asked Dylan.

Heather's headshake was so slight Dylan was not sure he saw it.

"Maybe they were talking about Rich finding out about the reserve?"

Heather said nothing.

"What's wrong?"

"I don't know," she said, half to him, half to herself. "What are these bastards up to? And what the hell is 'Schedule B'?"

Dylan leaned back in his chair. He studied Heather's aquiline profile. "I have no idea."

She turned her face to him. Heather was a beautiful woman; he had known that since he had first laid eyes on her. He had admired her quick wit and intelligence, but he had never before realized just how strong a woman she was. He placed these thoughts back in the "Heather" file in his mind and returned to the business at hand.

The next several videos were more mundane and much longer than the first. It didn't take them long to understand they were watching regular meetings between Art and Ivan, or Art and Christine—though why they were special enough to be recorded and archived remained unclear.

"You know what surprises me?" said Dylan as they took a break. "How Art defers to Christine's opinion."

"I think she's a pretty scary person. Maybe he's afraid of her. I doubt he's just being polite. I always wondered how she got into the tech biz."

"Being in finance is different. You have to know the financials backward and forward, but you don't have to be a technical genius."

She nodded absently. "Rob is proof of that."

There was no trace of hidden meaning. She just said it, plain and simple. That absence of resentment on her part told him she was over Rob. But it also dawned on him that he really didn't know anything about their relationship.

"What happened with you two?" he asked, and was shocked at his impudence. "Not that I have any right to ask."

"He has bad habits," she said. But she didn't look at him.

His face reddened, and he started another video. "This next one is dated the day before the IPO."

"He made some bad choices," said Heather, her tone subdued.

"What?" It took Dylan a moment to realize she wasn't talking about Art. "Oh."

"I didn't like them," she added.

Dylan withdrew his hand from the track pad. "What kind of choices?"

"Women, for one. He's an attractive guy, and he knows how to use it. He flirted all the time. I wrote it off as harmless, until it went beyond that." She stared absently into the distance. "He was careless. Tony knew. I assumed he told you."

Dylan shook his head. "No, he didn't. I don't know why, but I never wanted to know about Rob's personal life. Or yours."

"Or anybody's."

Dylan fell silent. This was exactly the reason he didn't have these personal discussions, he reminded himself—why he always moved past the moment with a shrug and a self-effacing smile, his standard technique for smoothing over a rough patch.

"Let's see what's next," he said, and tapped the track pad.

"I've seen this one. You won't like it."

They sat in silence for the next five minutes as Art and Christine discussed firing Rich. While Dylan watched the video, he felt Heather staring at him, waiting. When the video ended, he got up and circled the room, staring at the floor, his mind wandering over what he had just viewed. "I knew it," he said, finally. "All that crap about Rich not being good enough for the job. Bastards."

"This is evidence, isn't it? They've admitted they hid the reserve, for one thing, and for another they were trying to hide the fact. Plus they bloody well lied to you."

"I guess so. I don't know. I mean, we stole this, more or less. Can that be used as evidence?"

"There's nothing in there about who killed Tony or why. There's got to be a clue somewhere."

Dylan brought up the next video, dated the day of the IPO. They watched the scene unfold as Ivan crossed the room.

"Close the damn door," Art barked.

Ivan closed the door and sat down across the table from Art.

"So what did you find?"

"I have good news and bad news. Which do you want to hear first?"

"I thought by now you'd know better than to ask a question like that. Just tell me the bad news."

Ivan took a deep breath. "Your hard drive was definitely accessed. And thoroughly."

"All of it?" said Art, the muscles of his jaw worked back and forth and tensed.

"Yes. All of it. They spent hours going through it."

Art slammed back into his chair. "And the files?"

Ivan nodded slowly. "I'm afraid they've been compromised."

"So what the hell is the good news, anyway?"

"I know who did it," said Ivan.

"You do?" Art was suddenly re-energized.

"Yeah. It wasn't easy, but he used Verizon FiOS. A friend of mine just happens to work there, so I called in a favor."

"And?"

Ivan continued. "Well, we had to trace it, of course. Turns out it was routed from the W Hotel on Lexington where these guys always stay. So, after slipping a couple of Benjamins at the hotel, I got a look at who was registered there last night."

"Jesus, Ivan," Art said, his tone filled with anger. "Congratulations on being a world-class sleuth—okay? Now just tell me who the damn person was, will you?"

Ivan frowned. "It was Tony Caruso."

Art looked completely dumbfounded. "Tony?" he said. "Are you sure?"

"Quite sure."

Art stood up and walked around his office. "Why would Tony do this?" he said.

"My job was just to tell you who did it. Not figure out why. I may not know why Tony did it, but from a technology perspective, he was probably the person in the firm most capable of figuring out how to. He's even better than Sandeep at getting into this stuff."

Art resumed pacing around his office. "Where is Tony now?"

"He's been tied up in meetings most of the day. But I caught Sandeep in the hallway and told him I was looking for him. He said Tony wasn't feeling

170

well and was going to go home. Sandeep wanted to know what I wanted, but I didn't tell him. He did not seem pleased. I think his insecurity is showing."

"Who else knows about this?"

"No one. Just you and me."

"No one else? You don't think he got help from Sandeep? Did you get any help from anyone else in your group?"

"No. Tony and Sandeep don't talk much, and I handled it all on my side. I even went to the hotel myself. And I didn't identify what company I was with or who I was looking for."

"Are you absolutely sure?"

"Art, I swear to God, no one knows but you and me."

"What about the detection of an intruder into our network?"

"That's an automated system. I was the first one in this morning, so I'm the one who detected it. And then I followed protocol. I erased the log for it and came directly here to see you."

"So only you and I know about this?"

"That's what I'm saying."

Art went back to his chair and sat down. "Okay. I'll take care of this."

"Fine." Ivan looked relieved.

"Can you find out what e-mail messages Tony has sent and received in the past forty-eight hours?"

"Yes. That shouldn't be a problem."

"Good. And can you access his voice mailbox and listen to his messages?"

"Of course."

Art stared silently at Ivan. "All right. Now listen to me carefully. You're not to talk to anybody about this."

"Of course."

"I'm serious, Ivan. Dead serious. You're not to discuss it with a soul. Not your friends, not your family. No one, not even your computer security buddies. I don't care how proud you are about figuring out it was Tony. You are never to breathe a word of this to anyone. Ever."

"Okay, Art. I got it."

"And if you ever do—" Art said, pointing his finger at Ivan.

Suddenly, the screen went black. Heather reran the last few moments, but again the video ended at the same point. "I don't know what's wrong. Somehow this video is damaged."

"This is incredible," said Dylan, ignoring her comment. "My God, they really did it. They killed Tony to cover up something."

"Dylan—"

"Okay, you're going to tell me it's not proof. But it's a motive, Heather. A real motive."

"Dylan!"

He looked at her and found her face full of concern.

"If they killed Tony, they could kill you. Or me. Remember?"

Fear assailed him. "I won't let them hurt you."

She gave a short laugh. "That's very noble of you."

"I mean it," he said firmly. "We've got to take precautions."

Heather nodded her head in agreement. "Look, something is very clear to me. Whatever Art is doing, there's a method to it. He's cheating and lying to make a ton of money. But he's built a house of cards, Dylan, and it won't stand for long. All the things that have been going wrong? He's setting you up to take the fall when it all comes crashing down. He means to put the blame on you."

Dylan nodded silently. "I know. It fits the pattern. They'll claim Mo-biCelus was a cancer on their business and that Hyperfōn was a failure to begin with and someone in our group sold them out."

"We can't let them do it."

"They can't succeed if we can track down the leak to LC and prove it wasn't our fault."

"Well, I think we have a pretty good idea who did it. Fucking creeps!"

Dylan glanced at the clock. It was after nine. "Let's keep going. This is a gold mine." He opened the video from the evening after Tony's death.

"Did you hear Christine's message?" Ivan asked.

"You mean about Tony? Yes, I heard it. Very tragic."

"This doesn't have anything to do with us, does it?"

"Of course not!" Art bellowed. *"You heard the message. Tony was killed in an electrical accident up in Boston."*

"So did you talk to him before he left the office?" Ivan asked.

"No, I didn't catch him in time. But obviously that doesn't matter now."

"That's a pretty strange coincidence, don't you think?" Ivan asked.

Art locked eyes with the security chief. "I don't know what kind of crazy Slovak Intelligence shit is going through that mind of yours, but I had nothing to do with this. And I ought to kick your ass for even thinking it."

"The police will take his computer," Ivan warned.

"Shit. Can you prevent that? Claim it's private property, or—"

"They won't be able to find anything." Ivan said.

"Oh. Good. So what did you find out about his e-mail and voice-mail traffic?"

"Nothing."

Art leaned forward in his chair. "Don't mess with me, Ivan. You know what I mean."

"I checked our system. There's no evidence Tony forwarded any of the files he may have accessed to anyone else."

"Really? What about e-mails to Dylan?"

"I didn't see any e-mails. But there were voice-mails."

"Tell me."

"There was one voice-mail from Tony to Dylan. It was left yesterday at about four p.m. And there were two from Dylan to Tony later that night."

"What did Tony's message say?"

Ivan pulled an mp3 player from his breast pocket and hit the play button.

"Dylan! Hey, it's Tony. How come you're never there? Look, things are sort of crazy around here, y'know? I got sort of caught up in something big. Ha! So you're coming back to Boston tonight—right? Listen, stop by my place on your way home and I'll show you what I've found like I promised I would. And look, this is hush-hush, so don't tell anybody—okay? Heads are gonna roll when this gets out. Oh, and hey—I'll be online just after four for the IPO celebration. Promise!"

"Did you delete these messages off the system?" Art demanded.

"I couldn't. Johnson had already heard it and saved it."

"So? You could have made it look like a malfunction."

"That is too obvious and would only draw attention to us."

"That's what you think. Nobody notices how much shit just disappears. Trust me."

Ivan maintained a stony silence.

"Continue to monitor Dylan's e-mails and voice-mails. Let me know if you see anything unusual."

"Why?"

"Ivan, never mind why. Just do it. And get up to Boston and yank the hard drive from his computer!"

Ivan looked into Art's eyes, an expression of suspicion and dislike on his thin face. "I'll do that immediately," he said and walked out of his office.

Dylan leaned back in his chair. It wasn't what he had expected, but, of course, if Art had murdered Tony, he wouldn't be bragging about it. Even to Ivan. "He treats Ivan like shit," he muttered. Then he glanced up at Heather. "Not that he doesn't deserve it. And did you see the look on Ivan's face? He really doesn't like Art."

"I still don't trust him. I don't care who he dislikes. So what's next?"

"I don't know." His e-mail alert jingled softly. A priority message. He opened the message.

He glanced at Heather: *From Art*

He moved his laptop so Heather could read it too.

Dylan,

Pursuant to our previous conversation, and due to the fact that, despite our attempts to keep your dirty laundry out of sight, word has gotten out to the general public about the Hyperfōn scandal, I hereby notify you that Matt Smith will no longer be an employee of Mantric. I have attached a letter of termination written in your name. You will sign it and deliver it to Smith immediately. In case of your refusal, I have attached your letter of resignation. Your choice.

Art Williams,
CEO Mantric

Dylan looked at Heather as she read the letter. Her lips formed a small "o" and she looked back at him in disbelief. He picked up the Trac-fone and dialed Matt's home phone number.

"Matt, I'm going to be sending you a letter I got from Art. He's demanding I terminate your employment. I need you to sign it and send it back to me, but you need to trust me that everything will be fine, and you need to give me some time. I know that sounds odd, but Heather and I are getting close to solving several problems, Hyperfōn among them, and I think we're going to need your help."

"I can't say I didn't expect this. I just wasn't sure when it would happen. So what's up?"

"I can't give you any more information right now, but expect a call from Heather, and let's just keep this between ourselves for now."

Chapter 26

May 16, 7:30 a.m. Boston

The radio clicked on at 7:30, and the brash voices of the local radio jocks talking about the previous night's Red Sox game dragged Dylan awake. Beside him, Heather was still asleep. They had agreed that Heather would stay with him over the weekend, at least until they could find answers to the questions they grappled with.

He moved slightly, trying not to awaken her, and shut the radio off, then got out of bed. His morning ritual began with the hot shower doing its best to drown out the thoughts racing through his mind. Dylan stood under the hotter-than-usual spray of water, watching the steam building up, feeling its cleansing effect.

The movement of the shower curtain startled him. Heather poked her head around and greeted him. "Good morning. Do you mind if I join you?"

For the first time in several days, he smiled. "Not at all."

"Good. Got a washcloth?" she asked with a sly grin. "I'll scrub your back."

• • •

May 16, 9:00 a.m. Boston

Heather sat with her back to the wall in the Panera café on Lexington Street in Waltham and stirred her coffee slowly, all the while staring at the doorway. It was five past nine when a familiar face appeared.

"Rich! Over here."

Rich Linderman gave a little wave and wove his way through the crowd to the unbearably small round table where she sat.

She pushed a second cup of coffee toward him. "Cream and sugar—right?"

He grinned foolishly. "Aw, you remember."

"Of course. Thanks for making time to see me."

"Not at all. In fact, I'm glad you called. I was sorry we didn't have a chance to catch up at Tony's funeral. I've been thinking about you lately."

"And I've been thinking about you."

"Hey, I'm all right. Actually I just accepted a job at Fidelity in their finance department. I start next week."

"I'm glad to hear it."

"Yeah. I figure it's the kind of company where I can learn a lot. And I spent a lot of time with my new boss before accepting the offer. I really like him."

"I'm happy for you, Rich."

"Thanks. Look, Heather, I don't blame you guys for what happened. In the end, it's working out well. From what I hear via the grapevine, I may have gotten out just in time."

"I'll say." Heather crossed her legs and eyed him coolly. "Can we talk off the record, Rich?"

He frowned. "Sure."

"You can't tell anyone we met. And don't phone me at the office. Use the new number I gave you if you have anything to add later on."

"Christ, Heather! Okay, I'm in. What's up?"

"Do you recall seeing anything in accounting relating to a company called LC?"

"No, I don't think so. I mean, Mantric worked with a lot of companies, and I was only there a couple of months. Why?"

"LC is a competitor to Hyperfōn. Out of the blue they launched their own competing mobile business. We lost Hyperfōn as a result."

"I'm sorry to hear that. But no, I've never heard of LC."

"What about Hyperfōn? Was there anything about the account?"

"Rob and Matt handled it. We had team meetings, of course, but—" He shook his head. "What the hell is going on?"

"I can't go into details, Rich, but it looks like someone at Mantric may have stolen the Hyperfōn information and sold it to LC."

"Christ! Really? Is Christine involved?"

"I can't rule that out," Heather said cautiously.

Rich leaned forward. "Heather, nothing would surprise me about that woman. I've done a lot of thinking about it since I left. Did you ever hear about a company called Cendant?"

Heather shook her head.

"Check it out. It happened pretty long ago, but it was a huge scandal. It sounds similar." He met her eyes. "Seriously. Check it out. C-E-N-D-A-N-T."

"Thanks, Rich. I will. And I'm sorry I've been out of touch."

"That's perfectly understandable. Don't apologize at all."

"All right. Let's make a point to get together again. Soon."

He stood. "Sounds great. Take care of yourself, Heather."

"You too, Rich."

• • •

May 16, 9:30 a.m. Boston

Sarah opened the door and walked in. "You're in late today, aren't you?" She looked at her watch.

"Yeah," Dylan answered curtly. "What's up?"

Sarah sat on the corner of his desk. "I just wanted to quickly review your calendar today, but I can come back later if you like."

"No, that's okay. Sorry to be short, but I just have lots on my mind. What's on the calendar?"

She shrugged off his indifference. "Well, it's actually pretty light. You have a couple of calls to field, at ten and eleven, and then a video conference this afternoon at three."

"Okay." It hadn't escaped Dylan's notice that Sarah was trying hard to keep his schedule fairly open. He appreciated it.

"Oh—and you might want to spend some time going through your e-mails," she added as she turned to leave. "I've had a few people call wondering if you ever got them."

He frowned. Ever since joining Mantric it seemed like he received at least fifty e-mails a day. He used to be pretty good about staying on top of it, but he had recently fallen behind. "Okay, I'll do that this morning. Thanks."

"You're welcome. Door open or closed?"

"Closed, please."

She nodded and closed the door behind her.

Dylan turned back to his computer and called up his e-mails. He shuddered at the long list: over two hundred unread messages. As he started plowing through them, he noticed how many were a back-and-forth discussion of some particular problem. Most had been resolved without his involvement. It was as if he were already out.

He remembered his conversation with Matt and felt the anger rising in his mind. His thoughts wandered back to the weekend as he and Heather watched the videos over and over until they were almost memorized. He knew he would never receive Tony's e-mail. It was time to stop beating his head against that wall. He had secondary proof that Art and Christine were heavily involved in some scam, but no proof as to what it was. All he knew was that he would give anything to find it. He also feared they were involved either directly or indirectly in Tony's murder. Time to do some research. He opened up his web browser and Googled the Securities and Exchange Commission website: a vast archive of stock market history and data. In response to the great stock market crash of 1929 and the ensuing Depression, Congress had established the SEC in 1934 to protect investors.

As he looked through its site, Dylan noted that the primary mission of the SEC was to protect investors and maintain the integrity of the securities markets. If he could find hard evidence that Mantric was cooking its books to fraudulently boost its stock price, the SEC would certainly be interested. He wrote down the address of their Boston office.

Dylan searched through the site looking for the Office of Internet Enforcement, commonly known as the "Internet fraud squad." It had been created to combat the opportunity the Internet had created for stock swindling schemes. Dylan added the Washington, D.C., number of the director, Steve Markes, to the contacts list of his new Tracfone.

Then he went to www.fbi.gov.

Thirty minutes later he pushed back from the desk and walked out of his office. "I'm going down for a Coke," Dylan said as he passed Sarah's desk.

"I can get you one," offered Sarah.

"No, thanks, I'll get it myself."

Dylan left the office and took the elevator down to the second floor. When he arrived, instead of going to the cafeteria, he turned left and slipped into an empty conference room, where he pulled out his Tracfone.

"Hi," Heather said. "You okay?" The sound of an espresso machine roaring in the background and customers being called to pick up orders assaulted Dylan's ears.

"Yep." He heard clinking sounds. "Where are you, anyway?"

"I'm at a restaurant. Had my meeting. It went okay, but nothing much to report. He didn't work on that account. Just Rob and the team. And he knew nothing about LC."

"Okay."

"But he has suspicions. He says to check out a scandal involving a company called Cendant."

"I vaguely recall something about that company, I think. I'll check. Anything else?"

"Nope. Just doing research in my new and very public office while I wait for my eleven o'clock."

"Be careful."

"You too."

• • •

May 16, 10:30 a.m. Boston

Back at his computer, Dylan popped open his Coke and Googled Cendant. Over 100,000 hits. He read the detailed report about the company and its "irregular accounting practices" over the course of three years. Once it was discovered, Cendant's stock dropped in market value by fourteen billion dollars in one day. It also triggered one of the largest shareholder lawsuits in history.

Dylan scanned the report until he reached the section that indicated that the CFO had kept a schedule the management team used to track the progress of the fraud itself. Dylan pushed back quickly from his desk, and his mind rushed over the details. "Holy shit," he said out loud. "Schedule B!"

• • •

May 16, 11:30 a.m. Boston

"Hey, Heather."

Heather, lost in her laptop, jumped when she heard her name.

"Whoa! Didn't mean to scare you!"

"Hey, Matt. Sorry. I guess I was pretty absorbed in my work."

Matt sat down in the chair that Rich had occupied earlier. "I like your new office. The décor. The staff. An upgrade."

"Agreed." She smiled. She had always liked Matt, and hated what had happened to him.

"Did you get booted too, or are you just playing hooky?" he asked with a lopsided grin.

"I needed the air. After Friday—Jesus, Matt, I'm sorry. Dylan did not want to send that letter to you."

"Hey, I understand. Dylan wants to get to the bottom of this LC mess, and he can't do it if he resigns, so I had to be the one. I believe him." He shrugged. "Besides, I've been expecting this for days. Things just aren't right there, Heather. But hey—I already wiped my office computer," he joked.

"It's all so incredible. I just wanted to see you face-to-face and for you to know that, somehow, all of this is going to work out."

"Look, Heather. I'm done with Mantric. I don't care about being fired. Except for one thing. All I honestly care about is finding the SOB who sold us out to LC and proving it wasn't me or anyone on my team. If they hadn't fired me—"

"You'd have worked it out eventually?" Heather cut in.

"Well, I think so. I felt really close to discovering something, something I mentioned to Dylan about coding—" he faltered.

"Matt, I think you have it exactly right. I think you were fired because you were on the verge of working it out. I need you to tell me everything you did after your conversation with Dylan on Friday."

Matt's eyes widened. He nodded slowly, collecting his thoughts.

• • •

May 16, 2:00 p.m. Boston

"How did it go?" Dylan asked, holding the Tracfone close to his ear.

"Okay." Heather whispered. "He's a little upset, but not as angry as I expected."

"That sums Matt up. Did you get his itinerary from Friday?"

"Yeah. He didn't tell Rob he had been fired. Rob told him to go home, eat something, pull down the blinds, and go to bed, and he'd send him the files when he woke up and checked in."

"Hmm," Dylan said, gathering his thoughts.

"He said he went out like a light and woke up at about six. He found an e-mail from Rob saying, and I quote, 'Bad news, Matt. Got an e-mail from Art saying I was to have no further communication with you about company business. What's going on?'"

"What did he say to Rob?" Dylan asked, his mind racing over the turn of events.

"He said he didn't want to get Rob in any trouble."

"Okay. Now with Matt out of the picture, we'll leave LC to Rob, and we can focus on the real issue—proving who killed Tony and why."

"Agreed. Have you discovered anything more that might finger Art or Christine?"

"I followed up on Rich's suggestion and checked out Cendant. According to what I read, the company was formed in 1997 by the merger of CUC and HFS. One was a direct marketing company and the other was a franchiser."

"And?"

"Well it turns out they had inflated their earnings by 500 million dollars over the previous three years. That triggered one of the largest shareholder lawsuits in history. Cendant agreed to pay two-point-eight billion dollars to settle, effectively admitting their management team had issued false and misleading statements and sold a large portion of their stock at inflated prices. And get this. The CFO was not only deliberately falsifying the company's quarterly and annual financial results, he actually kept a schedule that the management team used to track their progress."

He heard a slight gasp. "A schedule? Schedule B?" Heather asked.

"That's right."

"Jesus. Do you think Art and Christine would be stupid enough to actually keep a schedule like that?"

"Nixon was stupid enough to tape-record his conversations, wasn't he?"

"Okay. In fact, if we use Cendant as a template for what's happening here, I think I can add to the picture."

"I'm all ears."

"I did a little work myself while I was waiting for my appointments. I've built a spreadsheet model. You know, loading all our consultants by rank, the billing rates they charge, and an estimate of the average hours they should be billing. I started with our San Francisco office. Based on the number of consultants there, I calculated that they should account for about ten percent of our revenues."

"And?"

"It wasn't even close. And, since I've been out there a lot, I happen to know there are a number of consultants who aren't working on any projects at all."

"Christ."

"There's more. Then I did the same exercise for all of our offices. I even used a very conservative estimate of the hours they are billing by rank, a good fifteen percent below what we've been told. I plugged those numbers in and totaled it up."

"Let me guess. That wasn't even close either."

"Not by a country mile."

Dylan was stunned. He wanted to ask her if she was sure she'd run the numbers right. But of course she was.

"Dylan, do you remember when we were at Docks and I told you how enthusiastic those investment bankers were about our stock?"

"Yes."

"Well, I checked out all the major investment sites and message boards. You wouldn't believe it. There are tons and tons of postings playing up Mantric and how hot we are and how high our stock is going to go. There are even rumors being posted that some of the big firms like IBM are taking a look at acquiring us."

"*Acquiring* us?" he said skeptically. "I haven't heard anything about that."

"That's my point. It's as though someone is spreading rumors on purpose."

"Maybe they are. Maybe that's another part of the whole campaign." Dylan sat back and rested his head on the sofa, then jerked back upright. "Heather, does this mean what I think it does?"

"It means we're on to them."

"Yeah. Only we just don't have the damn evidence. And, if we are correct, the bigger question is: Did Tony know? If he did, then we have strong evidence of a motive for his death."

"Maybe it's time to talk to the cops."

"Maybe. Or maybe it's time to let in some sunshine on these guys and expose the truth."

"And how are we going to do that?"

Dylan paused. "Heather, I have an idea."

"What?"

"I need to think about it a little more. And I'm going to need help."

"You know I'm here."

"Someone from outside the office. You still have the key to my place?"

"Of course."

"Good, I'll meet you back there by five o'clock to discuss it. It's time we turned those bastards' own tactics against them."

Chapter 27

Dylan arrived early at the Boston office. He seated himself at his desk amid the quiet of the morning; the normal buzz of activity was absent. He opened his laptop and watched the stock market prices stream across the bottom of the screen. Mantric's stock soared to an all-time high of $101.75 a share, and for Dylan that meant that, on paper at least, he was now worth over sixteen million dollars.

He shook off the thought and forced his mind to refocus on just two things: business and Tony—and how they crossed paths. He obsessed about Art and Christine's probable involvement with Tony's death, and the ongoing Hyperfōn fiasco continued to raise its ugly head and beckon him.

He expected to hear from Art at any moment, a curt letter demanding his resignation—or maybe from Christine, unapologetically nasty as she fired him and laid the blame on Art. He was staring at the streaming figures on the monitor when his screen flashed, letting him know a caller wanted to speak to him on the LAN. It was Ivan. He got up, closed his door, then reseated himself. He clicked "accept," and Ivan's grim face appeared.

"Good morning, Mr. Johnson," Ivan said, his accent more chopped and precise than normal.

"Morning," Dylan said, his tone barely civil. "What do you want, Ivan?"

"I would like to discuss the Hyperfōn situation with you."

"Would you? Okay. Go ahead."

Ivan cleared his throat. "I would prefer to do this in person."

"Well that could be difficult, because I'm in Boston, and—"

Ivan cut Dylan off. "Yes, I know. As am I."

Dylan caught himself short, wondering why Ivan was in Boston. He cursed under his breath. "You know you can have your secretary call my secretary and—"

"Mr. Johnson, please. Will you come to Tony's office?"

Dylan noticed a subtle change in Ivan's expression. Not threatening, but more pleading. He gave a curt nod. "I'll be right there." He signed off and left his office.

The sound of his steps echoed as he walked through the empty hallway. He recalled the last time he had gone to Tony's office—he'd found Ivan dismantling his friend's computer. He hesitated outside it, then opened the door.

Ivan sat in a chair behind the desk, arms folded and head bowed. Dylan glanced around. The empty office, now stripped of any evidence of its former occupant, contained only a desk and two chairs. A cold and empty feeling swirled through the pit of his stomach. He stepped in and closed the door.

Anger bubbled up from his gut like bile. "So why do you give a fuck about Hyperfōn?"

Ivan raised his head and regarded Dylan as an unwelcome pest. "I don't. I had to say something to get you here." He glanced around the room. "Where we can talk."

Dylan snorted. "You're kidding. *Now* you're worried about someone snooping in my office, after what happened last week and what's been happening for months?" He shook his head in disbelief. He pulled up a chair and sat in silence, waiting for Ivan to take the first step.

"We have a big problem," Ivan said.

"Really? What a brilliant revelation!"

"You refer to what happened last week. You are speaking of Mr. Smith's firing?"

Dylan cast an icy stare across the desk.

"I did nothing, Mr. Johnson." Ivan looked at him with a pained expression. "I don't think you appreciate the difficulty of my position." He rose and walked to the window, his back to Dylan.

"I think I do. You're playing both sides for your own benefit."

"Not benefit. Survival." He turned around and faced Dylan. "This is a difficult time, Mr. Johnson. The moral issues are . . . ambiguous."

"Right. Because it's hard to decide whether or not to turn in a murderer."

"Sometimes, yes, but not in this case. Unfortunately, I do not have any substantive information leading me to identify the murderer."

Dylan scrutinized Ivan's face. He saw questions in his eyes. Was he lying about knowing who murdered Tony? Was he wondering what Heather had seen? The man's granite face left little room for answers. Only his eyes displayed fear—and perhaps a bit of sadness.

"So what *did* you want to talk about?"

Ivan hesitated for just a second. "I wanted to see if you have made any progress in your investigation of Tony's death."

"Nothing that points away from Mantric, if that's what you mean." Dylan tried to stay one mental step ahead of Ivan, but felt the man's breath on the back of his neck.

"Have the police told you anything?" Ivan asked.

"I'm actually avoiding the police. I guess you know about that."

"You guess wrong, Mr. Johnson. The people I am avoiding are not the police."

"Well, if you lie down with swine—"

"You criticize me?" He lifted his chin. "You are such a successful young professional, aren't you, Mr. Johnson? With the world in the palm of your hand. Money is your god. You think you are so different from Art Williams, from Christine Rohnmann, from me? How closely have you examined your motives? Because from where I am sitting, you are well on your way to becoming a second Art Williams." His tone was not rude, just stating the facts as he saw them.

Dylan bristled: he knew that Ivan's angry words might well be true. Again, he thought he saw a moment of fear, crossed with desolation. "What does Art have on you anyway, Ivan? The way Art talks to you— his condescending attitude. It's pretty clear he's holding something over your head."

Ivan returned to the desk and sat down, leaning in toward Dylan. "You couldn't even begin to imagine my situation."

"Fine. So again I ask, what do you want?"

Ivan's jaw clenched. "I want to ask you to warn me when you make your move."

"What move?"

"Please, Mr. Johnson, don't bother to try to cover it up."

"Okay, so you want a heads-up if I know when something is coming down."

"If you want to put it that way."

"So you can what? Take off? Warn Art?" He heard the anger in his words.

Dylan watched Ivan's gaunt face. He realized Ivan was on the verge of a disclosure; he just didn't know if it would benefit him or not. He decided to push. "I notice I didn't get a heads-up from you about Matt."

"I didn't know Art would ask you to fire him. I'm not hearing as much as I once did."

Dylan wrinkled his brow, confused. "Okay," he said slowly as he organized his thoughts. "So—what? All you want me to do is promise to give you warning if I discover something? You're still on my suspect list, you know, and pretty close to the top."

Ivan remained emotionless and let out a long sigh. "I did not kill Tony, but I have nothing other than my word that I can give you. While I realize he was a close friend to you, he was nothing more to me than an employee. I mean no ill—I just had no history with him. My time with Mantric is coming to an end, one way or another. I'm just asking for a favor. Whether you grant it or not is up to you."

Dylan lowered his glance toward the desk. The last thing he expected from Ivan was the request of a favor. The sound of silence, that mind-numbing experience of the total absence of sound, wrapped itself around him and squeezed. His photographic memory recapped the entire conversation but could not provide an answer to the question: Should he trust Ivan? All he had to go on was his instinct, his ability to judge this man. And, in Ivan's case, his head told him one thing, and his gut another. He took the chance. "Okay. Consider yourself warned."

Ivan raised one eyebrow and leaned forward in a conspiratorial manner. "Something is in the works?" he whispered, more as an aside than a direct question.

Dylan nodded.

Ivan stood and walked to the window. He clasped his hands behind him. "Hmm. Your goal is to—what?—find evidence of wrongdoing, or proof of who killed your friend?"

"It's all the same to me."

"Perhaps not. Do you plan to do this alone, Mr. Johnson?"

"Actually, I've lined up outside help."

"And what about inside help?"

Dylan's heartbeat increased, and suddenly the temperature of the room seemed to rise. "What about it?"

Ivan paced across the room, the image of a man trying to make a key decision. "You wonder what Mr. Williams had on me?"

"Yeah."

Ivan walked over to the window and looked out. "My country doesn't exist anymore." He stopped and took a breath, released his breath through his nose. "In my line of work, situations occur and people turn quickly to save themselves. I do not have pleasant memories of my actions. Let us just say political strife, when it reaches high levels, results in actions people do not forget."

"So what does Art have on you?"

"When the revolution came, fortunes changed hands, memories were long, and my actions in one regime were remembered by the second. I had worked for the wrong side, you see. I fled with a price on my head and eventually found my way to your country. I am skilled at my job, and contacts introduced me to Mr. Williams. Unfortunately for me, they informed him of my past, and he has maintained a file on me. This was several years ago, but even then he was planning. He has the ability to look into the future and plan for his own good fortunes. I would not play a game of chess with him if I were you. He is always several steps ahead of his opponent."

"How did you ever get a green card?"

Ivan did not answer.

Dylan immediately realized the answer. "You don't have one, do you? Art somehow fixed it up so you could stay, or got you a fake identity. Is that it? Is that what you wanted to find? His file that proves you're an illegal alien?"

Ivan's eyelids flickered. "Yes."

Dylan stopped and thought. "But you had access to all the computers, all the files. You could have deleted that information any time, and he could not have said anything to you because he would have been complicit in your illegal status."

"His file on me was not on any computers. He had a paper file I've never found, and he would have manipulated the information to keep the authorities away from his involvement. I won't be able to rely on Mr. Williams's sponsorship any longer." He turned to Dylan and changed the subject. "You won't see me again, Mr. Johnson. I admire your desire to fight for justice for your friend. You show commendable passion." He picked up a sheet of paper from the desk and scribbled directions on it. "Perhaps this information will be of some value to you." He handed Dylan the paper and turned to leave. He stopped at the door and turned around. "One more thing, Mr. Johnson. Those videos Ms. Carter saw? They were my insurance plan. Mr. Williams knows nothing about them."

• • •

May 17, 6:00 p.m. Boston

The medical examiner's report on Tony Caruso, ruling the death to be a homicide, was released at eleven o'clock that morning, more than two weeks after his death. The Mantric employees' cell phones rang non-stop throughout the day, and Art sent out another emergency voice-mail to the U.S. staff expressing his distress, his support of Tony's father in this difficult time, and the unsubtle implication that, if true, it certainly had nothing to do with Mantric. Dylan wondered if the news caused Art to put off firing him for another day. If so, he owed the Boston medical examiner a big thank-you.

Dylan was in his kitchen pouring a second cup of coffee just as the Tracfone rang. It could be only one of three people, and he hoped it was Heather. "Hello?"

"Hi," she said. "Are we putting our plan into action today?"

"Yes. I'm taking the eight o'clock shuttle to New York this evening. Sorry I didn't call you. Are you okay back in your apartment? You're welcome to stay here if you prefer." The sound of hope echoed in his voice, and he wished he were not so obvious.

"No, I'm fine. Did you see the news?"

"If you mean about Tony's death, yeah, I saw it." A moment of silence echoed between them. "Where are you on the spreadsheet?" he asked.

"I spent most of the day reviewing the information with Rich. He really is quite good with numbers, and even better at explaining them. I'm comfortable once we solidify the information, even if it has nothing to do with Tony's death. With these numbers and the videos, we will have a solid case against Art and Christine and their illegal business practices."

"Good. I'll be at my hotel in New York. I need to organize our plan. Monday will be an ugly day at the office." He hesitated for a moment, and then added, "Listen, Heather. I had a meeting with Ivan this morning."

"You what?" Her tone became defensive. "Why didn't you call me and tell me?"

"I needed to have some time to myself to digest the conversation, but, if you have a few minutes, let me tell you now."

Chapter 28

Mantric's senior mobile technologists gathered in the conference room to prepare for the week. Tony had been running those meetings, but now the task fell to Sandeep, the technology chief, who ran the meeting from his sanctuary in the New York office over their secure videoconference system. The agenda focused on a discussion of next-generation mobile computing operating systems and the impact they might have on Mantric's clients.

The mundane discussion bordered on tedium, and Sandeep nodded periodically but said nothing. He kept a close eye on the morning's stock prices as they scrolled across the bottom of his laptop display. Mantric, he noted, was down a few points, to 100. Sweat trickled down the side of his face and disappeared under his collar as he watched the Mantric price tumble down to 91.

The sounds of the voices in the distance became muffled, drowned out by the sound of blood surging through his head. He stared at the stream of information displayed on the screen; with each moment, the Mantric price dipped further.

"Oh my God," he said suddenly. He rose quickly, sending his chair skittering across the floor, where it banged into the bookcase at the far side of the room. "I'm sorry. This meeting is adjourned."

• • •

In the cafeteria of the Park Avenue headquarters, assorted members of the staff helped themselves to the daily fare of croissants and fruit. Rachel, telling herself she deserved a treat given the goings-on of the past two weeks, had just picked up a Danish when an outburst arose at one of the tables.

"Holy shit!" said Jack Krone, a notoriously fussy man from the marketing department known for his ability to write extremely witty headlines. He never swore.

"What's happened? You're going to have to be more specific if you want me to join in the fun," Rachel quipped. She licked a bit of cheese Danish from her little finger as she wandered toward his table.

"This isn't funny!" said Jack, pointing at his laptop. Rachel leaned forward and looked over his shoulder and her eyes widened. "Jesus! That's true," she muttered.

Stephanie Mathers entered the cafeteria bearing a half-grapefruit. "What's going on?" she asked.

Jack took a deep breath. "Our stock is nose-diving so fast it's hard to keep track of it. Look at this," he said, pointing to the bottom of his screen.

"*What?*" Stephanie gasped. She leaned close over Jack's shoulder and squinted at the screen. "Quick," she said, poking Jack. "Open CNBC and see if there's anything there about the market. Maybe there's something else going on that's driving this fall. Maybe something happened that's affecting the entire market."

Jack quickly opened CNBC. There it was, right on the home page: "*Breaking News: 'Mantric Leaders Accused of Financial Irregularities.'*"

Stephanie read the details.

"Numerous financial news websites have received information from un-named sources within Mantric (NASDAQ: MNTR) that the firm's senior management has been falsifying its financials to boost its stock price in an effort to sell their shares at a highly inflated price. In addition, it is reported Mantric, a recent darling of the investment community, has at least on one occasion, and perhaps more, actually sold its own clients' secrets to other firms to generate additional income. While CNBC has not been able to verify this information, the sheer volume of accusations being made on reputable investment websites, including our own, has alarmed investors and resulted in a sharp drop in Mantric's stock price. CNBC is investigating these charges and will provide continuous updates."

Stephanie stopped and shot straight up. "Oh my God! This can't be true," she said to the half-dozen horrified Mantric employees who had gathered around them. A wave of panic began to build like a tsunami.

May 18, 10:00 a.m. New York

Dylan entered the New York office unnoticed. He avoided people and hurried to his office, wondering who would be the first to call him. He looked at the screen of his computer and shook his head. From behind closed doors, he heard Rachel as she rushed back to her desk and picked up the phone. Her voice had risen an octave.

"Have you heard the latest?" Rachel called to another party. "Apparently there's breaking news on CNBC about us falsifying some financial information to jack up the value of our stock! They say it's been done by people inside the firm!"

Dylan walked quietly to the door and pressed his ear against it to listen. He assumed she was talking to Michelle, Art's secretary. He heard only one side of the conversation, but he knew the word was making rapid rounds throughout the office.

"You can say that again! When Mr. Williams finds out—well, somebody's living on borrowed time!"

Dylan's company cell phone vibrated in his pocket. He walked as far away from the door as he could and eyed the caller I.D.: Joe Ferrano. "Hello, Joe," he said, his voice low.

"Dylan, what the hell is going on?"

"What?"

"You haven't heard?"

"Heard what?" He wondered how fast the story would make the rounds, and he knew he would get a good read from an outsider like Joe.

"Are you kidding me? The news is everywhere! On CNN, on CNBC, on every financial and technology industry website. Check it out. It seems your boss and his cronies have been cooking your books!"

"Really. When did you—?"

"Two minutes ago. Dylan, it also says you guys are padding your pockets by selling out your own clients."

Dylan was silent.

"Before all of this, the news about what happened to Hyperfōn was already getting out on the street. It won't take people long to figure out our company was one of the ones your firm sold out! Jesus, Dylan, are you even listening to me?"

"Yes, Joe. I am. But I can't talk about it over the phone."

"I see." There was a pause then a change in tone. "Dylan, are you okay?"

"I think so."

"You don't sound it. Can I help?"

Dylan stopped and shook his head. "Joe, I'm really grateful for that offer. After all that's happened, I'd have thought you'd be the last person on Earth to offer me help."

"Look, Dylan, I'm not saying I'm not still pissed off at what happened. I am. My company got screwed. But I don't believe for a second you're involved. I warned you about Art Williams's reputation. And I like you, Dylan. You're a talented and hard-working guy. I didn't get where I am by luck. I'm pretty good at reading people, and we've worked together long enough for me to know you've been snookered as well as me. Hell, you remind me of me at your age."

Dylan bowed his head. From across the room, he could see the computer screen blink with an urgent message from Art. He ignored it. "Thanks, Joe," he said, choking on his words. "I'm sorry you're involved in this mess."

"Yeah—me too."

Dylan paused and took a deep breath. "Listen, Joe. Do you think it's crazy to pass up a fortune for the sake of a good friend?"

"Hell no! Wait. How big a fortune?" Joe chuckled.

Dylan returned the chuckle, then said, "I have to go. Thanks for calling, Joe. Maybe we can get together sometime. Outside of work?"

"Sure, Dylan. Call me when you can. And remember that offer of help remains open."

Dylan disconnected his phone without further comment. He felt like a ghost, sitting in his office, silent, while at every level the Mantric staff found themselves in a world crashing down around them. In an eerie reversed image of the day the company had gone public, they huddled before their monitors and over their smartphones watching the numbers dance, spiraling down from the heights just as quickly as they had risen just a short time earlier: 61, 53, 51, 44, 37, 27 . . . 12.

Dylan sat in the dim office, lit only by the morning light coming through the windows. He went to his computer, ignoring Art's urgent message, and dialed two numbers. Within moments the screen divided in half, with Heather's face on one side and Matt and Rich on the other.

He placed a headset on his head to ensure no one in the office could hear their conversation. "Are you ready?" he asked in a hoarse whisper.

"Yep," said Heather.

"Us too," echoed Matt and Rich.

"Okay, so let's go over this one more time."

Heather spoke first. "I'm going to call Christine and ask her if she has spoken to you. I'm going to tell her I got a frantic message from you on my voice-mail and I've not been able to contact you."

"And if she asks for any details?"

"I'll tell her that you said you spoke to Matt and Rich and they had some important financial information related to Hyperfōn, but you didn't leave any particulars."

"What if she pushes for more?"

"Then I'll act stupid, like financial things are so far out of my league, and I thought you might be contacting her."

"Good. Okay, guys." He turned his attention to Matt and Rich. "How about you?"

Matt spoke. "I'm going to call Rachel and ask for you. When she tells me you're not there, I'm going to ask her to give you a message— that I heard from Rich that he was supposed to meet with some high-end corporate lawyer about suing Christine and Art for unlawful termination. That the lawyer had found something in the paperwork that raised some legal questions in his mind. Then I'll tell her I am going to meet Rich and his lawyer to give a statement, and the lawyer said he might be able to help me too with the Hyperfōn situation." Matt chuckled. "Sorry to have to use Rachel this way, but she doesn't keep secrets very well."

"Well, that's what we're counting on. Okay, our timing has to be perfect." He lowered his voice to just barely a whisper. "It's 11:30 and Rachel has left. She'll be back from lunch in about thirty minutes. Just keep calling until you get her. I'm staying put until I hear her side of the conversation. You let Heather know once you've completed your end of the deal. Heather, you make your call to Christine as soon as you hear from Matt."

Rich's face appeared on the screen. "Are you sure about the timing of this thing?" he asked.

Dylan took a deep breath. "Nothing is guaranteed, but, if I know Rachel, she'll hightail it to see her good friend Michelle, Art's secretary. And I have no doubt Michelle will waste no time telling Art. By that time, either Art will call Christine, or she will have already called him. All they need to know is where your supposed meeting will take place. Be sure you give the name of some restaurant far enough away that traveling to and from it will give me enough time."

"What about Michelle?" Heather asked. "How are you going to get past her?"

"One thing I've learned is that when Art is out of the office, she takes advantage of his absence and runs an errand or two. She keeps a close eye on his calendar and knows when she can wander and when she can't. He won't be gone ten minutes before she's out somewhere."

There was a moment of silence before Heather asked, "Are you sure the information Ivan gave you is correct?"

"No, I'm not sure of anything, but for some reason, I trust what he said. I haven't seen him today, and I suspect he is long gone."

Matt piped up, "Well, be careful. If they come back before you're finished, you'll really be finished!"

Dylan raised his eyebrows. "That's an understatement. Listen, everyone, no more contact until tonight. I'll get back to you and let you know what's happened from this end. Good luck!"

Matt and Rich disconnected. Heather remained. "Dylan, please be very careful. Now that we know Ivan taped all of those meetings secretly, your safety may really be in question. We know from that one damaged video that Tony knew something—something he was getting ready to tell you about. If they did not kill him, I'm sure they had their fingers in that pot. Either they made Ivan do it, or they hired someone else." Her voice began to rise.

Tears filled Dylan's eyes as his memory reran the details of that video. The last day of Tony's life. There was something about the video he could not put his finger on, but he was certain it held the key to Tony's murder. "Wish me luck." He disconnected the call and turned his computer off.

He looked at his watch. Twelve-oh-five. Suddenly he heard a rustling outside the door. He hurried over to a dark corner behind the door and waited, holding his breath. He watched the doorknob turn and the door open just a few inches. Then he heard the phone on Rachel's desk ring. The door closed, and he heard Rachel answer the phone.

"Oh, hi Matt. No, he's not here. I was just going to check his office calendar when you called."

Several moments of silence followed. Dylan tiptoed to the other side of the door and gently opened it just enough to see Rachel's back. She had cradled the phone between her left shoulder and ear while she scribbled notes. Dylan could not see her face, but the speed with which she wrote, her head bobbing up and down in frantic silence, spoke volumes.

"My goodness! I see. Yes, I'll tell him as soon as he comes in. Oh no, I won't tell anyone. Yes, I promise to give him the message immediately."

Dylan softly closed the door and moved to the shadows in the back of the office, but Rachel did not enter with any notes for him. He waited for one minute, one minute that seemed like an hour, before he opened the door again. Rachel was nowhere to be seen. A quick scan of the cubicles across the hallway told him the employees were still gathered in small clusters, either in someone's cubicle or in the cafeteria or the conference room, watching their world collapse. He hurried out the door toward the stairwell, yanked the door open, and raced, two steps at a time, up two flights to the senior executive floor. He leaned against the wall next to the door and bent over, grasped his knees, and took a deep breath. Then he opened the door a fraction of an inch and listened to silence. He heard no voices, no sounds of movement of any kind. He slipped into the hallway.

Like the floors below, all life was focused on computers, smartphones, or tablets as employees watched their futures disintegrate before them. Dylan held himself close to the wall, eyeing nearby offices in case he needed a quick hiding place.

"What the hell is this all about?" Art's voice boomed from around the next corner.

Dylan rushed into an empty office. He placed his ear close to the door.

"I swear, Christine, between this damned news leak and your handling of Linderman's termination, we have a real mess that I have to clean up."

"*My* handling of his termination? You're the one who wanted him out. You're the one who told me to do whatever it took to get rid of him, and fast!"

"Don't try to shove this off on me. Everything was working as it was supposed to until that blunder." Art's deep voice continued to rise.

"Keep your voice down!" Christine demanded.

Dylan listened through a moment of silence, wondering if they had taken the elevator or were still nearby. Then he heard Christine continue. "Let's take a deep breath. Did Michelle tell you where Matt was meeting with Rich and this lawyer?"

"Yes. It's a restaurant about fifteen minutes from here."

"So we go there and do what? Do we confront him with his lawyer standing there?"

"I don't know what we do yet. I just feel like we have to get there. We can act surprised—be nice. You *do* know how to be nice, don't you?"

"I don't like this, not at all. I don't think we should leave."

"Fine. You stay here and bury your head in that damned computer, like you always do."

"I'll go with you, just to make sure you don't do something else stupid. But I think we need to discuss what we're going to do about Dylan."

Dylan pushed his ear harder against the door and held his breath.

"I'll fire him, of course."

"On what grounds?"

Art remained silent for a moment, and Dylan imagined him running a hand through his hair while he considered the question. He waited, wondering what Art was up to. Then he heard Art on the phone: "Michelle, call the garage and get the limo ready." Then Art turned his attention back to Christine. "We need to discuss this on the way to the restaurant. We have to be together on this, Christine."

Dylan noted Art's tone had changed.

"Of course, you're right." She said nothing for several moments then asked, "What about Dylan, and Tony's death?"

Dylan's eyes opened wide as he listened to Christine. *Where is she going with this,* he wondered?

"What about it?" Art asked.

"Well, now that the world knows Tony was murdered, someone has to take the fall." Christine lowered her voice, and all Dylan heard was garbled whispering.

"What are you talking about?" Art said, his voice now clear. "He has a rock-solid alibi for that day. He was in New York—remember? He didn't even get back to Boston until after Tony was killed, and he has a bucket full of receipts and airline personnel who can verify his alibi. Why would you even think that?"

"Well, where were you when Tony was killed?" Christine asked.

"I was also here in New York. You might recall we had just returned from the road show, and the IPO occurred that Monday."

Christine's manner became sour. "Yes, and it's just a short shuttle trip up to Boston, isn't it? We worked on our notes that weekend, but Tony was murdered that following Monday. Seems like plenty of time to me—"

Art cut her off; his tone took on a cold, steely note. "Do not even attempt to go there, Christine. If you did not see me, please remember I did not see you either. Besides, what motive would I have for murdering him?"

Dylan gritted his teeth as he thought about the video; he struggled to keep from opening the door. He was bigger than Art; he was stronger than Art; he was younger than Art; and it would be nothing for him to take the man out. He was about to open the door when he heard Christine's response.

"Hyperfôn," she said. "Everything started to go bad with the Hyperfôn sell-out to LC. If Tony found out and threatened to make it public, there would be a number of people who would have a reason to kill him, including you."

"You should be very careful, my dear, with such loaded accusations. Remember, you would appear on that list as well."

Dylan realized Art had not shared the results of his meeting with Ivan with Christine. The sound of the elevator door opening ended the conversation and left Dylan standing in the dark office, a trickle of sweat wandering down his back. He leaned his head against the wall and slammed his fist into the door. "Wake up, Dylan," he heard himself say. "Deal with this later. Finish what you started."

He jerked open the door, not caring if anyone saw him, and hurried down the hall toward Art's office. When he arrived at the door, he noticed that, as expected, Michelle was not there. He regained the momentum of his plan, looked both ways through the empty hallway, and quietly moved into Art's office. He did not turn on the lights, but walked on silent steps toward Art's computer that sat in the middle of an otherwise empty desk.

Dylan removed the slip of paper from his pocket and unfolded it, placing it next to the computer. He turned the computer on, and while he waited for it to boot up, he read the information on the note. Ivan's handwriting was stiff and large, and, although he mastered the verbal language, his ability to write in English left a great deal to be desired. The dim light emanating from the windows was little help.

The dual screens opened up in front of him, and he knew that following Ivan's directions would be challenging. He removed the flash drive from his pocket and slipped it into Art's computer. His attempts to follow Ivan's directions felt stilted and awkward. Typing and reading and watching where he was, all at the same time, frustrated him. He leaned in close, reading the directory that appeared before him; he scrolled down, opening one folder and then another without success. This was taking forever. He looked at his watch. Twenty minutes had passed. He stopped and listened to noises outside the office as a group of disgruntled employees passed, exchanging loud arguments.

He turned his attention to another folder in the long list and discovered it opened a gold mine. Only one document was in the folder, but it was titled "Schedule B." He moved it to the screen on the right while at the same time loading the file onto the thumb drive. It was sizable, and he made sure the small light on the flash drive was blinking on and off, copying the file. Dylan looked back at the right screen, and his heart raced as he scrolled across the spreadsheet. It showed the firm's financials from its inception through the IPO. It even had projections through the end of the summer. But then Dylan scrolled down the spreadsheet and noticed there was a second set of financials below it. These numbers were different. They were much lower. And below them was yet another set of numbers. Added together, they equaled the numbers at the top. This was definitely a file Art didn't want anyone else to see.

"What is he thinking?" he asked out loud. "To actually name the file 'Schedule B' is either incredibly stupid or I'm spending a lot of time copying the wrong file." The thought startled him. What if it were a decoy? Art is smart enough to do that, but Dylan couldn't stop at this point. He had to hope this was the right file. Once Heather and Rich saw it, they would know for certain.

Suddenly he heard the sound of Art's voice in the distant hallway. The light on the thumb drive blinked rapidly as the copying process continued, but Dylan had to get out of the office without being seen. Thankfully, the blinking stopped, and he ripped the drive from the port and quickly scanned the office. The only refuge was Art's conference room. He rushed over, hoping it was not locked, and to his relief the door opened when he tugged. He slipped into the room and gently closed the door just as he heard the office door open.

"Do you think Michelle got the name of the restaurant wrong?" Christine asked.

"She is very reliable. If anyone got the information wrong, it was Rachel."

From his hiding place, he heard Art's voice grow louder as it neared the conference room door. He prepared for the worst, but the voice passed. Dylan heard the sound of a cabinet opening and liquid sloshing into glasses.

"I don't like this, Christine. It just doesn't feel right."

"Well, right or not, we need to settle on how we're going to fire Dylan. Could he have been responsible for those news leaks? And if so, how can we use that?"

Art remained silent for a moment. "Considering what's going on, he should be on the front lines helping us to resurrect the image of the company—right? But he's not, is he? So let's start out small. We can accuse him of gross negligence and willful misconduct in the performance of his duties."

"Well that is one of the reasons for termination for cause in his shareholder agreement. But it's weak." Christine sighed. "I think we'd be better off just saying we know what he did."

Art responded, "And when he says, 'Oh? I did what?'"

"You say, 'You leaked false information on the Internet, where it got picked up by CNBC and everyone else. Why did you do it, Dylan?' You hit him right up front before he can deny it. I think he'll quickly realize he's in way over his head."

Dylan noted something unusual in her tone. It seemed to lack her usual brash confidence.

She continued, "He knows he's going down, but he's not going to bring us with him."

Dylan clenched his jaw and shook his head as he listened to their plan hatch. While his mind organized his thoughts, he remained stationary, fearing detection if he moved.

Art returned to the cabinet and refilled his glass. Whatever he was drinking increased his fury. "I've watched him poking around where he had no business. Bringing him and his little group into this company hasn't been fun."

"He just had to push, didn't he? Anyone else would have been thrilled just to take the cushy job that came with the acquisition and sit back and enjoy the ride and the money. If he hadn't demanded to be more involved with the financials, none of this would have happened."

Dylan listened to their banter as they worked to increase their confidence in their plan, but he recognized that when Christine spoke, Art seemed somehow diminished, always responding with anger. Dylan pondered the earlier conversation outside the elevator, and although there was no doubt in his mind about their complicity in the fraud, he wondered about whether or not one or both was involved in the murder. He did not doubt Art's motivation, but he was not sure about Christine. In his mind, she was clearly capable of murder, without remorse, but was it really enough that her lifestyle was in jeopardy to drive her to that extreme? Art was not smart enough to pull off the financial scheme without Christine. Dylan's normally organized mind flipped back and forth as he recognized he wanted Art to be the guilty party in both crimes. But a nagging thought itched at the back of his mind: Was Christine the mastermind and Art no more than her front man? Another item to be tucked away into the recesses of his mind.

He heard Christine growl, "Let's get it over with. We need to have something in writing, some confession for him to sign."

Art said, "With him admitting what he did? Do you think he'll do it?"

Dylan heard Christine rise from the sofa where she and Art had been sitting. "He may have his suspicions, but proving it is another matter, isn't it?"

"Yes, but this will be a world-class game of chicken, and I don't like to lose," Art said.

"So how do we plan on getting him to confess?"

Dylan strained to hear Art's answer. This was it, the point of no return.

"You and I know everything said on those websites is true, but the fact is Dylan has no proof. If he wants to make those accusations, he has to show the evidence, which he doesn't have. That's the answer. No evidence. So here's what happens. First, we fire him for committing libel and gross negligence and willful misconduct in the performance of his duties. We don't need to do anything more; we just hit him with that. Second, we demand he post a retraction to the same websites he posted to before, and maybe even agree to speak on CNBC admitting it was he who leaked the misinformation. He will tell them he was despondent over Tony's death and now recants all the things he said."

"And what do you say when he refuses, which I'm sure he will?" Christine asked.

"That's the beauty of this situation," Art answered. "We don't have to say anything. He has no evidence, only a cheap accusation with nothing to back it up. Like I said, we tell him he's committed libel. And we tell him we won't prosecute if he resigns."

Dylan's eyes focused on the sliver of light that reached under the doorway. He fingered the thumb drive tucked safely in his pocket and drew comfort in the fact he indeed did have the evidence. He heard the rustling of clothes and held his breath.

"Well then," Christine said, "I think we should prepare that termination letter."

The sound of movement across the room gave him a short-lived moment of relief.

"What's this?" Christine asked. "Why did you leave your computer open, and especially to this file?"

"What are you talking about?" Art demanded, rushing to the desk. "Holy shit!"

The sound of jostling and swearing reached his ears and faded away into the distance as the door slammed.

Chapter 29

Dylan rushed out of Art's office, to the surprise of Michelle, who sat at her desk, her mouth open but unable to speak. He raced for the first stairwell he found and bounded down the two flights with the speed of a jaguar. He yanked open the door and raced down the hallway and around the corner toward his office. He silently thanked his guardian angel when he arrived at his office and found Rachel's desk unoccupied. He rushed into the office, threw off his jacket, turned on the light, bounded to his desk and composed himself—with Art and Christine close on his tail.

Art rushed through the door and screamed, "Hey, asshole, that information is confidential and my personal property."

Dylan looked up questioningly. "Excuse me, Art? What's this all about?" His mind raced as he waited for the accusations.

Art growled, while Christine, arriving just a moment after him, reached for his arm to contain him. She turned to Dylan and said, "Didn't it ever occur to you what you've done is illegal? I will see to it that you go away for a long, long time."

Dylan sensed a level of insecurity in her tone. He leaned back in his chair, collecting his thoughts. "I don't know what you two are talking about. Why don't you sit down?" He watched the veins in Art's neck pulsate, his face red with rage.

Christine stepped in front of Art. "The truth, Dylan," she said in a sour tone, "is that you told a series of blatant falsehoods to a number of websites that was picked up by CNBC and spread like wildfire. Information that was damaging to this company's reputation. That's slander. You did this out of a vicious desire for vengeance when you realized you were going to be fired for incompetence!"

Dylan noted that the normally stern Christine was struggling with the accusation he knew she would make. The sound of silence echoed around the room, reverberating off the walls as Dylan took a calculated risk. He finally spoke. "Let me make sure I understand this. You steal millions, and, when I find the evidence of it, you have the audacity to call *me* incompetent?"

Art stepped back and took a deep breath. "Yes. Because you're the one that got caught."

"Oh, really? What proof do you have of anything I may have done?" Dylan asked, throwing right back at them the words he'd heard them exchange in Art's office.

Christine shot him a look that ranged from curiosity to wonder; she hadn't expected this response. She recovered quickly and stepped up to his desk. "Here are your choices, Dylan. We can fire you for committing libel and gross negligence and willful misconduct in the performance of your duties. You will be escorted off the premises right now, and then we'll sue you." She paused, wanting that threat to sink in. "Or," she continued, "you can go back to those websites and admit to leaking false information, contact CNBC and make a public retraction, and we'll make sure you get the medical help you need."

Dylan recognized the first step in their game of "chicken." "So you expect me to contact a bunch of websites and go on CNBC and admit to something I didn't do?"

"Yes—and don't think we don't know you were responsible." Christine snarled.

Art had taken a back seat; the game being played was now between Dylan and Christine. He looked up in defiance at Art and Christine. "So the story is, I made it all up and don't really have any proof?"

"Exactly. We'll give you a six-month payout. Enough to tide you over," Christine said with a shrug. She pulled herself up straight and stared into his eyes. Dylan saw defiance with just a tinge of fear in her body language. He found her a most daunting competitor. Art had become weak and pathetic, but Christine stood strong.

"Tide me over until what? Till I forget how you bought my company under false pretenses, then fired my staff and sold out my clients? Even murdered my friend?"

At the word "murder" Christine stalled for just a moment, then recovered. "Just realize if you don't take it, we'll destroy you both financially and professionally. You won't be able to work again. You'll lose everything. And you'll rack up a fortune in legal bills."

Dylan watched her closely. He thought she spoke just a bit too fast.

He took a deep breath and ran his fingers through his hair. The room fell into silence.

"You don't want to do this, Dylan," Christine continued, her tone changing to a dangerous purr. "If you try and bring us down, you'll bring yourself down too. You'll lose everything."

Dylan just leaned back and smiled a knowing smile.

With a worried look on his face, Art took a step towards Dylan and broke his silence. "Okay, look. We can make a deal. We'll cut you in," he said. "One third."

Dylan recognized the second level of "chicken," and he watched as Christine flinched at Art's offer. They both fell silent for too long. Dylan smiled again: his turn. "I'm more concerned with Tony's murder than I am with money." He turned to the weakened Art and used his ace. "Where, exactly, were you on May 2nd?" Dylan watched as Christine stepped backward, her eyes looking around as her mind raced at this new tack. Art choked.

"I was in New York. You might recall having had a conversation with me."

Dylan smiled. "See Art, that's the thing about technology. It's great because we can see and hear each other from anywhere on the planet. But the truth is we don't necessarily actually know *where* the other person is. Yes, I spoke to you, but no, I don't know you were in New York." He leaned forward and glared at them. "I'm sure one of you killed Tony." Dylan's eyes darted back and forth between them. "And you're going to pay for what you've done."

Art's eyes opened wide. "What?" he screamed.

Christine stiffened, then snorted. "Why the hell do you think we killed Tony?"

Dylan reached another level of the game. "Because he found out about your scams and about Schedule B and you wanted to shut him up."

Christine's face changed in a way Dylan had never seen before.

"Oh, Jesus," said Art, rolling his eyes.

"I am convinced one of you did it. Probably you, Art."

"Jesus, Dylan. We've been through this. I was in New York at the time."

"Even if you were, you had plenty of time to fly up to Boston after you left the floor. You used the IPO as a cover."

Christine frowned at Dylan, the furrows of her pinched face even deeper. She had been silent for several moments. She glanced sideways at Art, then focused back on Dylan. She moved closer and leaned in toward him. He noticed her lips quivered slightly. "Listen, Dylan. I can help you, if that's what you want. We'll hire the best detectives to find out who killed Tony." Her speech took on a quiet panic. "As for this scandal? That was Art. I didn't have anything to do with it. You'll never prove it."

Dylan had not expected Christine to throw Art under the bus.

"What the hell—?" Art clearly hadn't expected it either. He stepped forward and glared at Christine.

"The records are on his computer, not mine," she continued. "I'll deny everything, Dylan." She shook her head. "I'll say I thought what Art said about you was true, that you were crazy with grief and afraid to lose your job. I'll say I didn't know he was trying to squeeze you out."

"You fucking bitch," said Art. "If I—"

Dylan's mind ignored their squabbling. He heard their muffled conversation as if through a fog: Christine working on her story, Art furious at her betrayal, both of them squirming to find a way out of their predicament and neither of them the slightest bit worried about being tagged for Tony's murder. *They didn't do it*, he thought, realizing the truth.

Christine refocused her laser attention on Dylan. "Dylan, I'll back you all the way. I'll help you. I'm a good friend to have."

"I think you're going to be busy, Christine." Dylan looked at his watch. It was almost four o'clock. He punched the intercom on his phone. "Rachel, have those people from the SEC arrived? Good, send them in."

Chapter 30

Stars flickered in the deep purple sky of the late May evening as Dylan dragged himself up the stairs of his condo. He had e-mailed Heather, Rich, and Matt that he would take the seven o'clock shuttle and to meet him at his place in Boston by nine p.m. He knew Heather would let herself and the others in with the key he had given her. When he opened the door, he smiled—a tired, lackluster smile, but a smile nonetheless.

They all pounced on him at once. "Well?"

Dylan poured himself a drink, sat down, and relayed the events of the day up to the point where the SEC left with Art and Christine. "I don't know if they will be able to use these files."

"Why in the world not?" Rich asked.

"Well, I *did* literally steal them from Art's computer. They may be damning evidence, but obtained illegally. I probably need to start looking for a lawyer, just in case. But that's not why I asked you guys to meet me."

He placed his laptop on the dining room table and booted it up. While they waited, he excused himself and went into the bedroom to change his clothes. Heather's suitcase was on his bed, open. He smiled.

He returned to the dining room and winked at Heather. "OK, guys. I looked over this file just casually, but we need to give it a detailed review. I mean, item by item. We don't want to miss a thing."

The four of them gathered around the screen as Rich began scrolling through the file. They studied the numbers carefully and realized that the numbers at the top, the numbers given to Wall Street, were bogus. He scrolled down to see what they were doing to artificially inflate them.

"Jeez," Rich said, pointing to three lines of information. "They were doing a lot. They booked some of the revenues from clients when the work was sold, not delivered. That's illegal. And look here," he continued, his voice taking on an air of excitement. "They actually did take a reserve of three million for the MobiCelus acquisition without disclosing it. It looks like they used it to bolster the firm's financials right before the IPO."

Rich became like a man driven to find water in the desert. Dylan, Heather, and Matt all moved back and let him take over.

"He's a lot better than Christine said he was," Heather whispered to Dylan.

"Yes, and he might just be our savior in interpreting this information." Dylan breathed a heavy sigh. "But there's more."

"What do you mean?" Heather asked.

"You'll find out in a few minutes." He said nothing more, but sat back and let Rich do his work.

"Hmm," Rich said under his breath. Everyone closed in.

"What is it?" Matt asked.

"Here, look at February. It shows a mysterious infusion of ten million dollars in cash that was spread across February and March to inflate our numbers. Another mysterious infusion of fifteen million dollars in cash was scheduled to dramatically inflate our numbers in April."

Everyone remained silent, unsure of what they were seeing, but afraid to break the spell.

Rich continued, "Looks like from the very beginning, Art and Christine set up Mantric as a way to make themselves extremely rich. This is a classic pump-and-dump scheme. They are deliberately hyping the firm's stock and falsifying its financials to drive up the price of the stock so they can then sell it at a huge premium."

"Anything else?" said Matt.

"Hell, yeah! This shows they orchestrated a massive spamming campaign with the media and investors. Oh, and look—there's a list of payoffs to their law firm Daley and Hahn and their accounting firm Hickman and Ross to make everything look legitimate. Jesus! Everyone was in on this scam."

He scrolled further down and saw that large amounts of Mantric shares were scheduled to be sold every month, starting with the IPO. "Aha! So that's how Art and Christine were planning to get their money out! Through the corrupt bankers and into offshore accounts."

Dylan moved further back, away from the table, while Heather and Matt had closed in toward Rich, reading over his shoulder. Rich moved to the next page of the spreadsheet to see an infusion of ten million dollars in February attributed to LC. Then he saw that another infusion of fifteen million dollars in cash had been scheduled to happen in March. It was attributed to Bendeta Corporation, a direct competitor of another one of Dylan's mobile computing clients. Rich stopped and lifted his hands off the keyboard as if it were on fire. Everyone stared at the screen then slowly turned toward Dylan.

"That's why Tony was murdered."

• • •

Later that evening, Dylan sent Matt and Rich home with specific directions not to speak to anyone about the contents of Schedule B. They knew the SEC would want to talk to all of them, and it was important that they present a unified front as to what they knew and what it meant. Matt and Rich would each spend the rest of the next day once again going over the details, while Heather and Dylan undertook an unpleasant task of a different sort.

Chapter 31

Dylan rose early and put the coffee pot on, then returned to the bedroom. Heather mumbled in a state of half-sleep, and Dylan remained still, watching her. The discoveries of the night before seemed to fuel their desire to find comfort in each other. Dylan replayed the passion of the previous night over and over, trying to capture the intensity of Heather's love. Dylan's life had revolved around the thrill of establishing his own business. Until recent weeks, Heather was an unreachable star, and not until last night did Dylan awaken to the full sense of her passion. She cried in his arms as they talked about the day and closing the final chapter—confronting Tony's murderer. They shared the sadness of remembering Tony, his childish pranks and his adult brilliance. And she fell asleep in his arms, a tear wandering down her cheek.

Dylan looked at the clock. They'd slept late and had not set an alarm. The clock turned over 8:35. He lay down next to Heather and kissed her eyes.

"Mmmf," she mumbled as she stretched and lifted her head, her eyes still closed, awaiting a kiss.

"Morning," he said, kissing her lips.

"Umm—hmm," she returned. Suddenly her eyes opened wide, a look between fear and anger washed across her face. "Oh, what time is it?" Then she looked into his eyes, her glance deteriorating to a dark sadness. "We have to do this thing, don't we?"

"Yep. Coffee's on. I don't think we should let this go any further. Let's get it over with."

"Shower?"

Dylan smiled. "We'll never get this done if we follow *that* routine!"

"I know," she answered. "But just a quick shower?"

• • •

May 19, 10:00 a.m. Boston

The Mantric office was quiet; all employees were away for the day and would not return until after the investigation was completed. Dylan sat at his desk and keyed in a number at his computer. He moved close to the screen when Rob's face materialized in front of him.

"Dylan, sorry I couldn't meet with you guys last night. Are you okay?" Rob asked.

Dylan shook his head slowly. "No, Rob, I'm not."

"Me either. The CNBC report and all of those accusations. It's all crazy. I can't believe it!"

"I can believe anything now."

Rob's expression grew concerned. "Dylan. You look very strange. What's going on?"

"The SEC is investigating Art and Christine as we speak, Rob. It's all over."

"What are you saying?"

"I think I just said it, Rob. What you saw in the news. It was true. And the SEC has the proof."

"You mean Rich was right about the reserve for MobiCelus?"

"That's only the beginning. There's been massive fraud. It's all coming out now."

"Oh my God!"

"It gets worse. They've been out to bring me down since the day we were acquired."

"Dylan, no!"

"'Fraid so. Turns out they authorized the leak of Hyperfōn to LC."

Rob shook his head in amazement. "This is incredible. Why would they do this?"

"Why do you think?"

"Greedy bastards!"

"Yeah. Well, at least we'll catch the guy who ruined Joe's business by stealing his Hyperfōn model. That's something."

"That's great. Who was it?"

"We don't know yet." Dylan paused and drew a breath. "Christine finally told the SEC the secret accounts are detailed on her computer in her office in Boston. You said nobody on our staff ever showed signs of unusual income—right?"

"Right. Nothing. I can't imagine who it could be, except, well—"

"Well what?" asked Dylan.

"Shit. I asked Matt to look into that. He might have buried that information himself or deleted it. Jesus, Dylan. Matt must have been the one responsible for selling out Hyperfōn, and Tony must have discovered him!"

"That's a strong possibility. We'll know for sure tomorrow. The SEC is sending their people up to Boston to investigate."

"Right." Rob swept his hair off his face. "Sorry, Dylan, but this is an awful lot for me to absorb."

"Yeah."

"When are you coming back from New York?"

"It's ten o'clock now. I'll hop a shuttle around noon. I think we should get together, don't you? There's a lot to discuss."

"Absolutely. Just call me when you land and we'll work something out."

They ended the connection. Dylan sat back and took a deep breath.

• • •

May 19, 11:30 a.m. Boston

Rob closed his laptop and packed it into his bag. He walked through the halls of Mantric's Boston office. The place looked like a ghost town. The news of the last few days—Tony's murder, the news about Mantric's corruption, the plummeting stock price—had emptied the building like a poison gas. He walked through the empty halls to the elevator, but instead of pushing the down button, he continued past it to the corner office: an office once occupied by him, but confiscated by Christine shortly after the acquisition.

He quietly turned the knob only to find the door locked. Rob reached into his pocket and pulled out a key, one he had not returned when Christine moved in, and opened the door. The blinds, closed tight, allowed only dim light into the room. Rob bypassed the light switch and walked to Christine's desk.

Reaching down beneath the desk, he pulled the computer tower out from its space, unscrewed the pins that held the cover on the side, then slid it back. Reaching inside, he pulled the cables off the hard drive and lifted it out of the computer. With a quiet chuckle, he placed the hard drive in his laptop bag and stood up straight.

"Don't go yet," said a voice.

Rob jumped backwards, crashing into Christine's side table, sending a vase of roses tumbling to the floor. A shadowy figure rose from the conference table in the middle of the room and approached him. Rob blinked in the dim light.

"Dylan?"

Dylan switched on the light to see Rob standing on a jumble of scattered roses, clutching his laptop bag to his chest in a pair of gloved hands.

"Yeah."

Rob's glance cascaded around the room. "You were in New York!"

"It's easy to fool someone, isn't?" Dylan strode over to Rob, grabbed his shirt and slammed him against the wall. "You bastard. You fucking bastard! You sold us out."

"Dylan, I don't know—"

"Don't!" Dylan said, cutting Rob's sentence off short. Dylan towered over Rob by almost half a foot and easily carried an additional twenty pounds of muscle. He pushed his left arm against Rob's throat to hold him in place and pointed a shaking finger in Rob's face. "Don't even think of denying it."

A look of terror crossed Rob's face. "Dylan, what are you talking about?"

"God damn it, Rob, I know everything." He leaned forward, pressing his face to within two inches of Rob's. "And you've just removed any doubt I might have had by taking the bait and stealing Christine's hard drive." He moved his arm away from Rob's throat, grasped him by the shirt, and pulled him away from the wall, spinning him around. He gave Rob a final push that sent him sprawling across the room.

"Help me out here, Dylan." Rob's voice shook. "I really don't understand what you're talking about. I just didn't want the police to get our files, so. . . ."

"Fuck you! Selling out our Hyperfōn work to LC for ten million dollars?"

Rob's face went pale. "What?"

"I've got the files, Rob. The spamming campaign, the cooked books, the payoffs for our mobile computing clients' software, the offshore bank accounts. Everything. You must have known when LC approached you that you couldn't do this without help. I'm sure Art and Christine jumped at the idea of selling out Hyperfōn for some quick money. They certainly had no loyalty to Joe. Getting millions of dollars instantly from LC was a lot better than waiting for revenues from Hyperfōn. Now I understand why you defended them and their decisions so often. I should have seen that tide turning, but I didn't."

"There must be some mistake," Rob pleaded. "I really don't know anything about any of this."

"You're lying," Dylan said, crossing the room in three bounding steps and pulling Rob's collar tight around his neck. "It was right in front of my nose all the time, but I didn't see it. I know you gave the Hyperfōn plan to LC, Rob. You didn't remember that while Hyperfōn was our client, way before Mantric, we built our own tags into the system. That was your biggest mistake. That's the mistake that will take you down. No one from Mantric knew of those tags, only you. It was you, not Matt, who was in charge of checking the records between LC and Mantric to see if there was a connection—to see if any of our people had a windfall they couldn't account for. But you didn't check yourself, did you? You had access to the Hyperfōn model while we were still at MobiCelus. And the second you heard I wanted Matt to look into it as well, you sent him home to sleep. He was working too hard, you said. He needed some time to rest, you said. So considerate of you. And then you called Art and told him he had to fire Matt. But I never saw it because I trusted you."

Rob's eyes widened, his mouth opened, but the words didn't come.

Dylan pulled the collar even tighter, choking Rob. "God damn it, Rob! Just take the responsibility and admit it, for once in your life!"

Rob's face turned red, and he gasped for air. He nodded, and Dylan relaxed his grip.

"Okay," Rob said, struggling to speak. "You're right. I did hand over the Hyperfōn plan."

"That's a start." Dylan stared hard at Rob. "And now tell me about the Bendeta Corporation."

Rob froze for a moment. "Okay," he gasped, sagging against the wall. "I won't deny I was supposed to do that too, but I didn't do it yet. Listen, this wasn't my fault! Art told me to do it. He told me there was big money in it, and if I didn't follow his orders he'd kick me out onto the street. He was holding Hyperfōn over my head."

"You little fucker," Dylan screamed. He grabbed Rob, pulled him forward, then pushed him back, hard. There was a dull thud as Rob's head smashed against the wall. "Why, Rob? Why did you do it?"

Rob slumped down onto the floor. "For the money. I was broke and I needed the money."

Dylan looked away for a moment then rushed back and kicked him in the gut. "Ten million! Ten—fucking—million!"

Rob let out a moan and gasped to catch his breath.

"You bastard! You actually squandered all the money you got when we were acquired? So you did this to keep up the ridiculous lifestyle you created for yourself? Christ, all you had to do was live within your means until the legitimate payday came when your stock vested. You're pathetic." Dylan made another motion towards Rob, who instinctively put up his arms to protect himself from further attack. "Stand up, you piece of shit."

Rob didn't move.

"I said stand up."

Rob slowly took his arms down and stood.

"You think money is that important? It was just something to have because you didn't have anything else. Tony was the boy genius, Heather was the talented designer with the amazing computer skills, and I'm the one who brought in the clients. *We* all drove the business. All you had was your good looks and your precious Harvard MBA. All you could do was *add*."

"Dylan, please."

"You wanted to be the rich guy, the guy who made money. You wanted lots of money, and you didn't care how you got it." Dylan clenched his fists.

"I'm sorry." Rob's mind rushed through answers. "It was Heather, man. She has such expensive tastes. Everything has to be the best. You don't know what I went through trying to please her. I was addicted to her, I know. But listen, she's out of my life now. I'll make it up to you. I'll do whatever you say. Whatever it takes."

Dylan stared at Rob, unable to respond to his lies about Heather, angry enough to kill Rob. "You can't give me what I want." Dylan's words were slow and precise. "And the funny thing is I think I'd be better off if Tony really had just died in a stupid, idiotic accident. I could have grieved, and healed, and maybe after a decade or two had the satisfaction of knowing it was so like Tony to die like that."

"I think the police are wrong about that," Rob spoke in a rush of words. "I'm sure it wasn't murder. How could it be?"

"You tell me. You were there." He watched Rob's handsome face stiffen, his blue eyes flicker. But there was no telltale tick or sudden flush. He did not move at all. "No comment?" he demanded.

Rob licked his lips. "I'm not sure what to say. Are you asking me what I think?"

"No. I'm telling you I know you did it."

"Okay." Rob held up his hands. "Dylan. I know you're upset. And I know you have every right to be. But I was at the office at the time, remember?"

"No you weren't."

"Dylan, we conferenced that afternoon. You know where I was. We've been over this."

"I know, and I missed it. I assumed you were in your office, the way I always assume whoever I'm conferencing with on the VPN is where I think they should be, where they were the last time I talked to them, where they tell me they are. The way you thought I was in New York when actually I was here, in Christine's office."

"Dylan, I really was in my office. But even if I wasn't, even if I was at home, at an Internet café, or anywhere else, I was talking to you on the VPN at four. Didn't you tell me the time of death had been established between 3:30 and 4:30?"

"Yeah."

"So how could I be both on the VPN and killing Tony at four o'clock?"

"You joined the conference from Tony's computer. It was on when you got to his place. It was on when you left. It was on when I got there. You killed him, logged out of his account, and logged into yours. My God, when I think I was talking with you—what? Ten minutes after you killed him? With him lying there on the floor?"

Rob brushed a shaking hand through his disheveled hair. "That's— no. Dylan, really, I think you're being delusional." Rob searched for words, tried to sound confident.

"How could you do it, Rob? How could you be capable of such a thing?" Dylan grabbed Rob by the front of his shirt and pulled him forward until Rob's face was within inches of his own. "Tony was our friend!" He smelled the scent of fear on Rob's stale breath.

Rob's eyes flashed, but he did not resist. "I'm not going to fight you."

"Tony was on to you, wasn't he? He asked Heather's advice about how to handle a sticky problem. And I thought he was talking about Art when he said he had evidence about something big, but it was you. You selling out Hyperfōn. How did he find out?"

Panic continued to build; Rob grasped for an answer that didn't come. "I don't know. I found him there. He was already dead."

Dylan's eyes flashed in disbelief. "Right. And for some bizarre reason you didn't call the police."

"I panicked. I had a guilty conscience. I thought they'd think it was me."

"I'm sure you did. Did he ask you to come over to talk to you? I bet he did. That was Tony. He always believed people had their reasons for what they did. I bet he even offered to help."

Rob looked away, breathing heavily. He said nothing but scanned the walls, searching for some scrap that would convince Dylan of his innocence.

"Let me guess. He made the mistake of telling you he hadn't told anyone yet. And you saw that as your way out. You saw a way you wouldn't have to lose everything. Once you saw how easy it was to make millions without losing your job or your reputation—without earning it—you just couldn't stop, could you? And the only person who stood in your way was Tony!" Rob turned his face away, but not before Dylan saw the spasm of anger cross his face. Dylan released him and stepped back. "How did it go down, Rob?"

Rob turned slowly, his demeanor changed. "One day he said he knew something was wrong, something he wanted to talk to me about. There was something in the way he looked at me, the way he spoke, that told me he knew it all. I knew then I had to find out more, that I had to do something to convince him not to say anything. I stopped by to find out what he knew."

"And? Come on! Don't fuck with me, Rob!" Dylan demanded.

Rob stood up straight. "We were supposed to meet at a restaurant, but I didn't want to talk about it in public, so I went to his house early. As soon as he answered the door, I saw by the look on his face he knew why I was there. He told me about looking at the Hyperfōn account, and it took him no time at all to put two and two together. He knew I was living beyond my means, and when he told me I had to tell you about this—Dylan—I got *angry*. I was tired of being the one person in the group who had to hang onto everyone else's shirttails. I wanted out of this group, and Hyperfōn was my ticket. I shoved him and he fell, hitting his head. He was unconscious, so I stripped an electric cord from his workroom, wrapped it around him, and plugged it in. The bare end of the wire electrocuted him. I thought it would look like an accident." Rob, bereft of all emotion, turned and stared at Dylan. "You just don't understand, Dylan. He was in the way."

Dylan stepped back from Rob, unable to speak for several moments, and then he turned his head and called. "Did you get it all?" he asked.

"What?" Rob said.

Heather stepped through the slightly opened door with an mp3 recorder in her hand. "Yes, absolutely everything." She walked over to Rob and just stared at him.

"What are you doing here?" Rob asked.

"Getting to the truth." She drew back her open hand and struck him across the face, forcing him backward into the wall. She turned back to Dylan. "We need to call the police. Right now."

Chapter 32

June 15, 8:30 a.m. Boston

An early summer storm had raged up the Atlantic coast, bringing showers quickly followed by intense heat and oppressive humidity. Small pools of water shimmered on the road below.

Dylan and Heather sat on Dylan's rooftop deck, their feet propped up on the railings. Heather, her hair in a ponytail, was dressed in a flowing brown cotton skirt and a peach-colored top that left her arms and most of her shoulders bare against the blazing heat. She looked a lot like the college girl who had caught Dylan's attention several years earlier. Dylan wore his favorite khaki shorts, an old MIT T-shirt, and Top-Siders without socks.

Every once in a while, a slight breeze wafted across the roof, causing just a hint of relief from the heat, but little more than that. Sweat trickled down the back of Heather's shirt. She focused her attention on a man walking a dog on the brick sidewalk below.

Dylan took a long sip from a large glass of iced coffee. A cold drop of sweat from the glass wandered down his hand and meandered in a crooked path further down his arm to his elbow. He wiped his arm on his shirt, opened up his iPad, and started reading the business section of Boston.com.

"Hey, listen to this one. *'Mantric's stock scraped along for the last week at pennies a share due to the frantic efforts of a host of mid-level managers as they attempted to salvage what little remains of the company. Yesterday, Art Williams and Christine Rohnmann, once the darlings of the technology world, were formally charged with fraud, causing the once proud MNTR symbol to quietly disappear from the list of public companies trading on the NASDAQ.'*" He closed the cover of his iPad and adjusted his sunglasses.

Heather turned to him. "I feel sorry for Stephanie and Sandeep and those left behind, but they really need to just give it up and move on."

"At least one person is never going to be allowed to move on," he said, his voice edgy and angry.

Heather nodded slowly, knowing he was talking about Rob. The betrayal was still raw for both of them. She decided to change the subject and snatched Dylan's iPad. She flipped through various news sites and scanned the financial pages. "Wow! The press really has whipped itself into a frenzy over this. It's amazing how they've filled their pages with self-righteous claims of the inevitability of something like this. They're so angry, they're blaming Mantric for the NASDAQ's seven consecutive days of decline."

Dylan nodded. "Yep. And in another week, Mantric will become old news when some new scandal feeds their insatiable appetites."

Dylan had spent the first few days of the collapse being interviewed by an Assistant U.S. Attorney named Morgan Banion. Her interest in the story peaked when he provided details on the information in Schedule B, but waned when she deemed that any other information was not pertinent to the case, or more accurately, to her success.

He watched Heather out of the corner of his eye. She was engrossed in the iPad. He reached up and caught an errant curl that had skittered across her face, and moved it behind her ear. She smiled.

Dylan thought about the world of things that had happened in the past few weeks. He'd lost almost everything except for his condo, which luckily he had enough cash to cover. Heather lost her own condo in Cambridge and ended up collecting unemployment. Dylan offered her his extra room. She agreed, with absolutely no interest in the "extra" room. Their future was uncertain, and they both agreed to take life as it came, clinging to that understanding.

He realized their relationship would never really go back to what it was just a few months earlier, especially when the two other people they had been closest to were now gone from their lives. So much of what they thought they had known about the world had been completely overturned. At least their shared experience had bonded them together; moreover, Dylan knew he wanted to be with her. He grinned as that errant tress wriggled away from her ear and blew across her face again.

"Did you see where Art and Christine failed to post bond of one million each?" said Dylan.

"Frankly, I'm surprised. I thought for sure Christine or Art or both of them would be able to snatch such a small amount out of one of their 'off-shore' accounts!" She looked at him out of the corner of her eye and laughed. She pulled the hair away from her face and attempted to, once again, anchor it behind her ear.

He laughed too and topped off their glasses. They turned their attention to well-dressed men and women six stories below, who had places to go and money to make. "It seems odd not to be part of that bustling crowd," he said, leaning his arms on the railing and staring down at the activity below. "To have nowhere to go and nothing to do."

"You give any thought to doing another start-up?"

"I don't know. Guess I'd need to find another catchy name."

A warm breeze wafted across his arms.

"It was Tony's idea. MobiCelus."

"So it was." He half-smiled, remembering.

She flashed him a dazzling smile, placed the iPad on the deck, and stretched. "I'm going to have to do something soon. I'm running out of all the money I don't have."

"Me too. I can't plan on living on my savings and investments forever." He took a sip of his cold drink. "Joe Ferrano called me Saturday. I filled him in on the details I could talk about. He's pretty shook up. He liked Rob." Dylan stopped and shook his head. It was still all so hard to believe.

Heather nodded, a sad look in her eyes.

Dylan continued. "So anyway, I told him what our lawyer is doing to try to keep us from being sucked any further into this mess. I told Joe we were beached. And get this—he said he wanted to help out somehow. As a favor."

"Really! What's he thinking?"

"He wondered if we had any new projects that he might be able to invest in. He might be able to recoup a lot of money, since LC is now in such hot water over the Hyperfōn situation."

Heather sat forward, an expression of interest on her face. "Us? He wants to partner with us?"

"Yeah. You're the one he really wants, but he figures he can use me somehow," Dylan smirked.

"Very funny. Tell me more."

"Joe's itching to figure out his next move. He called to ask if I had any ideas."

Heather raised an eyebrow. "A very good man."

"Yeah."

"So what did you tell him?"

"That we might have something. I was thinking about Tony's wireless electricity device. Mr. Caruso has inherited all of Tony's patents and, believe it or not, Tony had actually already filed one on it. What do you think about approaching Tony's dad and suggesting we try to commercialize it? He'll have a rough time without the money Tony used to send him, not to mention the evaporation of the Mantric stock. This could make his life a lot easier. Plus give him the satisfaction of watching his son's work see the light of day."

"So," Heather said, scrunching her nose. "Remind me of what this thing is?"

"Well, as Brandon Wist explained it to me, it's not totally complete, but it looks like it can transmit power over short distances. But over long distances, the problem is that the power must be sent in a manner identical to the shape of the receiver."

"I'm sorry—you lost me."

"Well, basically the challenge is that the antenna receiving power via radio waves has to be perfectly matched to the correct frequency of the source transmission, or else all devices have to adapt one standard. Not exactly easy to do. I can tell by his sketch that Tony was still trying to figure out a way around this. But if we can finish what he started and make it work, it would really be huge!"

Heather remained silent for several moments, and Dylan knew her mind was throwing ideas around. Finally, she leaned in close to him and placed her hands on his knees.

"I won't claim to understand this stuff, but I like the idea of taking Tony's work to the next stage. But how do we do that?"

A small smile crossed Dylan's lips and quickly grew into a big grin. "I bet I know just the person who would have a clear understanding of how to crack this." Dylan got up and began pacing rapidly back and forth as a plan hatched in his mind.

"Who?" she asked.

He put his thoughts in order and rushed back to where she sat. "Brandon! He would be perfect."

"Are you serious?" Heather moved next to him. "From what you said about your meeting with him, he seemed pretty squirrely."

"Yes, he was that, but when I left that meeting in New Jersey, I was certain his friendship and respect for Tony were genuine. And he has a double-major in computer science and electrical engineering, not to mention the fact that he's got the curious mind of a madman!" Dylan laughed and threw his arms around Heather. "Brandon will do it. I just know he will."

Heather nestled into Dylan's arms. She looked up at him and nodded in agreement. "Let's not forget the rest of the team. Matt and Rich would be ideal team players, and I'm sure they would jump at the chance to work on this project."

Dylan caught her enthusiasm. "We could work together. With our combined skills, we can make anything succeed."

"I'm in, and we should snatch up Matt and Rich right away! I was very impressed with the way Rich understood the infamous Schedule B. Let's call Joe and see what he thinks."

Dylan reached into his pocket and pulled out a piece of paper folded over several times. "I think you should see this. I got an e-mail this morning. The reply address was a fake, but—well, there's no mistaking who it's from." He handed her the paper. "Somehow, when I read this, I realized it was truly over." He took a deep breath. "Go ahead. Read it."

Heather unfolded the paper and read:

"I started monitoring Tony's e-mails after April 1st. I pulled this one, intending to delay it until we could take steps to circumvent the problem. I didn't realize he was talking about Rob. And then Tony was gone, and if I'd shown it to you, you would have thought I had done it. I didn't show it to anyone. I did my job until I couldn't stand to anymore."

She looked up at Dylan and said one word, "Ivan?" then continued reading.

"Date: May 2
"To: djohnson@Mantric.com
"From: tcaruso@Mantric.com
"Subject: FW: Our Ivy Boy

"Hey Dylan. Look, man, this is hard to write, but we've got trouble. This is no time to beat around the bush, so I'll just say it. Looks like our Ivy boy has been making a mess of things. Turns out he's been spending money before he has it and never manages to get out from under. Jerk. Or poor guy. Maybe both. Anyway, I heard from a guy who's a pretty bright dude that somebody from Mantric was looking to sell some inside information, so I did a little snooping. Shh, don't worry, nobody'll ever know. Anyway, now I'm sure, so the question is what to do? I figured I'd better talk to you first. Of course we'll stand up for him, but this is gonna cause a hell of a stink at Mantric. Well, I needed to get that off my chest so we can celebrate this afternoon when our stock goes through the roof. The sky's the limit, man! T."

Heather returned the paper to Dylan, who slowly ripped it into tiny pieces and threw them to the wind.

"Dylan!" she yelled, stunned he would destroy a message from his best friend.

"It's OK, Heather. Tony would approve. He was a big fan of Bertolt Brecht. One of his favorite quotes was 'Do not fear death so much but rather the inadequate life.'"

"That does sound like Tony." She hugged Dylan.

"Yes it does. So let's call everyone and see if we can't bring Tony back!" He smiled a sad smile, but he knew he would sleep well that night.

CPSIA information can be obtained at www.ICGtesting.com
Printed in the USA
BVOW020429020312

284245BV00007B/8/P